Badly
Done.
Emma Lee

Also by Leah Marie Brown
You'll Always Have Tara
Dreaming of Manderley

The It Girls Series
Faking It
Finding It
Working It
Owning It

LEAH MARIE BROWN

Badly Done, Emma Lee

LYRICAL PRESS
Kensington Publishing Corp.
www.kensingtonbooks.com

LYRICAL BOOKS are published by

Kensington Publishing Corp.
119 West 40th Street
New York, NY 10018

All Kensington titles, imprints, and distributed lines are available at special quantity discounts for bulk purchases for sales promotion, premiums, fund-raising, educational, or institutional use.

Special book excerpts or customized printings can also be created to fit specific needs. For details, write or phone the office of the Kensington Sales Manager: Attn.: Sales Department. Kensington Publishing Corp., 119 West 40th Street, New York, NY 10018. Phone: 1-800-221-2647.

First Printing: November 2018
ISBN-13: 978-1-5161-0115-3
ISBN-10: 1-5161-0115-4

eISBN-13: 978-1-5161-0118-4
eISBN-10: 1-5161-0118-9

10 9 8 7 6 5 4 3 2 1

Printed in the United States of America

To the Emma Lees of the world—the hopeless romantics who believe in meet-cutes, soul mates, and silly love songs, the intrepid who dare to venture beyond their comfort zones in search of happily ever after.

And to my agent, Ethan Ellenberg, and my editor, Esi Sogah. Thank you for helping me achieve my happily ever after.

"Silly things do cease to be silly if they are done by sensible people in an impudent way."
—Jane Austen, *Emma*

Prologue

Emma Lee Maxwell, beautiful, clever, and amiable, with an overly indulgent father and a prodigiously large circle of friends, seemed to unite some of the best blessings of existence and had lived nearly twenty-three years in the world with very little to distress or vex her.

On the day Emma Lee was born, the angels gathered in heaven to witness the hallowed event. All births are hallowed events, but Emma Lee's was perhaps more hallowed than most. For, on the day Emma Lee took her first breath, her mother took her last.

And so, the celestial gathering decided to bestow upon the tiny orphan a bounty of divine gifts, including beauty, amiability, joy, and intelligence. They created a most magnificent and congenial child.

The little orphan, our most unexpected heroine, grew to be a beautiful, clever young woman with a doting father, indulgent sisters, and a life free of any real expectation. As a result, Emma Lee's slender shoulders formed unblemished by the burden of expectation.

Indeed, Emma Lee knew the unadulterated joy of leading the fun, fanciful, feckless life of the truly blessed. Idle days filled with sunshine and shopping. And at night, when she rested her golden head on her satin pillow, neither care nor want threatened her peaceful slumber.

Alas, dear reader, do not operate under the misapprehension that our heroine is a wholly divine manifestation tumbled to earth, for Emma Lee Maxwell has, like all mortal creatures, a unique combination of vexatious flaws.

Emma Lee, precious, golden-haired Emma Lee, possesses the singularly challenging traits of the youngest child: manipulativeness, selfishness, attention-seeking, immaturity, and an overweening desire to please others, particularly those fortunate enough to orbit around her celestial body. Emma Lee, with her angelic countenance and form, suffers the worst of afflictions: vanity.

Vanity working on a willfully pampered girl, produces every sort of mischief, to (mis)quote a sensible nineteenth-century English novelist. And this is where our story well and truly begins, dear reader, when vanity run amok propelled our heroine on a crash course with her destiny . . .

Chapter One

Emma Lee Maxwell's Facebook Update:
Did you know Seal proposed to Heidi Klum (Queen) in an igloo he had built in a remote part of the Canadian Rockies? Epic, right?

It's official: I am a crap best friend. Not just moderately crappy, but fantastically crappy. Yep. That's me. Emma Lee Maxwell, Charlestonian by birth, Clemson grad, unemployed, aspiring matchmaker, craptastic best friend.

I am stuck in bumper-to-bumper traffic on Meeting Street *and* my best friend's engagement party starts in ten minutes *and* I am supposed to be giving the opening toast.

"Pardon me"—I say, leaning forward and tapping the taxi driver's shoulder—"are you fixing to hang a left on Charlotte Street?"

He squints into the rearview mirror, fixing me with a weary, yellow-eyed gaze.

"You going to the Gadsden House, right?"

"Yes, sir."

"Meeting to Calhoun to Bay Street."

"Would you mind taking Charlotte to Alexander to Calhoun instead?" I hold his gaze and smile a big, toothy smile, the same smile that won me a place on Clemson's All Girl Cheerleading Team. "I'm due at my best friend's engagement party in nine minutes and I can't be late. I just can't."

His gaze softens.

"I gotchu, girl. Trust in old Charles."

"Thank you, Mr. Charles," I say. "I sure do—"

The car behind us beeps its horn and old Charles takes off like a pony at a polo match. We are flying down Meeting Street, whizzing past John Street, Charlotte Street, Henrietta Street . . . and then the car in front of us comes to a sudden, violent stop, crashing into a truck. Old Charles hits the brakes with surprisingly quick reflexes and we lurch to a stop.

The box on the seat beside me—a gift-wrapped silver picture frame I found at George C. Birlant antiques—falls to the ground with a sickening thud. I pick up the box, tears pricking the corners of my eyes when I hear the rattle of broken glass, and check the analog clock on the dashboard.

Eight minutes.

Lexi is counting on me. I can't let her down.

Traffic has stopped moving in both directions. I lean forward in my seat and look down Calhoun. Traffic isn't moving on Calhoun either.

"I am sorry, girlie," Charles says, frowning. "There are more cars than palmetto bugs at a picnic."

"The Gadsden House is only a ten-minute walk from here. If I run, I might-could make it. What do you think, Mr. Charles?"

"What do I think? I think you should go."

I reach into my purse, pull out the full taxi fare and tip, and hand it to old Charles. Then, I grab my purse and my gift box. I climb out of the car and start walking briskly toward Calhoun.

Mr. Charles beeps his horn and I look back.

"Run, girlie. Run like a scalded haint!"

For a moment, I wonder what Miss Belle would say if she could see me running through downtown Charleston like an ill-bred chicken with her head cut off. Miss Belle Watling taught comportment and etiquette at Rutledge Hall, the private all-girls academy I attended for the first seventeen years of my life. Poor Miss Belle passed when I was at Clemson. She was having lunch at The Grill, excused herself, and was discovered a quarter of an hour later, dead on the lavatory, her orthopedic hose around her ankles. A most undignified ending for a stickler for Southern morals and manners, even if she did expire wearing her polka-dot-lined picture hat and double strand pearls.

I best stop thinking about what Miss Belle would do if she saw me hightailing it in heels and start thinking about what Miss Lexi will do if I am a no-show at her engagement party. After all, I introduced my best friend to her fiancé, Cash William Aiken III. It was my first official foray into the highly pleasing world of matchmaking. Just thinking about my success sends a double-espresso-strength shot of adrenaline surging through my veins, and I start running down Calhoun Street, past the old Episcopal church and the Charleston County Public Library.

I clutch my purse and Lexi's gift and run like I'm a scalded haint—whatever that is—until I reach the Saffron Bakery, where the scent of buttery Florentine cookies hangs heavy in the humid evening air. By the light of a flickering gas lantern, I tuck my hair behind my ear and dab the dew from my brow; according to Miss Belle, Southern ladies never perspire. We glisten with dew.

My iPhone was vibrating all the way down Calhoun, so I pull it out of my purse to quickly check my texts.

Text from Madison Van Doren:
Cash's brother is hot—in a *Southern Charm* meets *Duck Dynasty* kind of way. Will you introduce me? Do you think he would consider shaving the sideburns and putting on a pair of socks? Where are you, btw? You're late.

Text from Roberta Hearst:
Procreation is highly overrated. Fatigue, nausea, constipation, hairy nipples (WTH?). Give Lexi my love and tell her I would rather be at her engagement party than stuck at home on bed rest. Text me all the deets. I want to know everything.

After typing my responses, I walk the short distance from the bakery to the Gadsden House, a magnificent eighteenth-century carriage house with a brick façade and wide, inviting side porches. It was the perfect setting for an engagement party, which is why I'd suggested it when Lexi's momma phoned asking for my help. Lexi and her people are from Virginia, but Cash is Charleston born and bred.

Ravenel. Calhoun. Middleton. Aiken. Maxwell. Pinckney. Ashley. Barton. Some names have cachet in Charleston, and Aiken is one of them. I know what you must be thinking: You best pray for good weather, Emma Lee Maxwell, because you've got your nose so high in the air you would drown in a rainstorm.

I swear on my Kappa Kappa Gamma key I didn't

mean that in a highfalutin, snobby way. It's not about strutting around town thinking your sh*t tastes like sherbet. It's about having roots that go deep into Charleston's sandy soil. It's about the pride that comes from flipping through the pages of *Colonial South Carolina: A History* and seeing your ancestor listed as a founding father, someone who helped shape your hometown in a significant, lasting way.

I get the same warm-all-over, puffed-up-with-pride feeling when I imagine myself ten years from now, a successful matchmaker, with stacks of leather-bound albums bulging with photographs of perfectly matched couples. Couples I brought together—same as I brought Lexi and Cash together.

Some might argue that being a matchmaker isn't as important as helping to write the Constitution of South Carolina, but I strenuously disagree. No disrespect to my nine-times great-granddaddy, Benjamin Josiah Maxwell, but connecting soul mates is as significant an accomplishment as drafting a state's governing document. Love Matters. Maybe if the world spent more time focusing on the heart and less time focusing on the hate, we wouldn't be in this school shootings/terrorist attacks/gender divide/racial divide/North Korean Missile Scare meltdown. All's I'm Sayin'. Hashtag that.

I walk through the open wrought-iron gates into the courtyard, lit by strands of fairy lights strung overhead and crowded with guests already clutching glasses of champagne. Round tables covered with crisp white linen tablecloths and decorated with bouquets of ivory patience garden roses, white peonies, and white hydrangea in mercury glass containers have been arranged beneath the oak trees. A string quartet is playing Debussy's "Clair de Lune" from their perch on the upper porch, the soft, sweet notes falling gently like morning rain, mixing with the tinkling laughter and clinking glasses.

I deposit my present on the gifts table and pause to take it all in—the candles glowing in hurricane lanterns, the cicadas chirping in the trees, the scent of magnolias perfuming the air—and my heart aches with the sublime perfection of this moment. It literally aches, y'all. Tears flood my eyes. If I don't get a handle on my emotions, I am going to be doing one of those ugly, mascara-running, just-watched-a-Hallmark-Christmas-movie cries.

Cash and Lexi suddenly appear on the white-painted porch and I just about die. Die! My best friend is wearing an ivory fit-and-flare cocktail gown with a sweetheart neckline. The dress is perfection in lace. Per-fec-*shun*! I'm serious, y'all. It looks like something Reese Witherspoon—*Hail, Queen*—would wear in a rom-com about a warmhearted big-city girl who finds love with a wise-cracking, small-town boy.

Lexi notices me staring at her and squeals the way best friends do when they haven't seen each other for years— or several hours. She presses a kiss to Cash's cheek and walks across the porch, her heels tapping an excited staccato on the wood floor. We meet at the bottom of the stairs and throw our arms around each other. A thick lump forms in my throat, my eyes fill with tears, and I wonder if this is how thousands of mommas feel each September when they drop their children off for their first day of school. Joy and loss commingling until you don't know whether to laugh or cry. I give her an extra squeeze, blink back my tears, and let her go.

"You look amazing." I reach for the chiffon overskirt of her gown. "Is this lace or embroidery?"

"Appliqué," she says, beaming. "It's a Miiko Sashiko.

Can you believe it took three *petites mains* over two hundred and fifty hours to apply the flowers? Can you imagine being stuck in an atelier for that long, sewing a thousand fabric cherry blossoms?"

"Stuck in Miiko Sashiko's atelier? To dream."

Miiko Sashiko won *Project Runway* four years ago. Since then, she has become the golden child of couture, launching her own label and a line of bespoke leather handbags. She even designed the ethereal gown Hailee Steinfeld wore in her "LoveStruck" music video.

Lexi looks over at Cash.

"You don't think it makes me look like a Disney Princess?"

"What's wrong with looking like a Disney Princess?"

Lexi nibbles on her bottom lip and looks down at her feet.

"Lex?"

"Cash said I look like I should be sitting on a parade float, waving at the people on Main Street U.S.A."

"Is that a bad thing?" I scrunch my nose and look at her through narrowed eyes. "Who wouldn't want to be compared to a Disney Princess?"

Lexi laughs.

"Right?"

"Who would you be? If you could be a Disney Princess, which princess would you want to be?" Lexi opens her mouth to speak. "Wait!" I cry, holding up my hand. "Let's answer at the same time. Okay?"

"Okay." She laughs.

"On three?"

She nods.

"One . . . two . . . three."

"Rapunzel!"

Of course. Princess Rapunzel is spirited, social, and loyal. She fills her time with art and music and friends—*and* she has magical blond hair that's always snatch.

We laugh and hug again.

"We both know there's only one reason you chose Rapunzel," I say, pulling a face. "Flynn Rider."

Lexi sighs and looks at me through dreamy, lovesick eyes.

"It's true. Flynn is boyfriend goals."

"Alexandria Armistead, you can't have boyfriend goals. You have a fiancé now."

"Fine," she says, laughing. "The animated hottie is yours."

"Animated hotties are the best," I say. "They're heroic and dependable, and they never break your heart. Put that on a T-shirt."

"That's so *sad*," Lexi says, drawing the last word out. "Don't be sad, Emma Lee. You're going to meet your live-action hottie soon. I just know it. Ooo! Maybe over in England."

"I am not going to England to meet a man, Lex."

"What if he has Kit Harington's hair, Tom Hardy's voice, and Daniel Craig's Bond bod?"

Kristen Carmichael, Savannah Warren, and Madison Van Doren, three of our Kappa Kappa Gamma sisters, join us, and more squealing and hugging ensues.

"Did someone say Daniel Craig?" Kristen asks.

Kristen is working to get her doctorate in Sports Psychology. She's athletic, competitive, a total guys-girl, with a dirty sense of humor and Jennifer Lawrence's beauty.

"I was saying to Ems she might meet her dream man in England. A guy with Kit Harington's hair, Tom Hardy's voice, and Daniel Craig's body, circa *Casino Royale*."

"If we are building our dream man"—Kristen wiggles

her eyebrows, and I know what she is going to say before she says it—"can he have Orlando Bloom's—"

"Kristen Anne Carmichael!" Lexi cries. "Don't you dare finish that sentence."

Kristen has been obsessed with Orlando's *bloom* ever since the paparazzi released pictures of him paddleboarding stark-*nekked*. Orlando Bloom. Nekked as baby Jesus in the manger. I can't unsee that. Ever.

"Don't Kristen me. If Orlando Bloom walked into this courtyard right now and asked you to go paddleboarding with him, you know you would."

"I am engaged. To be married."

Kristen rolls her eyes.

Kristen doesn't believe in matrimony. It's my goal to match her with her forever mate after I have a few more successful matches under my belt.

"Daniel Craig and Tom Hardy disdain politics, but Orlando Bloom works with Global Cool to raise awareness about greenhouse gas emissions," Savannah says, flipping her long, sandy-blond hair off her slender shoulder. "I will keep Orlando, and trade Daniel and Tom for Leonardo DiCaprio."

Savannah Warren looks fragile, like one of the Olsen twins, but she's sharp and scrappy. Her granddaddy was a senator and her daddy created the Warren Institute, one of the most influential think tanks in the country. Not surprisingly, Savannah is passionate about politics, especially equality, climate change, and LGBTQ+ rights. When she gets too preachy, I remind her of the time she got crazy drunk on Irish Car Bombs and created her alter ego, Sugar Bush, George W. Bush's secret illegitimate daughter, who works as a stripper while she puts herself through college. Savannah couldn't dance her way out of a wet paper sack . . . neither could Sugar.

"Enough about Orlando Bloom!" Maddie says, rolling her eyes. "Can we please talk about Cash's brother? A little manscaping and he could join my BOMC."

Madison Van Doren, Maddie, grew up in Greenwich, Connecticut. She's the sixth child of Winston Van Doren IV, heir to the Van Doren chemical and glass fortune. In college, she changed her major more times than her hairstyle. Eastern Asian Art History, Automotive Engineering, Economics, Anthropology. She dated a bunch of random guys and even flirted with lesbianism, which she confessed to me one Wine Wednesday, after *Rosé* and *Real Housewives*. Maddie's living in New York City and working as a barista in a coffee shop/tattoo parlor while she studies international education at NYU.

"BOMC?" Lexi asks.

"Boff of the Month Club." Maddie dips her chin, staring at Lexi through the thick black fringe of her blunt-cut bangs. "A new guy every month for twelve months. No obligations. Keep the ones I like, send the rest back."

"Maddie!" I cry, fanning my flushed cheeks with my hand.

"Madison Rose Van Doren!" Lexi hisses. "You best hush your mouth before my momma hears. Boff of the Month Club!"

Maddie laughs, a wicked little laugh that has me mentally making the sign of the cross for her naughty soul. I swear, *y'all*, Maddie is not a ratchet girl. She's just a little lost. Maddie's mom was the *second* Mrs. Van Doren. Maddie's story is tragically cliché: her billionaire father had been married to his first wife for twenty-five years when he met Maddie's mom, a stunning, five-foot-ten Black Irish model nearly thirty years his junior. Mr. and Mrs. Van Doren (the first) battled it out in divorce court, spending millions in litigation and generating dozens of sensational tabloid headlines. The children from Mr. Van Doren's first marriage, Maddie's half siblings, are successful captains of industry and philanthropy, movers and shakers from Manhattan to Malibu, who look down on Maddie. They consider Maddie to be the unfortunate product of their father's midlife crisis. Maddie's dad is too old to notice. Her mom is too self-involved to care. I swear, it breaks my heart.

"How about it, Ems?" Maddie fixes her bright gaze on me. "Will you introduce me to Cash's brother?"

I look from Maddie to Lexi. Lexi keeps her expression blank, a vacant, I'm-not-involved look in her eyes. What would Patti Stanger, *Millionaire Matchmaker*, do? Patti would advise Maddie to make a nonnegotiable list of the things she absolutely wants in a mate. I am not even sure Maddie knows what she wants in a man (or woman, *just saying*). How could she identify what she wants in a mate when she can't even settle on an identity for herself? One week she's the preppy WASP in summer-weight plaids and J.Crew twinsets; the next week she's Malibu Barbie, saying things like, *Yoga isn't really yoga unless you're wearing Lululemon Wunder Under Crop leggings*. This week, she's Beatnik Bettie writing slam poetry and musing about social injustice. God bless her heart.

"Are you talking about the tall ginger with mutton chops in the gingham shirt and khakis?" Kristen nods her head at the bar. "The one over there, slamming back his fourth Old Fashioned?"

"That's him," Maddie says.

"You don't want to go out with him," Kristen says.

"I don't?" Maddie frowns.

"Nope."

"Why not?"

"Yeah, why not?" I ask, interested.

"I heard him talking to another guest about crabbing."

"So?"

"He said he thought it should be an Olympic sport. Crabbing!" Kristen cries. "I don't care if you're wearing a snapback and your high school football jersey, lifting a crab trap out of the water isn't an athletic competition."

While my friends argue about the physicality required in crabbing, I search the courtyard for a more suitable addition to Maddie's Boff of the Month Club: someone more suitable than Cash's big brother, Chase. Chase Aiken is sweet, but he is dumb as a box of rocks. My daddy used to say, *If that boy had an idea, it would die of loneliness.* I watch him tip the contents of his old-fashioned glass into his mouth, crushed ice, maraschino cherry, orange slice, and all. He notices me watching and flashes a big, old smile, an orange rind where his teeth should be. Sweet baby Jesus and Forrest Gump, too! I can't possibly encourage someone as bright as Maddie to hook up with a man who lives on the special bus. I am not being mean, y'all. Chase lives on a converted school bus parked out behind his granddaddy's house on the Wadmalaw. It literally says Santee Special Education in big block letters on the sides.

I shift my gaze to B. Crav. Beauregard Cravath III— B. Crav to his friends—is a member of Charleston's ancient elite. The Cravaths are an influential political family with roots going clear back to the seventeenth century. B. Crav is an enthusiastic polo player. His Whitney Turn Up is the social event of the polo season, a raucous, Moët-fueled party with a guest list comprised of blue bloods from all over the world. B. Crav has serious connections that stretch far beyond our magnolia-shaded borders . . . He's also a philandering playboy who has tried to bed or wed every woman under thirty from the Mason–

Dixon to the Florida–Georgia line. He would chew my friend up and spit her out.

Hmm. Maybe one of the Barton twins. Truman and Tavish Barton, known around Charleston as *Those Barton Boys*—usually said in an exasperated tone on account of their wild ways—are wealthy, worldly, and definitely eligible. I narrow my gaze and study their carefully coiffed chestnut curls and ubiquitous bow ties. I reckon they're handsome-*ish*. They're also two of my sister's best friends, so . . .

The twins notice me staring and stroll over.

"Hey, dahlin'," Tavish says, giving me a side hug.

"Emma Lee Maxwell, as I live and breathe." Truman drawls out his vowels, letting them roll around on his mouth, savoring each one as if it were a drop of Old Fitzgerald Bourbon. "What's this I hear about you leaving Charleston?"

"That's right," Tavish chimes in. "Tara said you're moving to Hong Kong to write fortunes for a fortune cookie manufacturer."

"Wrong, Brother," Truman says. "Emma Lee is moving to Mars to be a space travel agent . . . or was it Japan to be a panda fluffer?"

"What's a panda fluffer?" Tavish says. "Is that even a job?"

"Oh, it's a job!" Truman cries.

"Pandas are frigid, lazy animals," Maddie deadpans. "Often, pandas in captivity must be induced to mate. The captivity center in Chengdu employs panda handlers who are tasked with introducing virile male pandas to sexually responsive females."

"That's right!" Truman grins at Maddie. "Who are you, dahlin', and why haven't we been introduced?" Truman looks at me through narrowed eyes. "I fear your future as a panda fluffer, Emma Lee Maxwell. What are you waiting for, girl? Introduce this virile panda to your friend."

"Eww." I wrinkle my nose up and shudder like I just caught whiff of something foul. "There are so many things wrong with that vulgar statement, I don't even know where to begin."

"Begin by introducing me to your friend."

Chapter Two

Emma Lee Maxwell's Facebook Update:
According to *Bride Magazine*, December is the most popular month for getting engaged. If you are reading this post **Jackson Harper** you have six months to find a ring and pluck up your courage, boy!

I know what my sister and her friends think: poor, vapid Emma Lee Maxwell. She's Life of the Party Barbie, fashionably dressed in designer heels and Lily Pulitzer dress, swirling from cotillion to Clemson, perpetually surrounded by her sparkly, perky squad. Life of the Party Barbie with an IQ as minuscule as her shoe size, clutching her BA in communications and public relations in one plastic hand and her daddy's credit card in the other. How will she survive without her father's cushy fortune? Is she capable of fashioning an independent life?

My sisters have always loved and supported me, but they thought I was one pink plastic door short of a Dreamhouse when I told them I wanted to move to the Cotswolds to start a matchmaking business. What else can I do?

I don't have a cushy trust fund to fall back on. Before she died, Momma established generous trust funds for both my sisters. Manderley and Tara might not be able to throw down with Paris Hilton, but they'll never know the shame of watching their Lexus be towed away.

Daddy was my trust fund. Daddy provided me with luxuries—luxuries I took for granted, like shopping trips to New York and a shiny convertible Lexus. Daddy provided me with the security that comes from having an encouraging, generous parent.

Was. Provided.

It's difficult to think of Daddy in past-tense terms. I reckon it will always be difficult. When you're not ready to say good-bye to someone, your mind fools you into believing the parting didn't happen. You hear them calling your name, smell the scent of their pipe, catch their reflection in a store window, even though they're gone.

Two months ago, Daddy was sailing off the coast of Sullivan's Island with Aunt Patricia, Momma's sister, when a wave created by a boat passing too close at too high a speed knocked them overboard. I was hosting a pool party to celebrate graduating from Clemson and moving into the guesthouse when the sheriff arrived to inform me of their deaths. Life of the Party Barbie, in her Vitamin A bikini, sipping a blueberry margarita, got a brutal lesson in what life is like in the real world. I would have collapsed right then and there if not for Lexi wrapping her arm around my waist.

A few days later, Daddy's lawyer phoned to tell us Daddy owed a whole mess of back taxes and the IRS was seizing his property. All of it. Black Ash Plantation, the home built by my six times great-granddaddy, the home where I was born and my momma took her last breath.

Daddy's beloved sailboat. My momma's antique writing desk and all her books. Even my Lexus.

Gone. With the wind.

Like Daddy and Aunt Patricia.

I miss my comforts but not nearly as much as I miss my kin.

I'm not gonna lie, y'all. Grief looked mighty ugly on me. I am not a pretty griever, nothing like Demi Moore in *Ghost*. I was not sitting around making pottery and shedding Swarovski crystal tears. I spent a few weeks on Tara's sofa, bingeing on Raising Cane's chicken-and-crap television, missing my daddy something fierce, and fretting about all the time I had wasted letting him baby me when I should have been learning how to Adult.

That's when I had my epiphany. I was eating a three-finger chicken combo meal and watching a documentary about dating. The narrator said 80 percent of *singletons* polled admit they frequently visit bars in hopes of finding a date, even though their chance of meeting their forever mate in a bar is less than 5 percent. A pretty brunette named Bree admitted she has been clubbing three times a week for the last two years but hasn't found a decent guy.

I thought, *What the hell? Doesn't she know the definition of insanity is doing the same thing over and over and expecting a different result?*

The interviewer must have thought the same thing because he asked her why she kept going to clubs in search of love, and do you know what Bree said? She was *comfortable* in the clubs, surrounded by her friends. So, then it cut to a cute hipster guy named Evan, who said all his friends were into online dating, but he wasn't down with meeting a girl in such an *impersonal* way. Which, I thought, was smart of Evan because I read a statistic on

PopSugar's Twitter feed that said online dating site users have a .03 percent chance of finding lasting love (Evan must follow @popsugar, too).

Point zero three percent! That's insane, right?

I felt bad for all those misguided online daters, eagerly clicking Yes and swiping right. And poor Bree, wearing out her Louboutins, dancing with sweaty strangers, hoping for love. She just wants to feel *comfortable* and *connected.*

Single people want to feel comfortable and connected.

That thought kept playing in my head, like a YouTube video on loop. I don't know why, but suddenly I started humming the matchmaker song from *Mulan.* Ohmygod, I thought, I should be a professional matchmaker. I'm good at making people feel comfortable and connected.

If I learned anything from my daddy and my Aunt Patricia, it was to fill my life with passion and purpose. Daddy was passionate about so many things: parenting, sailing, eating biscuits and peach jam, smoking pipes. If Daddy didn't feel passionately about it, he didn't do it. Aunt Patricia was the same way about her travels and the friends she collected along the way, like souvenirs to be treasured. So, right then and there, I opened my MacBook and composed a list of my passions.

Emma Lee Maxwell's Passions:

- Reese Witherspoon (Queen)
- Eating Raising Cane's Chicken
- Clemson (go Tigers!)
- The color red
- My sisters
- My friends

- Making people happy
- Bringing people together

And there it was, my passion and my purpose: bringing people together. Staring at the flickering cursor on my MacBook screen, I suddenly realized what I wanted to do with my new Adult life. I wanted to bring people together. I wanted to help give couples their happy endings—don't be dirty, y'all. I wanted to be a professional matchmaker.

A few days later, I met Isabella Nickerson at B. Crav's Whitney Turn Up, an annual event that allows a mess of blue bloods to sip Moët and pretend to watch Charleston's finest polo players ride around knocking a small wooden ball with a long wooden mallet. It turns out, Miss Isabella went to boarding school with Momma and Aunt Patricia. We got to talking. I told her about my idea to become a professional matchmaker, and she told me about her intention to see her three unwed sons happily married.

If only you lived in England . . .

It turns out, Isabella (and her bachelor sons) live a few kilometers from Wood House, the cottage Aunt Patricia bequeathed to me in her will. Some might look at it as a happy coincidence, but I think it is divine intervention, like Momma and Aunt Patricia are looking out for me, taking over where Daddy left off. I could almost hear their celestial voices whispering, *Go to the Cotswolds, Emma Lee. Live in Wood House and start your career as a matchmaker by finding wives for Isabella's sons.*

Someone touches my arm and I startle.

"Emma Lee?"

Lexi's momma is standing beside me, staring at my

untouched bowl of she-crab soup. I got so tangled up and turned about in a labyrinth of memories, I completely missed the first course of my best friend's engagement dinner.

"Is there something wrong with the soup?" Mrs. Armistead frowns. "It's too heavy, isn't it? I told Alexandria nothing good could come from serving a cream-based soup on a warm spring night, but . . ."

"Are you kidding?" I grab my spoon, dip it into the bowl, and lift the tepid crab soup into my mouth. "Serving she-crab soup at an engagement dinner is positively inspired."

"It is?"

"Sure it is." I rest my spoon on my soup plate, cross my hands neatly on my lap, and smile at my best friend's anxious momma. "Did you know she-crab soup, at least the version we eat here in Charleston, was created by a butler working at the Rutledge House?" She shakes her head and the worry lines marring her otherwise blemish-free face start to fade. "I reckon you already know John Rutledge served in the Continental Congress and was the governor of South Carolina, but I'll bet you didn't know he built Rutledge House as a wedding gift for his bride."

"You don't say?"

"True story!" I shift my gaze across the courtyard to Lexi and Cash and a shiny, buoyant bubble of pride forms inside me. *I introduced my best friend to her soul mate.* "She-crab soup was invented in a house built by love. Knowing that, why wouldn't a bride serve it at her engagement party?"

"Emma Lee Maxwell, you are a veritable treasure!" She laughs and shakes her head. "Honestly, how do you come up with this stuff?"

"My sister, Tara, is a chef. She's got a whole mess of food trivia rattling around in her brain. Don't get her started or she will go on and on about the history of bisques and biscuits and"—I shrug—"I guess some of it must have stuck in my brain, too."

Mrs. Armistead fans her face with her hand. Her upper lip and brow are glistening with dew.

"A chef? Does she have a restaurant here in town?"

"No, ma'am. Tara works at WCSC Channel Five, the CBS-affiliated television station for the Lowcountry. She films news pieces about Charleston's food scene and a weekly cooking segment."

"I knew that." She sighs and resumes fanning her face. "I swear, the stress of planning this wedding is killing what's left of my menopausal brain."

My cheeks flush with heat at the word *menopausal*. Oh. My. God. Dying like Hazel Grace in *The Fault in Our Stars*! Doesn't Mrs. Armistead know Southern women never discuss their nether regions? I swear, my sister Manderley still refers to a man's naughty bits as his *little Elvis*, and my sister Tara calls her you-know-what *Mount Pleasant*, which was mighty confusing to me growing up, because Mount Pleasant is also the name of a town outside Charleston.

Mrs. Armistead squats down beside my chair so she can look me in my mortified eyes. I swear, if she asks me to go and fetch her a box of Estroven for Menopause Relief, I will drown myself in my bowl of she-crab soup.

"When Alexandria said she wanted me to host the engagement party here in Charleston instead of Richmond, I about cried. I didn't know how I was going to make her Antebellum-Splendor-Meets-Enchanted-Garden theme happen from four hundred miles away." She wraps her clammy palm around my arm and gives it a good squeeze. "This evening would have been less enchanting without your help, Emma Lee."

"It was nothing, really."

"Nothing?" Tears fill her eyes. "It was your idea to hold the dinner at the Gadsden House. You suggested the florist and the caterer. Have you thought about being a wedding planner?"

"No."

"Alexandria told me you have your heart set on being a matchmaker, but maybe you should consider being a matchmaker *and* a wedding planner. 'From first date to I do.'"

"You think?"

"Absolutely." She lets go of my arm and stands up. "Now, are you all set to give the toast?"

Toast? A sour taste fills my mouth and I suddenly feel nauseous. The she-crab is crawling around my stomach, looking for a way back out.

"Good heavens," she says, squeezing my arm again. "You've gone green, dear. Are you nervous?"

"I am not nervous."

I graduated from Clemson University (Go Tigers!) with a degree in public relations and communications. Speaking in public doesn't give me she-crab belly. Speaking in public when I'm pretty sure my cue cards are sitting at home beside a half-consumed glass of rosé, now that's a different story.

"You'll be fine, dear."

She pats my cheek and hurries back to her place at the head table. Tavish Barton is watching me from across the table, one corner of his mouth twisted down in a knowing smirk. I plaster a big old smile on my face and try to recall the things I put in my purse. *MAC Viva Glam red lip-*

stick. Hourglass Lippie in Forbidden Apple. NARS Matte Lip Pencil in Dragon Girl. Tin of Altoids. iPhone. Key to Tara's condo. Cab fare. Cue cards?

I lift the cloth napkin off my lap and slowly fold it into a neat rectangle. I am cool as cucumber slices floating in ice water. I am calm, composed, and confident. Standing, I lift my Tyler Ellis Candy Clutch by its slender gold chain, toss the napkin on the seat of my chair, and walk casually across the courtyard, waving and saying "Hey y'all" to various guests. I thank the string quartet for the beautiful music and walk into Gadsden House with the poise of a pageant queen.

"Hey, Emma Lee."

"Good to see you, Emma Lee."

"How you been, girl?"

Sweet Jesus! Why is it when a girl wants to be alone she can't say boo without scaring up an Aiken? My daddy used to say they had more kin than sense. Remembering Chase smiling at me with his orange rind teeth, I'd have to say Daddy was right.

I slip into the empty banquet room and hurry over to the fireplace, my heels tap-tap-tapping on the polished wood floor.

Please, please sweet Jesus, let my cue cards be in my purse.

I sit on the marble hearth, open my purse, and look inside at the tubes of lipstick, tin of mints, iPhone, and house key resting neatly against the red velvet lining.

Oh. My. God. This is not happening.

So. Not. Happening.

I close my eyes and will the cards to be there. *Be there. Be there.* I open my eyes and cry out when I realize the cards have not magically apparated into my purse.

I close my eyes tight. *Think, Emma Lee. Try to remember what was on the cue cards. Think. Think. Think. Think pink ink.*

In my mind, I see my large loopy handwriting scrawled over three-by-five cards in bold pink ink, but I can't see the words. Other than a pink happy-face daisy doodled in the corner of one of the cards, I can't remember anything I wrote.

What would Manderley do?

There's only one woman I admire more than Reese Witherspoon (hail): my big sister, Manderley. She is calm and terribly clever. She was editor of Columbia University's literary magazine. She's brilliant with words. Absolutely brill. She will tell me what to say. I pull my iPhone out of my purse and start clicking.

Text to Manderley Maxwell de Maloret:

I am supposed to give a toast at Lexi's engagement party and I forgot my cue cards. My mind is emptier than a whorehouse on Sunday morning. Help!

I have just enough time to pop an Altoid in my mouth and dab a little Viva Glam on my lips before Manderley's response hits my phone.

Text from Manderley:

People love meet-cute stories. Tell them the meet-cute story.

Text to Manderley:

OMG! You're brill, Mandy! One more thing: what's a haint?

Text from Manderley:
Emma Lee Maxwell! You were born and raised in Charleston. You should know a haint is a ghost.

I told you, my big sister is brilliant.

Chapter Three

"Someone wise told me to start this toast off by telling the meet-cute story." I smile at Lexi and Cash, standing beside their three-tiered engagement cake. "For those of you who don't know, meet-cute is a screenwriting term used to describe a situation that brings two characters together in an entertaining, unusual, and perhaps even cosmically destined way. So, here goes . . ." I pause for dramatic effect. "The first time I saw Lexi, she was holding a big old hypodermic needle."

The guests laugh.

"What?" I scrunch up my nose and look around the courtyard as if confused. "Were y'all expecting a different meet-cute story?"

"I think they meant *our* meet-cute," Cash says.

I wave my hand dismissively, and the guests laugh again.

"We were freshman at Clemson. Lexi was volunteering at the blood drive and I was a donor. She jabbed that big old needle in my arm, and I swear my ears started buzzing, my vision narrowed. I passed out like a preteen at a Taylor Swift concert, y'all. I woke up flat on my back with Lexi arranging my hair and brushing bronzer on my cheeks. I knew then, we were destined to be best friends and soul sisters. I mean, any girl sweet enough to remember to brush bronzer on your face after you've passed out is a keeper, right?"

Laughter ripples around the courtyard.

"That's always been my mantra," Truman cries.

The guests laugh even louder. I smile real big and wait for them to fall silent.

"My daddy used to say"—tears fill my eyes, but I blink them away—"'Emma, darling, beauty is only skin deep, but ugly goes down clean to the bone.' Now that I have reached the wise old age of twenty-four, I disagree with my daddy. Beauty goes clean to the bone, too. I know this because Lexi's bones are about the most beautiful bones a person could have." I reach for my champagne glass, hold it out toward Lexi and Cash, and wait for the guests to raise their glasses. "Sadly, not everyone will find and marry a beautiful person, but you, Cash Aiken, you have found a truly beautiful person, clear down to her bones. I know you will share a long, happy life—just as I knew you would make the perfect couple. So, to Lexi and Cash."

To Lexi and Cash.

Cheers!

The quartet begins playing "Marry You" by Bruno Mars, and the guests rush to hug the happy couple. I drain my champagne glass and join my friends, who are congregating around the makeshift bar.

"That was a fab toast, Ems," Maddie says.

"Did you tell the quartet to play this song?" Kristen asks.

I grin. "Marry You" is one of Lexi's favorite songs.

I was tempted to have them play "Tale As Old As Time," the theme song from *Beauty and the Beast*. Lexi *loves* that movie. She knows the entire film by heart and even sings the "Bonjour" song in all the different voices. After Cash's comment about her dress, I am glad I went with Bruno instead.

"You did all right, girl," Truman says.

"Thanks a mil, Truman."

"Hear, hear," Tavish says, raising his nearly empty champagne glass. "In fact, I think Emma Lee's toast deserves a toast of its own."

I roll my eyes.

"To Emma Lee Maxwell, may your journey to England to be a sheep farmer's mail-order bride go off as seamlessly as this evening," he says, winking at me. "Cheers!"

"Cheers to Emma Lee," Kristen cries.

Someone gasps, and I turn to find Miss Ida Mae Rawlins staring at me with her mouth agape. Her lipstick has bled into the fine wrinkles around her mouth like tiny tributaries off a giant coral-hued lake. Miss Ida Mae was sweet on my daddy way back before he married my momma, but Daddy wasn't sweet on her. The matriarch of the Aiken clan, Miss Virginia, is standing beside Miss Ida Mae.

"Emma Lee Maxwell, is this true?" Miss Virginia asks. "I knew things were difficult since your daddy—"

"—God rest his soul," Miss Ida Mae interjects.

"Amen," Miss Virginia says, hastily making the sign

of the cross. "I heard things were difficult on account of your daddy owing all that money to the IRS, but I had no idea it was this dire."

I shoot Tavish the stink-eye. He gives me one of those highly infuriating Barton boy shit-eating grins and finishes his champagne in a single swallow.

Miss Virginia is president of the God Love Her Club. She's one of those Southern women who believe adding *bless her heart* or *God love her* to negative remarks will make them sound more genteel and compassionate. *She couldn't bake a decent peach cobbler if Paula Deen showed her the way, bless her heart.* She can gossip like all get-out. So, I widen my eyes and play dumb.

"Is what true, Miss Virginia?"

Miss Virginia and Miss Ida Mae exchange looks, and I can almost hear the silent conversation taking place between them.

Go on, ask her.

If I ask her, she will know we were eavesdropping.

We were eavesdropping. Don't be a ninny; ask her.

"We couldn't help overhearing the toast," Miss Ida Mae says, her powdery parchment face staining with color. "Are you moving to England? Truly?"

"Yes, ma'am."

Miss Ida Mae gasps.

"Emma Lee Maxwell," Miss Virginia says. "You are not selling yourself in matrimony to a . . . a . . ."

"Sheep farmer?" Savannah offers.

The two old misses nod their heads.

"She sure is!" Savannah says. "A widowed sheep farmer in Sheffield paid ten thousand dollars and two bags of wool for Emma Lee."

"Ten thousand dollars?" Miss Virginia gasps.

"That's right," Savannah says. "He set up a GoFundMe

and his seven kids went door to door selling their home-
made sheep milk cheese to raise the bride price."

"He wanted her . . . *baaad*."

Maddie bleats the word *bad*, and the Barton boys burst
out laughing. Kristen and Savannah join in, hooting like a
pair of owls.

You know the lemon juice concentrate that comes in
the plastic lemon-shaped container you get in the produce
department? ReaLemon? Well, Miss Virginia looks like
someone spiked her champagne with a whole mess of the
stuff. My daddy used to make lemonade using ReaLemon,
sugar, and water that was so tart, one sip made your lips
all puckery.

Miss Virginia clutches Miss Ida Mae's elbow and
leads her away, muttering something about those Barton
boys and their friends "from off."

From off is local lingo used to describe people who are
not from Charleston, specifically the Charleston Peninsula, where the folks with ancient names and old fortunes
reside. Miss Virginia lives in the Aiken-Winter House, a
three-story Federal on the Battery, which is the oldest and
most exclusive area on the peninsula.

I should be angry at my friends for tweaking the nose
of the doyenne, the grandest dame, of Charleston society,
but I reckon giving hoity-toity Miss Virginia Aiken a hard
time was their way of showing their loyalty.

"Ignore that old crab," Maddie says, grabbing my hand
and lacing her fingers with mine. "Don't let her steal your
light, sunshine."

Maddie is the most sensitive of my Kappa Kappa
Gamma sisters. Growing up the way she did, shunned by
her half siblings, she gets my struggle. She knows how difficult it has been since Daddy passed and the news of his
precarious financial situation was made public. One day,

I was helping organize the Spring Cotillion and planning what I would wear to the Victory Cup; the next, I was standing on the lawn at Black Ash, watching my daddy's belongings auctioned off like junk at a flea market. People I thought were my friends stopped inviting me to their charitable and social events.

That sort of humiliation either scars or shapes a body.

Chapter Four

Emma Lee Maxwell's Facebook Update:
"Someone you haven't met is wondering what it would be like to know someone like you." I saw that on a T-shirt the other day. It's exciting to think the next person you meet might be that special someone, the one who has been looking for you all along, isn't it?

Two months ago, Manderley was working a thankless job in Cannes with no prospects of romance on her horizon. Then she met Xavier de Maloret, a handsome French aristocrat who looks like David Gandy, that gorgeous model in the Dolce & Gabbana ads. Now, my sensible, bookish big sister is a glamourous jet-setter with a crazy hot husband. Isn't that romantic?

I hope Tara meets her someone special soon. My heart aches imagining her here all on her own—without Daddy around, warning her to watch her rebel ways, without me raiding her closet. I thought Grayson Calhoun, her on-again, off-again boyfriend, was going to ask her to marry him, but instead, he popped the question to Maribelle Cravath.

I glance over at my sister, sitting in the driver's seat, her long, toned legs looking fab in white skinny jeans, and my vision blurs with unshed tears. Maybe I am making a mistake. Maybe I shouldn't leave Charleston. I shift my gaze to the new Burberry trench folded in my lap—a generous bon voyage gift from Manderley after I told her Mrs. Nickerson said a proper, classically stylish raincoat is a staple of every British woman's wardrobe—and the clouds of doubt melt away.

I thought my sensible big sister was going to laugh when I told her I was thinking about moving to the Cotswolds so I could live in the cottage our aunt left me in her will. I thought she was going to tell me to stop talking nonsense and waddle about being a matchmaker.

But she didn't.

Go after your dreams, darlin' Emma Lee, she said. *Move to England and become a matchmaker, if that's what you truly want. Tara will be just fine. Daddy would want you to follow your dreams.*

So, I am. Even if that means saying good-bye to the familiar—like the sweet old woman who sells "bald" peanuts out of a cart. Daddy bought me a bag every time I went with him to his favorite barbershop over on Broad Street. After he died, she took to giving me the bag for free. If I close my eyes, I can almost smell the warm, salty husks.

"Did you remember your passport?"

"Yes, Tara."

"What about your iPhone charger? I want you to call me as soon as you land and when you have arrived at Wood House."

"Yes, ma'am."

"And you remembered to make your train reservations from London to the Cotswolds?"

"Mrs. Nickerson said she would send Knightley to pick me up."

"Knightley?"

"Her son."

"That's awfully generous of them."

"Isabella said it was the least she could do for the niece of one of her oldest and dearest friends. Besides, Knightley is some bigwig publisher. Apparently, he splits his time between London and the Cotswolds. So, it's not like it's a big deal for him to let me hitch a ride."

"Even so, be sure to thank him and Mrs. Nickerson."

"Please, Tara," I say, feeling as chastened as I did when Miss Belle told me I put too much sugar in my tea (*as if* you can put too much sugar in tea). "I'm Southern born and raised. I know how to do gratitude. I went to the Candy Kitchen and bought a big old box of pecan pralines for Isabella and a bag of bourbon balls for Knightley."

Tara slows to a stop at the intersection before the entrance to the Charleston International Airport and turns to look at me. I wonder who she sees when she looks at me. The knock-kneed little girl who used to follow her around, always two steps behind? The flighty teenager who forgot to return the clothes/shoes/makeup she borrowed?

I lift my chin and smile. I am not that little girl anymore. I don't need my big sisters chasing me around with a safety net just in case I take a leap too far.

"Are you sure about all this, Emma Lee? When was the last time Aunt Pattycake lived in Wood House? What if it hasn't been cleaned? What if it is infested with vermin? What if—?"

"Don't get your feathers all ruffled up, momma hen," I say, laughing. "Mrs. Nickerson said Aunt Patricia gave her a key to Wood House years ago, so she could look after it while she was away. Mrs. Nickerson sent her maid to clean the cottage and stock the larder, which I assume is a pantry."

When I was a little girl, I struggled in the pronouncing of my aunt's name. I took to calling her Aunt Pattycake instead of Aunt Patricia. My sisters still use the name when they talk to me, as if they are reluctant or incapable of letting me grow up.

Tara turns into the airport and drives slower than molasses. She pulls up to the curb outside the ticketing and check-in terminal and turns on her hazard lights.

"Are you sure you don't want me to come in with you, just in case you have any problems at the ticket counter or with security?" She snatches her press pass and station badge out of the cup holder and fiddles with the lanyard, anxiously weaving it around her fingers. "I don't mind."

"I'll be okay, Tara," I say, holding her hand. "I promise."

She looks at me with teary eyes.

"Are you sure?"

"I am mighty sure." I give her hand a little squeeze. "Are you going to be okay? You seem sad."

Part of me wishes she would break down in tears and beg me not to go, even as another part is itching to get out of the car and head in the direction of my future.

"Don't worry about me. I am just fine."

"You're sure?"

"Now who's being momma hen?"

We laugh. I open the door and climb out. I walk to the back of the car, lift my suitcase out of the trunk, and am waiting on the sidewalk when Tara joins me, holding a big shiny black box.

"Here," she says, handing me the box.

"What's this?"

"A proper going-away present."

I squeal because I know what is inside the big shiny black box with the red bow. The pair of glossy Hunter Wellington rain boots I might have mentioned wanting.

"Ooooo!" I lift one of the boots out of the box. "Military red wellies! How did you know this is the color I wanted?"

"Hmmm, let's see," she says, laughing. "Maybe I saw something on your Instagram, Twitter, or Facebook feeds. Or was it your Pinterest board? Wait! I think I might have figured it out when you changed the screen saver on my computer to a collage of red rain boots."

"You're the best, Tara. The best!"

I kick off my heels, shove them into my carry-on, and slide my feet into the boots. The bright red rubber looks lit as hell with my dark skinny jeans.

"Your Mrs. Nickerson said you needed proper raingear. Well, I couldn't have you showing up at Northam-on-the-Water in your six-inch red suede Louboutins, now could I?"

I laugh and throw my arms around her, squeezing her real hard, as hard as when she let me borrow her J.Crew twinset on my first day of high school.

"I love you more than my Kappa Kappa Gamma ring, Tara."

"Really?" She pulls away, a surprised look on her face. "You love me more than your sorority president's ring? And all it took was a pair of overpriced rain boots? Sweet!"

I smile.

"It's not just the boots," I say, even though there's a big old lump of emotion clogging my throat. "I love you because you are supporting me in my dream to become a matchmaker, even though, deep down, you think it is the silliest idea ever."

"I wouldn't say it's the silliest idea you've ever had," she says, grinning. "Perming your hair the day before your senior prom was a much sillier decision. Shoot! Letting that no-good, faithless, dirty-dog Jake Churchill take your virginity was a sillier decision."

"Tara Faith Maxwell!" I look around to see if anyone heard, my cheeks flushing with heat. "Hush your mouth. A lady never discusses her intimate relations in public. Didn't you learn a thing from Miss Belle?"

Tara rolls her eyes. You know how well-bred Southern girls are raised to be quiet and pleasing? Well, Tara decided early on she would be the opposite of the well-bred Southern lady. In high school, she had a reputation for scandalous behavior. She danced with boys outside her social circle, went to subversive political meetings, and thought for herself. She did just about everything Miss Belle told her students not to do.

"Fiddle-faddle!" Tara says. "Miss Belle was a priggish old dinosaur in polka-dot dresses and pearls."

"God rest her soul," I whisper.

"God rest her raised-pinkie, cucumber-sandwich-eating soul!" Tara laughs. "I hope she's sipping unsweetened tea with Jesus at the big cotillion in the sky."

I imagine Miss Belle correcting St. Margaret's poor posture and chastising St. Paul for wearing a hair shirt, and I can't help but laugh out loud.

Another car pulls up to the curb. The moment when I will have to say good-bye to my sister and walk into the terminal, away from the familiars of my old life, is approaching, and I still have something else to say to her.

"Tara?"

"Yes, Ems?"

"I know you're worried I haven't thought this plan through, that I am oblivious to the practicalities involved in moving to a different country and starting a new business." She opens her mouth, but I hold up my hand to stop her. "*How many lonely singles does Emma Lee think there are in the Cotswolds? What makes her think they will want to hire an amateur matchmaker from America? Did she apply for a work visa? What if the business is a bust? How will she pay the inheritance tax on Aunt Patricia's cottage?*"

"Well," Tara says, smiling, "I might have thought a few of those things."

"Aunt Patricia left just enough money to cover the inheritance tax, so that's settled. I don't know how many singles there are in the Cotswolds and I don't know if they are going to want some strange American meddling in their love matters. Maybe I am crazier than Miley Cyrus on a wrecking ball, but I would rather spend my life saying *oops* than *what if*." I grab her hand and give it a squeeze. "A little voice is whispering at me to take this risk, Tara. Maybe it's God. Maybe it's Aunt Patricia's spirit."

"Sweet Jesus! You're hearing voices?"

I am about to stomp my foot and pitch a big old hissy fit when Tara starts laughing. I stick out my tongue. She laughs harder.

"Stop fretting about my future, you old mother hen, and start fretting about your own!" I grab my carry-on in one hand and my suitcase in the other. "I'm gonna be just fine. You'll see."

"You're sure?"

"I got this one, girl! I got this like Jay-Z's got ninety-nine problems, like Lily Pulitzer's got shift dresses, like—"

"Okay, okay." She laughs. "You've got it, but if you don't get going, you're going to miss it."

"'Bye," I say, raising my hand and blowing her a kiss.

I walk through the sliding doors, rolling my suitcases behind me, my shoulders back and head held high, feeling more confident with each step.

A woman toting a covet-worthy patent leather Lady Dior breezes by me and I suddenly realize I forgot my purse in Tara's car. I turn around and hightail it out of the terminal and, sure enough, Tara is still sitting in her car, staring out the windshield like she knew I would be coming back.

I wrench open the passenger door and duck my head inside the compartment.

"Oh, sweet baby Jesus!" I reach down and lift my purse out of the passenger footwell. "Can you believe I almost forgot my purse?"

Purse. Passport. Tickets. Money. Pretty much every damned thing required for a transatlantic flight. No wonder Tara has been clucking like a mother hen!

"Can I believe you almost forgot your purse?" she says, looking at me over the tops of her sunglasses. "Is that a rhetorical question?"

Chapter Five

Emma Lee Maxwell's Facebook Update:
At JFK International Airport, y'all! Two-hour layover and then I am on my way to London Town! I'll be in the Cotswolds by teatime tomorrow. Get ready Northam-on-the-Water singletons, you're about to meet your match!

I snap a selfie beneath the yellow neon gate sign displaying my flight's information and post it along with my Facebook update, before taking a seat facing the people movers. My Kindle is loaded with reading material—funny rom-coms by Sophie Kinsella and Lindsey Kelk, historical romances by Sophie St. Laurent, a creepy vampire romance by Elle Jasper—and I have the latest *People*, *Vogue*, and *Tatler*, a British magazine that focuses on high society, but I would rather people watch. I like creating love stories for the people I see when I am crowd watching. I imagine where they are going and who they are going to meet. Sometimes, I match a stranger with another stranger and create a story for them. An hour later, I have made two dozen successful matches and imagined all sorts of happy endings (the PG kind, y'all). So, I pull my iPhone out of my pocket and scroll through my notifications and texts.

Text from Madison Van Doren:
I hooked up with that Barton boy after you left the party. It was incredible, but he hasn't returned any of my texts. What should I do?

Text to Madison Van Doren:
My daddy used to say, "A girl should be like a butterfly: pretty to see, but hard to catch." Be a butterfly, Maddie. Make him work to catch you.

Text from Alexandra Armistead:
Thank you. Thank you. Thank you. Everything was perfect last night, Emma Lee! The toast. The food. The fairy lights. Everything, except . . . NM.

Text to Alexandra Armistead:
I don't think so! Don't you try that never-mind business on me, Alexandra Armistead-soon-to-be-Aiken. Except what?

Text from Alexandra Armistead:
You're going to think I am silly, but I'm still a little hurt Cash didn't like my dress. It seems like ever since we got engaged, he's stopped giving me compliments. Tell me I am being a ridiculous, clingy fool.

Text to Alexandra Armistead:
Girl, please! You need to grab him by his ears and shake him like he's a new bottle of OPI nail lacquer.

Southern boys can be as backward as an unbuttered biscuit sometimes. Just tell him how you're feeling, Lex. Smooch.

Text from Savannah Warren:
   Did you know the government funded a study on the impact of marriage on poverty and illness? Turns out married people are wealthier and live healthier. Who knew?

Text from Manderley de Maloret:
   Bon voyage, darling Emma Lee! I am proud of you for having the courage to take this big step.

I snap a selfie with the collar of my Burberry trench flipped up and my lips puckered together and send it to my big sister with a sincere message of gratitude—for her generous gift and her emotional support.

Text from Truman Barton:
   Your girl, Maddie, is hot, but she's gone all Lisa on me, and shit. Can you tell her to chill?

Text to Truman Barton:
   Lisa? The crazy-ass woman who stalked Idris Elba in *Obsessed*?

Text from Truman Barton:
   Yaaas!

Text to Truman Barton:
   So, you don't like her?

Truman texts back to tell me he does, in fact, like Maddie, but she's been blowing up his phone with lovey-dovey messages ever since they hooked up. So, I text Maddie and tell her to stop being a Lisa. She promises she will take my daddy's advice and play hard to get. I suspect that will be mighty difficult because she's already slept with, and stalked, Truman.

I send Tara a text letting her know I am safe and rela-tively sound in the JFK international departures terminal and then send Roberta a mess of pictures I snapped at Lexi's engagement party.

Roberta Hearst—Bertie to her friends—is a Kappa Kappa Gamma big sister; she was in a class ahead of the rest of us. She married her college sweetheart the week after graduation and moved to his hometown, Guyton, Georgia. She's on bed rest because she's pregnant with twins.

"You're a busy young lady."

I was so caught up in my messages, I didn't notice when an older gentleman in a supernatty tweed blazer took the seat next to me. I slide my phone back into my pocket and smile.

"Not too busy to get to know my neighbor," I say, holding out my hand. "I'm Emma Lee Maxwell."

"It's a pleasure to meet you, Emma Lee Maxwell." He has a strong British accent and an even stronger grip. "William Amor, at your service."

"Amor? As in, the Spanish word for love?"

"Yes."

"How romantic!"

"You think?" He laughs. "My ancestor was Robert de Almore, a Breton soldier who fought alongside William the Conqueror. Robert married a Scottish lass named

Fiona, who bore him twelve children. They lived near the village of Aviemore, in the Scottish Highlands. Robert, it seems, was a wee bit of a lothario, though. He was rumored to have fathered more than fifty children with women from local villages and even a nearby convent."

"He sounds like a modern-day Casanova!"

"Quite right." He chuckles. "I suspect the surname was changed from de Almore to Amor because of Robert's numerous romantic peccadillos."

A chime sounds over the loud speaker, and a woman with a posh British accent begins speaking. *Good Afternoon. This announcement is for passengers traveling on flight BA723 to London Heathrow. We will begin boarding in twenty minutes. Please have your boarding pass and passport ready for boarding at gate 75. Thank you.*

I reach into my purse, pull out my boarding pass and passport, and double check my flight number.

"Are you on flight BA723?"

"Yes."

"Headed to London?"

I slip the boarding pass and my passport back into my purse and smile at my inquisitive, nattily dressed friend.

"I am going to the Cotswolds, actually."

"The Cotswolds, you say? Ah, but that is an area of particular charm and beauty, a splendid choice for a holiday."

"I'm not on holiday," I say. "I am moving to Northam-on-the-Water to start a business."

"That sounds rather exciting. What sort of business?"

"Matchmaking."

"Matchmaking? I didn't know young people still used matchmakers. I thought they used Timber."

"Timber?"

"My grandson uses a dating application on his smartphone called Timber. He looks at pictures of potential dates and swipes his finger across the screen to let them know he fancies them."

"Tinder! You're talking about Tinder."

"Tinder? Is that what it's called?" He shakes his head. "Timber. Tinder. It's quite sad, really. I tell Johnny that he can't judge someone's character by glancing at their photograph. To dismiss someone solely because of their appearance, it's a shallow approach to something that is meant to be meaningful."

"Johnny is your grandson?"

"Grandson and bane of my existence." He sighs. "He dropped out of Oxford a few credits shy of a degree in English language and literature because he said music was his true passion. Now, he spends his days helping his friend launch an indie book business and his nights singing in pubs in pants that are too tight and a velvet jacket that is entirely too pink."

"He sounds like my kind of friend."

"Hmmm. Does he, indeed?"

"Sure," I say. "You've described someone who is artistic, passionate, courageous, and loyal. It takes a lot of courage to leave a straight, secure path in pursuit of a passion."

His face softens.

"He is a good lad. He just needs a nice girl like you, to focus him. I don't see a wedding band on your finger," he says, nodding at my hand. "Is there a Mr. Maxwell pining for you somewhere?"

"No." I laugh. "The longest and most affectionate relationship I've had was with my hairstylist: six years and one regretful flirtation with red lowlights."

He chuckles. "Why is that?"

"I have commitment issues."

He laughs.

I laugh, too, even though I'm dead serious. You don't know the mental distress I suffer when I am faced with situations that require dedication to a long-term goal, like dieting or saving money. Shoot, I couldn't commit to raising a stray dog, let alone marrying a man. Kristen, the psych major, said commitment issues have psychological underpinnings, usually caused by a traumatic event or early childhood stress. I reckon losing my momma when I was a baby was the traumatic event, and growing up watching my daddy struggle with his grief was probably the early childhood stress.

"Why don't I give you my grandson's contact information? Maybe you could meet for tea. Who knows, maybe you could even find him a wife." His cheeks flush with color and he clears his throat. "Was that too forward of me? I suppose it was. I suppose a pretty girl like you doesn't need an old man introducing her to his grandson. I am sure you have plenty of friends already."

"Friends are like fabulous shoes, Mr. Amor; you can never have too many."

The chimes sound again and the woman with the posh British accent invites all Executive Club and Business Class passengers to form a queue. Mr. Amor reaches into his suitcoat pocket and removes a pen and small spiral notebook. He opens the notebook, writes on a blank page, and tears the page from the book. Then, he puts the notebook and pen back in his pocket, lifts a leather weekender off the ground, and stands.

"It was a pleasure to meet you, Miss Maxwell," he says, handing me the slip of paper. "Call Johnny, won't you, dear?"

"Definitely."

He shuffles away, taking his place at the back of the queue.

I stick the folded paper in my pocket and grab my carry-on. I can't help but feel Aunt Patricia's hand in my meeting Mr. Amor. Amor. Love! And he has a grandson he wants me to meet and match. *Thanks a mil, Aunt Patty-cake.*

Chapter Six

Emma Lee Maxwell's Facebook Update:
A simple *hey there* could lead to a million things.

Miss Isabella said Knightley would be waiting in the arrivals area just outside customs and immigration. She told me a whole mess about her oldest son. She said he is a bigwig at a publishing company, that he is quiet, bookish, and hardworking. *Knightley*—she said, beaming with pride—*portrays good judgment and high moral character. He is the most sensible and reliable of my sons. All who know him hold him in the highest esteem, despite his occasional lapses of severe judgment and sharpness of tongue.*

On the strength of Miss Isabella's description, I am expecting the adult male version of Hermione Granger, from the *Harry Potter* movies, or Dorky David, the nerdy law student in *Legally Blonde*. The Knightley Nickerson of my imagination is a wiry man with a receding hairline and round glasses with thick lenses.

So, when I breeze through the sliding doors, rolling

my suitcases behind me and clutching a big old box of bourbon balls, I am looking for a man in a wool pinstripe suit and oxfords, toting a walking stick umbrella with a chestnut crook. I scan the throng of people waiting in the arrivals area—an elderly couple, limousine drivers holding handwritten signs, a family wearing matching bright orange T-shirts, a hottie in a leather jacket and Ray Bans leaning against the railing, but no Dorky David.

I maneuver around the crowd and that's when I see him sitting on one of the molded plastic seats: a wiry man in a pinstripe suit holding a smartphone, his gaze fixed on the screen, a grim expression on his pale face. I move closer—close enough to observe him without drawing attention—and notice he is wearing scuffed oxfords and a cheap tie with an oily stain. It appears he hasn't had a decent shave in days, the hair at the top of his head is, indeed, thinning, and are those tobacco stains on his—

He looks up from his phone, notices me staring at him, and smiles. I roll my bags closer, and the stench of stale cigarette smoke assaults my nose. Sweet Patti Stanger and all the cherubs in heaven! Now I know why Miss Isabella enlisted my help in finding her sons suitable mates.

"Knightley Nickerson?"

He stands and stares at me. Not at me, exactly, but in my general direction. Poor wonky-eyed Knightley Nickerson with his scuffed shoes and aroma au cigarette! Finding him a wife won't be easy, but I am determined!

He takes a step closer and then walks right by me.

"Wait!" I say, grabbing his arm. "You're Knightley Nickerson, aren't you?"

Someone standing behind me clears his throat.

"I believe you are looking for me."

I let go of the wonky-eyed faux Knightley and turn around to find a tall, broad-shouldered man in an impeccably tailored three-piece suit of gray Glen check. *This* Knightley is well-groomed, with thick, wavy black hair.

"Shut up!"

His mouth quirks in a brief smile.

I want to die, y'all. Last year, the ground gave away in Greenwood, South Carolina, and formed a big old sinkhole. Why, why can't the ground give away now, so I don't have to stand here staring at gorgeous Knightley Nickerson with my heat-flushed cheeks?

"Sorry," he says, lowering his voice. "Was I too loud?"

"What? No! You're perfect." His lips quirk again and the flush moves down my body, from my cheeks to my shiny red rubber-encased feet. "I mean, your voice was perfect. You weren't too loud." I thrust the box at him. "I'm Emma Lee Maxwell and these are your balls . . . *bourbon balls*! I mean, I brought you a box of bourbon balls to thank you for picking me up from the airport. They're a Charleston specialty."

His eyebrow lifts and it's only then I realize he is holding a Costa coffee cup and a white, waxy paper bag.

"It's a pleasure to meet you, Emma Lee Maxwell," he says, taking the box of candy and handing me the coffee cup and bag. "I thought you might be hungry after your flight. I hope you like orange scones and black coffee."

I take the bag without saying a word because I am too mesmerized by his brownish-green eyes, his thick, fringy black lashes, and the deep timbre of his voice.

"By the by, when you meet my brothers, you might want to open with a handshake and a hello. In England, *shut up* is considered an informal greeting, usually reserved for family or close friends."

He's teasing. Sensible Knightley Nickerson is teasing me, and I am just standing here like Helen Keller at a rock concert. He tucks the candy box under his arm and then reaches around me and lifts my suitcases as if they are paper bags filled with fluffy orange scones. I catch a whiff of his cologne, a woodsy, mossy scent that reminds me of a sun-dappled forest. Sun-dappled forest? Where did that come from? Lexi would just die if she could hear me waxing poetic about Knightley Nickerson's cologne—and eyes, which, coincidentally, also remind me of a forest.

A tendril of steam curls up from the hole in the coffee cup lid and tickles my nose. Coffee. Scones. Airport noise. Snap out of it, Emma Lee, before you make an even bigger fool of yourself. You're in an airport, not a mossy forest.

"Where are my manners?" I raise the coffee cup and paper bag. "Thank you for bringing me breakfast. You're very considerate."

We start walking.

"Considerate?" He chuckles. "Don't tell my mother. She believes I am too obsessed with my career to fuss over niceties, like scones and coffee. She might misinterpret the gesture."

"Misinterpret?"

We follow the signs pointing to short-stay parking.

"I don't mean to frighten you off, Miss Maxwell—"

"—Emma Lee."

"Emma Lee." He clears his throat. "I think my mother has designs for us."

"Designs?"

I look at him with a dazed and bewildered expression, my eyes wide, mouth agape, because Isabella doesn't want him to know she hired me to find him a girlfriend. Knightley, Brandon, and Bingley Nickerson are my first clients—they just don't know it yet.

"I think she is hoping we will fall in love and get married."

"What?" I laugh. "Don't be ridiculous. She hardly knows me."

"Since her return from Charleston, I have heard of nothing but Emma Lee Maxwell." He looks over at me and my stomach does a loop-the-loop, like it did when my high-school boyfriend scored a touchdown at the homecoming game and pointed the football at me. "You have enchanted my mother, Emma Lee, and that is no easy feat."

"Your momma is the kindest person I have ever met," I say. "I am glad she is enchanted with me, because I am enchanted with her."

Returning a compliment with a compliment is a Southern thing, instilled in every little girl before she's old enough to strap on her first pair of Mary Janes and head to Sunday school. Saying I am enchanted with Isabella Nickerson is not one of those reciprocal compliments. I *am* enchanted with her. Not because she knew my momma and has promised to tell me loads of stories about her. Not because she is my first official matchmaking client. She's stylish and sophisticated, but also maternal and motivating. She's the sorta momma I always imagined my momma would have been if she had lived.

We enter a glass skywalk spanning the distance between the airport and a multistory parking garage. I gaze out the window at the leaden sky, the steady drizzle pattering the glass, and say a quiet prayer of thanks for my Burberry trench and shiny red wellies. I peek out of the corner of my eye at Knightley walking beside me. Sweet Jesus! He sure is gorgeous—even in profile.

"You're wrong."

He looks at me.

"I am? About what?"

"Your momma wouldn't be surprised if she found out you brought me coffee and a pastry." I take a sip of the coffee and shiver as the warmth hits my belly. "*Kind* is the first word she used when she described you."

"Is that so?" He raises an eyebrow. "What else did she say about me?"

Hmmm, let's see. Your middle name is Phillip. You're allergic to ginseng. You broke your collarbone playing polo. You're a workaholic. You haven't had a serious girl-friend in four years. You have a flat in Marylebone, but you spend most of your free time at Welldon Abbey, the Nickerson family seat two kilometers from Northam-on-the-Water. You have two wolfhounds you named after characters in your favorite novels.

"Not much."

"Not much?" He chuckles. "I find that rather difficult to believe. Brevity has never been my mother's strong suit."

We exit the skywalk through sliding doors and step into the parking garage. The damp cold slithers and snakes its way up the sleeves of my coat, and the flesh on my arms goes all goose bumpy. Tara tried to talk me out of wearing a sleeveless blouse, but I shushed her because I thought it looked prep with my new trench. Now, I'm wishing I wouldn't have been such a stubborn chick. I should have listened to momma hen and pulled my J.Crew Tippi sweater over my blouse.

"She said you were into competitive archery when you were younger"—I shift the coffee cup and scone bag to one hand, so I can button my coat with the other—"and that you had dreams of going to the Olympics."

I don't repeat the story she told me about the time Knightley was trying to teach his then-girlfriend, Jane

Bleddyn, how to shoot, and Jane accidentally shot one of his dogs, because I got the sense Isabella didn't care for Jane much.

"That's it?" He slants a knowing look my way, his lips curling in a playful smile. "*Have I told you about my son, kindly Knightley? He used to fancy archery. Full stop.*"

I laugh. "I don't think she referred to you as kindly Knightley."

"I suspect the conversation sounded more like, *My first-born, Knightley, is bloody brilliant. He won the spelling bee when he was in primary school, aced his A-levels, and graduated from Oxford with distinction. He is six-foot-three, weighs two hundred pounds, and has an O positive blood type. He is nearly perfect, though he occasionally demonstrates a sharpness of tongue and has an annoying tendency toward officiousness. Oh, and he has two left feet. A complete disaster on the dance floor.*"

I laugh, imagining Knightley, in his bespoke Savile Row suit and starched shirt, trying to Whip and Nae Nae on a dance floor. Deep down, though, I suspect this hand-some bachelor is as smooth on the dance floor as he is in an airport parking lot.

"You laugh," he says, directing me to a sleek navy BMW, "until she drives you to Harrods to register for china and cut-lery. You're not the first woman my mother has attempted to embroil in her thinly veiled matchmaking schemes. If you're not careful, she will have you wed to one of my brothers before the year is out."

"Are you so opposed to marriage?"

He pops the trunk and turns to look at me, his brown-green gaze fixing on my face. "I'm not opposed to mar-riage, just matchmaking schemes. Some things should be organic, don't you think?"

"Hello," I say, thrusting my hand at him. "I'm Emma

Lee Maxwell and I'm a professional matchmaker. Pleased to meet you."

Professional-*ish*.

His lips quirk in a grin.

"My mother told me about your ambition to start a matchmaking business in Northam-on-the-Water. You do realize most of the people living in the Cotswolds are in their late forties and married?" He lifts my suitcases into the hold. "I wish you every success, though I am afraid your pool of potential clients will be quite small."

"Every pool begins with a single droplet," I say, smiling my biggest, brightest Colgate smile. "I am confident I will find a droplet in Northam-on-the-Water."

Or three droplets.

He slams the trunk and looks down at me, his eyes twinkling, his lips curved in a wry smile, like he is an indulgent adult and I am a silly, simple child. I expect him to pat my head and coo hollow praise: *What's that? You want to be a fairy princess and solve the world's problems with pixie dust and strawberry cupcakes? Aren't you a clever girl.*

He doesn't pat my head or coo hollow praise. He nods and steps around me, unlocking the passenger door with a push of his key fob. I can't help but wonder what kindly Knightley, with his Oxford distinctions, thinks of a Clemson grad with aspirations to be the next Patti Stanger, minus the sleazy reality show and gold-digger clients.

He opens the passenger door.

"Knightley?"

"Yes, Emma Lee."

"Is it okay if I call you Knightley?"

"Of course."

"There were a lot of people in the arrivals terminal. How did you know it was me?"

He grins. "Your rubbers."

"My what?"

"Your boots."

I climb into the passenger seat and then look down at my feet, smiling at the light reflecting off my shiny red toes.

"What about my boots?"

"They're awfully shiny, aren't they?"

"They're new."

"And red."

He says it like it's a bad thing.

"What's wrong with red boots?"

"Nothing, if you are the flashy sort."

"I do not need a pair of flashy red boots to get people to notice me, Knightley Nickerson!"

He grins, and my heart does another one of those loop-the-loops. "No, you don't."

He slams the passenger door, leaving me to wonder if wearing flashy red rubbers is a good thing or a bad thing. Great! Mr. Distinction is in my head now. Making me doubt my boots, my move to England, myself.

Chapter Seven

While Knightley maneuvers his BMW through the airport parking lot, I make like Taylor Swift and try to "Shake It Off." Kristen would tell me to focus on my strengths and visualize myself doing them successfully. I close my eyes and mentally see myself in my Clemson cheer uniform. I take a deep breath and do a standing backflip, sticking the landing like a pro (in my head).

'Cuz the haters gonna hate.

If I could stand in Death Valley—Clemson Memorial Stadium, not the *real* Death Valley—and shout cheers to eighty thousand spectators, I can stand a snooty Brit throwing a little shade my way.

I open my eyes and stare out the rain speckled windshield at the people in the parking lot, passengers pulling wheeled suitcases. Gray and black blurs on a drab gray canvas. I squint, peering between the raindrops. There does seem to be a shocking profusion of drab colors. Gray raincoats. Black umbrellas.

I peek out of the corner of my eye at Mr. Distinction, in his gray Glen check suit, his long fingers curled around the gray leather steering wheel.

Flashy.

What's wrong with being a little flashy?

If you want to be heard in the back of the stadium, you better raise your voice, darlin'! Besides, I would rather be a single flashy splash of red than fifty shades of gray.

Thinking of fifty shades of gray makes me think of the movie *Fifty Shades of Grey*, which makes me think about the awkward way I presented Knightley with the bourbon balls, like I was some kind of pervert. *Here are your balls.* Lawdy! Why didn't I think that gift through? When I was standing in the Candy Kitchen, inhaling the addictive scent of chocolate, pralines, and caramel, I didn't imagine a little old box of bourbon balls could make me feel so much shame.

I replay the scene in my head, like a movie, only this time, I imagine the white-gloved ghost of Miss Belle floating between us, practically hear her gasp when I say the word *balls*.

"What made you decide to become a matchmaker?"

I blink until the ghost of Miss Belle disappears.

"There wasn't a big enough demand for fortune cookie writer."

He laughs, and for a moment I forget about the drizzly rain and drab skies. There is only sunshine and warmth and the unexpected joy I feel at making him laugh.

"Seriously," he says, his gaze flicking my way. "Why would a woman with a degree in public relations decide to become a matchmaker?"

"Life is filled with a whole mess of pain. I like the idea

of doing something that brings people pleasure, and I imagine falling in love is the most pleasurable experience ever."

Knightley stops at a traffic light.

"You imagine?" He looks at me, his brown-green eyes sparkling. "Haven't you ever been in love?"

My cheeks flush with heat. A Southern gentleman would notice the color rising on my cheeks and avert his gaze. Knightley is not Southern. He stares at me, a teasing smile tugging the corners of his lips, and prickles of embarrassment make their way up my body.

"Me? In love?" I force a laugh. "I've not met a man worthy enough of my love. I have high expectations, Mr. Nickerson."

"Is that so?" He chuckles. "Care to share them, Miss Maxwell?"

"Them?"

"Your expectations."

The light changes. Knightley shifts the car into gear and we are off, speeding toward a motorway on-ramp.

"Well, let's see," I say, keeping my tone light. "He would have to be tall, muscular, and handsome, with an impeccable wardrobe and impeccable manners. Honest. Charming. Compassionate. Spiritual. Close to his mother, but not in a creepy, codependent way. He should know how to do manly things—"

"Manly things?"

"Shoot a gun, ride a horse, pitch a tent."

"So, you are looking for a cowboy? You do realize you are relocating to the heart of England? I am afraid you won't find too many gunslingers in Northam-on-the-Water."

"Ha, ha," I say, resisting the urge to stick my tongue out at him. "My daddy knew how to do manly things, like change flat tires and fix leaky sinks. Resourcefulness is a manly trait."

"Right, resourcefulness," he says, shifting into a higher gear. "What else?"

"He should be successful."

"Rich, then."

"Do you measure success in dollars?"

"I don't," he says, changing lanes. "Do you?"

"Dollars don't hurt, but if I've learned one thing since my daddy died, it's that wealth is not the most important thing, and it certainly isn't a fair measure of a man."

I look out the window, at the blue directional signs bearing names to strange places, and feel a pang of homesickness, for Charleston, my daddy, my sisters. Knightley clears his throat, and I wonder if my candor has made him uncomfortable. I am about to say something flippant when he covers my hand with his, a compassionate gesture that surprises me as much as it excites me.

"I know about your father's boating accident," he says, pulling his hand away. "I am sorry for your loss."

"Thank you."

"I was at university when my father died," he says, pronouncing university as if it begins with *ew* instead of *u*. "Massive heart attack. Totally unexpected. I couldn't concentrate on my studies, barely finished my exams. I thought I would go barking mad with grief."

"Grief *is* a kind of madness, isn't it? An incomprehensible, all-consuming madness that makes you wail one minute and rage the next."

"Grief is a kind of madness." His deep voice and British accent make the words sound more poetic. "Beautifully expressed, Emma Lee."

I don't know what to do with his compliment, so I pretend I didn't hear him and go right on talking.

"It sure enough made me a lunatic, laying all up on my sister's sofa, eating fried chicken and watching television twenty-four-seven."

An awkward silence fills the compartment. *Sure enough. Laying all up.* First, I dazzle him with my beautifully expressed thoughts on grief and then I go all Southern on him—and not the genteel, finishing-school Southern, but the stereotypical Southern, the kind that drives a rusted-out old Chevy, the kind that goes frog plinking in Stumphole Swamp, the kind that says, *I'm fixin' to dig up some grub, lessen you wanna go to the Cracker Barrel.*

Knightley clears his throat.

"Aren't professional matchmakers usually . . ."

"Toothless crones who live in remote villages and spend their time meddling and gossiping?"

"Toothless?" He laughs. "I was going to say older."

He has a fantastic laugh. Supermodel Tyra Banks coined the neologism smize, which means to smile with your eyes. Well, Knightley laughs with his whole body.

"The top matchmaking company in the United States is owned by four women under thirty-five. In biblical days, a matchmaker was usually the oldest woman in the tribe. The matchmaker, or shadchan, would watch the unmarried women as they gathered around the well and then suggest matches. Today's matchmakers are savvy businesspeople who understand the importance of marketing, communication, and networking. Making a successful match is more than watching women water camels."

"Thank God," he says, chuckling. "Northam-on-the-Water has an abundance of charm, but an appalling dearth of camels."

I laugh.

"My aunt used to tell me wonderful stories about Northam-on-the-Water. The ivy-covered cottages, meandering footpaths, massive weeping willows dragging their limbs in the river, stone bridges. She said it is the Venice of England." I sigh. "I can't wait to see it."

"Northam is a village of outstanding beauty, but it's hardly idyllic. The villagers are reserved, though in no way disagreeable. Most visitors find them to be aloof."

"Pshaw," I say, waving my hand. "A stranger is just a friend you haven't yet met."

"How very American of you," he says, laughing.

"Thank you," I say, smiling. "Don't you worry about me. Meeting new people and making friends is my thing, darlin'. It's what I do best."

"What's your secret?"

I look at him, but he keeps his gaze fixed on the road.

"You're serious?"

"I am."

"My daddy gave me a brilliant piece of advice on my first day of elementary school. He said, 'Emma, darlin', be somebody who makes everybody feel like somebody.'" I shrug. "It's that simple."

"Your father sounds like he was a wise man."

"He was."

A silence stretches between us as my thoughts drift back to that day, standing beneath a magnolia tree outside Rutledge Hall, clutching Daddy's hand, listening to the melodic roll of his voice as he greeted the other parents by name. He had such a sweet, easy way about him. I remember thinking I wanted to be just like my daddy, sweet and easy, attracting friends like ants at a barbecue. I wanted people to say, *That Emma Lee Maxwell, she's more pleasing than a peach.*

"Isabella said you work in publishing. I imagine you meet loads of fascinating people in your line of work.

Writers, photographers, illustrators," I say, breaking the silence. "How glam!"

He quirks a brow. "Glam?"

"Glamorous."

He chuckles.

"Running a large publishing company is not glamorous, I assure you."

"Chatting up famous authors at book launches and swanky cocktail parties. That sounds very glamorous."

"Managing a team of publishing professionals can be more drudge than glamour, but helping authors bring their stories to a worldwide audience is vastly rewarding, and, occasionally, though not as often as I would like, a brilliant writer is discovered languishing at the bottom of the slush pile. Those undiscovered writers, the excitement and gratitude they feel when offered a publishing contract, before success has stripped them of their humility and passion for the craft"—he smiles and his eyes sparkle—"having the opportunity to discover those writers means more to me than attending glam cocktail parties."

"You help people realize their dreams."

He looks at me, smiling, and my throat goes dry. I haven't been on a date in six months. I am a little thirsty and Knightley Nickerson is one tall drink of water, y'all.

"I crush people's dreams, too," he says, looking back at the road. "We reject ninety-six percent of the manuscripts we receive."

"Let's not focus on that part. Tell me about the last brilliant writer you discovered."

"What would you like to know?"

"Was the writer a he or a she?"

"He."

"Fiction or nonfiction?"

"Fiction."

"What was the book about?"

"It was set during the French Revolution—"

"—Ooo, dark and morbid. Go on."

"A clairvoyant orphan girl living in a convent in Paris is able to communicate with the dead and uses her ability to save people from the guillotine."

"*The Foundlings*?" I look at him, eyes wide, mouth agape. "You discovered Griffin Hayes? Languishing in your slush puddle?"

"Pile." He laughs. "Would you believe he submitted *The Foundlings* to dozens of publishers before sending it to Nickerson Publishing? He said we were his stretch publisher."

"Stretch publisher?"

"He said we were a long shot because he felt his manuscript wasn't highbrow enough for our house."

"Are you publishing Tolstoy's lost manuscripts?"

"No."

"*The Foundlings* is a brilliant novel."

"You've read it, then?"

"Are you kidding?" I don't tell him I didn't make it past the second chapter. "Everyone has read it. Manderley read it from cover to cover, twice."

"Manderley?"

"My sister. She graduated from Columbia. She works in Hollywood, as an assistant to an award-winning screenwriter, even though we keep telling her she should be writing her own screenplays because she is crazy brilliant." Knightley Nickerson discovered Griffin Hayes. *The* Griffin Hayes. "Wait until I tell her you fished *The Foundlings* out of your slush puddle. She'll be pea green with envy!"

He laughs again.

"Tell your sister there will be more *Foundlings* books.

Griffin sent us the second book in the series after we offered him a contract."

"I didn't know it was a series."

"Nobody knows. We've kept news of the second book hush-hush, but we are sending out press releases tomorrow."

"So, this is insider information?"

"Yes."

"Ooo!" I rub my hands together. "I love insider information. Can I tell Manderley now?"

He chuckles. "Yes."

"Yay!" I clap. "Thank you."

I pull my phone out of my purse and hurriedly type a text to Manderley, my nails tap-tap-tapping the screen. Her response is immediate.

"She says she is pea green with envy." I look at him and grin. "Told you." My phone blings with another text. "She wants to know if there are more orphans at the convent who have special gifts, because she thinks Jacques might be clairvoyant, too."

"Sorry," he says, shaking his head. "I can't divulge details about characters or plot, but tell your sister her observation is rather astute."

I like the way he pronounces *rather*, replacing the flat A with an AW. *Rawther*. It's so posh, so British.

I send the text, slip my phone back into my purse, and look out the window. At some point during our conversation, Knightley pulled off the congested motorway and onto a narrow rural road lined on one side by thick, gnarly hedges. We are surrounded by rolling farmland, great patches of green stitched together like a quilt and spread as far as the eye can see. A thinning fog has settled at the bottom of the hills, and through it, I notice the ghostly silhouettes of spindly trees and the occasional thatched cottage, looking lost and forlorn in the vast landscape.

Charleston is hardly the big city, but this is straight-up country, y'all. Cow-milking, chicken-feeding, in-bed-by-sundown country. I am so glad I packed extra lip liner because I won't be popping into Sephora for refills. I'll bet the closest mall is two hours to the east, in London. Mall. Theater. Sit-down restaurant. No wonder more than 50 percent of Cotswoldians (Cotswoldites?) are single! There's nowhere for them to hook up. They need a matchmaker. They *need* me!

We come to a crossroads. I notice a wooden post with half a dozen signs pointing in all directions and read the strange names printed on them. "Lower Slaughter." "Little Rissington." "Clapton-on-the-Hill."

"'Nether Westcote,'" I say, reading a sign pointing in the opposite direction. "Doesn't that sound like the name of a character in a children's book? 'Nether Westcote's remarkable adventure began on the road to Little Slaughter.'"

"Hold on," he says, looking at me through narrowed eyes. "I thought you said your sister was the writer? It sounds to me as if you have literary leanings as well. Are you the Charlotte to her Emily?"

"Charlotte?"

"Brontë."

"Brontë. Right." Heat flushes my cheeks. "I am definitely not a Brontë."

"More of a reader than a writer?"

What do I say, y'all? Mr. Oxford, in his bespoke Savile Row suit, is looking at me with those soulful brown-green eyes, asking me if I like to read . . . *books*! Do I tell him the truth? That I haven't read a book since college because I have the attention span of a golden retriever in a yard full of squirrels? Do I admit I've never read a Brontë?

I don't do phony. Never have.

"Honestly? I don't read as much as I should."

Unless *InStyle* and *Cosmo* count as literature.

"What's the last thing you read?"

"'The Perfect Date.'"

"Mass-market fiction?"

"Excuse me?"

"Is *The Perfect Date* a paperback novel?"

"No," I say, laughing. "It's an article on PopSugar Love."

He glances over at me, his brows knit together.

"The website?"

"Yep."

I am suddenly and painfully ashamed of my literary ignorance. I should have read *The Foundlings* instead of using it as a coaster for my sweet tea.

"I meant book."

"Oh," I say, fanning my cheeks with my hand.

"Do you have a favorite genre?"

Nineteenth-century feminist poetry? Narrative nonfiction?

"Chick lit."

"Chick lit? Really?"

"What can I say?" I shrug my shoulders. "I like happy endings."

Knightley clears his throat, and I suddenly realize my inadvertent double entendre. I might not have had many boyfriends, but I hung around enough frat boys in college to know what *happy endings* means in street slang. Then again, Knightley Nickerson seems far too mature, too educated, to snicker at sophomoric street slang.

"Charlotte Brontë is, perhaps, a trifle too maudlin for you, then. I suspect you're more of an Austenite."

Heat flushes my cheeks again. I might be the only woman on the planet not to have read a Jane Austen novel. I look out the window before Knightley, the big-time publisher, reads the shame written all over my face.

"My mother is a rabid Austenite, hence my name."

Knightley? I don't remember a character named Knightley in *Pride and Prejudice*. Lexi downloaded a pi-rated version our sophomore year at Clemson because we had to write a two-thousand-word essay for lit class and had put it off until the day before it was due. I spent the whole seventy minutes focusing on Keira's bushy brows and unruly split ends. Why, sweet Jesus, why didn't someone on set think to spray an anti-frizz product in her hair?

"Knightley is her favorite Austen hero?"

Please God, don't let Knightley be the name of some fictitious village in one of Jane Austen's novels. Let it be a character. If you let it be a hero, I swear I'll read every night before bed—a book, not pop-culture blogs or fash-ion mags.

"George Knightley is, indeed, her favorite Austen hero."

Thank you, God!

"Why is he her favorite?"

"You will have to ask her. Be warned, though, if you show the slightest interest in *Emma* she will force you to join her All Austen Book Club."

Emma! So, Knightley is the hero in *Emma*. I make a mental note to download *Emma* to my Kindle. It might give me some insight into Mr. Oxford and his Austen-loving momma. And if I am going to successfully match Knightley with his perfect mate, I am going to need all the insight I can get!

Chapter Eight

Emma Lee Maxwell's Facebook Update:
Finding your soul mate is like shopping for a pair of jeans. Sometimes, it takes several tries before you find the right fit.

Northam-on-the-Water is as picturesque as I imagined it would be. It reminds me of the village in *Grantchester*, the PBS show about the sexy, jazz-loving vicar who solves murders. I caught pneumonia my senior year at Clemson. Manderley flew in and played momma hen. We sat around her hotel room in our jammies, eating cartons of Panera chicken noodle soup and watching *Grantchester*. Cozy mysteries aren't my thing—because I thought they were for people who knit potholders in their free time, eat at four in the afternoon, and fall asleep on the *davenport* watching their programs, but I'll admit *Grantchester* hooked me. The charming setting, the sexy crime-solving vicar—or maybe it was the NyQuil. Whatever, it brought out my inner senior citizen for a weekend and inspired a newfound respect for cozies.

We are driving down Northam-on-the-Water's main street, confusingly named High Street. Confusing because it is not the highest street in the village. Northam-on-the-Water is situated in a narrow valley nestled between two hills. High Street straddles the river that divides the village into two sections. Most of the village appears to be clinging to the hillsides, making High Street the low street.

Although I would hardly call it a bustling metropolis, Northam is larger than I expected, with dozens of shops and businesses situated in honey-colored stone buildings lining both sides of the river. Stone footbridges allow shoppers to cross from one side to the other. There is a tea room, Call Me Darjeeling, with a striped awning and lacy white curtains hanging in the windows, a small supermarket, a bakery, and a woolen mill. The pharmacy has an old-time wooden sign hanging over its door, "Curtis and Sons Apothecary" painted in loopy script. There is a restaurant called the Millhouse, with a working waterwheel, and an inn named Midsummer's Dream. Knightley stops at a traffic light outside a shop with an old-time glass storefront and a painted wooden sign affixed over the door. A silhouette of Queen Victoria's profile is painted on the sign.

"'Victoria's Candy Emporium,'" I say, reading the sign. "'First in Candy and Colonialism.'"

"Irreverent, isn't it?"

I giggle. "A bit."

"Deidre Waites can be rather irreverent, particularly when it comes to her love/hate relationship with Queen Victoria. She inherited the shop after her father died and her mum began losing her vision. She changed the name a year ago. She's quite brilliant, actually, and extremely unusual. She belongs to my mum's book club."

"I like irreverent and unusual people."

"She will be at the dinner party."

"Dinner party?"

"Didn't my mother tell you?" He chuckles and shakes his head. "She organized a small gathering tonight to introduce you to the villagers."

"Ooo! That sounds like fun."

He looks at me, eyebrow raised.

"Does it?"

"I love parties," I say, smiling. "Don't you?"

"As long as they're not too big or boisterous."

"Can a party ever be too big?" I look at him, wrinkling my nose. "I don't think so."

He laughs. "Now I see why my mother loves you. You're kindred spirits."

"Thank you," I say sincerely. "That's the kindest thing you've said to me."

My relationship with Isabella Nickerson began at a polo match and has grown through numerous phone calls and emails. Besides being warm, witty, and worldly, she is incredibly empowering, encouraging me to pursue my dreams. I understand why my momma and my Aunt Patricia chose her as their friend—I would have chosen her as a friend if we had gone to school together.

I look through the picture window, into the store, hoping to catch a glimpse of the irreverent and unusual Miss Waites but see only shelves of glass jars filled with colorful jawbreakers, glossy black licorice wheels, and candy-cane-striped peppermint balls.

An elderly couple cross the street, waving to Knightley when they recognize him in the car. They are each holding multiple leashes, a pack of West Highland terriers at their heels.

"The Swinbrooks," Knightley says. "They have a farm just outside the village where they breed champion West Highland terriers. Do you like dogs?"

"I've never had a dog."

He looks at me as if I said I was related to the Kardashians—shocked and a bit horrified.

"Is that true?"

"Yes."

"Tragic, that."

I am about to protest at his melodramatic choice of words when I remember something James Corden said in *Very British Problems*, a series on Netflix about British culture. Corden said his countrymen care for their dogs more than people. I assumed he was joking—I mean, he *is* a comedian. Now, I wonder. The crosswalk clears of people and pets, the light finally changes, Knightley shifts his car into gear, and we continue down High Street, past a clinic and a child care center.

A church with a brick turret and steeple stands at the end of High Street, flanked by a cemetery and neatly clipped green space, with a war memorial and wooden benches. It looks like a scene from an episode of *Grantchester*. As if on cue, the church door opens and a man in a black suit and a stiff white collar steps out.

"A vicar!"

"Vicar Ethan Parsons," Knightley says. "You will meet him tonight."

"This *is* just like *Grantchester*."

Knightley chuckles. "Ethan Parsons is no Sidney Chambers. He spends his free time in the garden cultivating his roses, not solving murders in smoky jazz clubs."

"You've watched *Grantchester*?"

I would not have pegged Knightley Nickerson, with

his bespoke suits and swanky London cocktail parties, as someone who watched cozy mysteries on *Masterpiece*.

"I've read *The Grantchester Mysteries* by James Runcie, the series the program is based on."

"Of course."

Books. Of course. I make a mental note to download *The Grantchester Mysteries* and Charlotte Brontë's novels. I hear Manderley's scolding voice in my head: *Lord knows you are smart, Emma Lee, but when it comes to literature, you are intellectually starved, practically anorexic. Consume something!*

Knightley turns right at the end of High Street, drives over a bridge spanning the river, and makes the first left after the shops, turning on a quiet residential road running parallel to the river. We pass a row of stone duplexes with glossy black-painted doors and flower boxes at each window and then single, detached cottages. Knightley pulls onto a gravel driveway—the last driveway before the road ends.

"Here we are," he says, switching off the engine. "Welcome home, Emma Lee."

I look out the window at the thatched-roof cottage.

"Are you sure this is my aunt's house?"

"Yes. Why?"

"It's stone. I always imagined it would be wood. Why else would it be called Wood House?"

Knightley's lips quirk. "I believe the cottage is named after the man who built it, Alistair Wood. Though your aunt was rather fond of Jane Austen's novels, something she shared in common with my mum, so perhaps Wood House is named after Emma Woodhouse."

My cheeks flush with heat and I make another mental note: download a book about the history of Northam-on-the-Water.

"Of course."

We climb out of the car. Knightley lifts my suitcases out of his trunk and I follow him down the drive until we reach a gravel path leading to a low stone wall with a wooden gate. I unlatch the gate and push it open.

Winter Hastings, the lawyer who handled the execution of my aunt's will, said the man living next door maintained the keys to her cottage and acted as caretaker in her absence. Isabella offered to pick up the keys and give them to Knightley because she said my aunt's neighbor doesn't like people visiting his home. *He's a massive germophobe, actually.* There is supposed to be a key to an old Jaguar stored in the garage, though Winter Hastings warned it might not be operable.

Knightley puts my suitcases down on the front step and fishes a ring of keys out of his inner suit-coat pocket.

"The keys to your castle, milady," he says, handing me the ring. "I hope you will be very happy here."

"Thank you, kind sir," I say, taking the keys.

I try not to react when his fingers touch mine, but my hand shakes as I slide the key into the lock of the heavy, scarred wooden door. I fumble with the key for several seconds, turning it to the left and right and left again, before I hear the tumblers turn. I pull the key out of the lock, lift the iron handle, push the door open. The powdery, perfumed scent of fresh-cut roses greets me as soon as I step through the door, and I notice a crystal vase filled with flowers on a table in the foyer. A small card is sticking out of the flowers. I step closer and read the welcome message scrawled on it in Isabella's neat hand.

"Your mother left me flowers," I say, pressing my nose into one of the blooms. "She's so thoughtful."

"She is excited you are here," Knightley says, depositing my suitcases in the foyer. "She asked me to tell you she had someone stock the refrigerator and make the house ready for your arrival, but if you need anything, just ring her."

"Thank you."

There is an awkward pause as we stand in the quiet cottage, trying to determine the best way to say good-bye. Do we hug? Kiss cheeks? Shake hands? Slap each other on the backs?

"Right," Knightley says, clearing his throat. "Would you like me to start a fire for you before I go?"

I look over my shoulder, at the fireplace in the living room, imagine Knightley Nickerson on his knees in his beautiful suit, arranging logs.

"I'm good," I say, even though the damp cold has seeped down straight to my bones. "Thank you, though."

"I will be back to pick you up tonight, around six."

"Six. Fab."

He turns and walks out the door. Just like that. No cheek kissing or hand shaking. Not even a slap on the back.

I close the door and count to three before running over to the window. I stare out the small rectangular panes of glass, watching as Knightley Nickerson strides down the path, his dark head held at a proud angle, the muscles of his broad shoulders visible beneath the checked fabric of his expensive suit.

If he looks back at the cottage, it means he likes me.

I hold my breath and count his strides.

One. Two. Three. Four. Five.

He is going to look back.

He walks down the path and through the open gate.

He doesn't look back. He doesn't like me.

I let out my breath in one loud, violent exhalation. I am about to step away from the window when Knightley stops, turns around, and looks back at the cottage. At the window. Where I am standing, gawking like a lovesick schoolgirl. It happens so fast, I don't have time to move away.

He doesn't know I am standing at the window. How could he know? It's not like he can see me. The window is very small and the room is dark.

Knightley smiles.

Oh my god! He sees me! He sees me creeping at the window, like some weird, thirsty creeper.

Great! This is the second time I have humiliated myself in front of Knightley-flipping-Nickerson and it's only been three hours since he picked me up at Heathrow. Wait! Make that three times. First, he catches me accosting some strange man. Then, I thrust a box of candy at him while referencing his genitalia. Now, he catches me creeping on him. He must think I am a nasty girl, a thirsty, nasty, red-rubber-boot-wearing creeper of a girl.

I should be embarrassed, but all I can think is, *He likes me. Knightley Nickerson likes me.*

Chapter Nine

Emma Lee Maxwell's Facebook Update:
Did you know when two people are in love and stare into each other's eyes, their heartbeats synch? Isn't that romantic? Sigh.

Once Knightley climbs into his car and backs out of the driveway, I collapse onto the overstuffed velvet sofa, kick off my boots, and take in the living room. The focal point of the room is the fireplace, made of honey-colored stone with a wood mantel stained the same color as the dark, rough-hewn beams crisscrossing the ceiling. The fireplace is flanked by floor-to-ceiling built-ins, the shelves loaded with leather-bound books and framed photographs, grainy black-and-white shots that illustrate my aunt's colorful life. Besides the velvet sofa, there are two armchairs, a pair of antique Chippendale side tables, and a large, tufted ottoman serving as a coffee table. A stack of glossy coffee-table books is arranged atop the ottoman, along with a silver tray and a porcelain tea set. The scarred wooden floor is covered with a thick Persian rug. Oil paintings in tarnished gilt wood frames hang on the walls, portraits of people long dead, a pinch-faced elderly man in a periwig, a pretty girl in a starched Elizabethan ruff, and a dashing soldier in uniform, his hand resting on the hilt of his sword.

The room is chic without being pretentious, which is how I would have described my aunt. Cultivated, but warm and welcoming. Sitting in this room, surrounded by her belongings, makes me feel happy. In her will, Aunt Patricia asked us not to waste time weeping at her passing. *Instead*, she wrote, *remember the joy I brought to your lives and pay it forward by bringing joy into the lives of others. That should be my legacy, and yours.* My sisters cried when Mr. Hastings read those words. I didn't. Aunt Patricia's words, her simple, selfless directive, freed my heart from the heavy burden of grief. Be happy. Be light. Lawd knows I miss my aunt and my daddy, but they would not have wanted me to sit around shredding Kleenex. They would have wanted me to get outta myself, think of others. So that's what I have been trying to do.

I wander around the cottage, checking in each room, opening every wardrobe. It might sound silly, but I have never lived by myself and I'm a little weirded out. I went from living with my daddy to living in the sorority house to living with my sister.

I open the door at the top of the stairs, expecting to find a master suite decorated in the same sophisticated style as the living room, but that is not what I find. Not even close. To say my aunt went in a different direction with the décor of her bedroom would be like saying Kylie Jenner has had a little plastic surgery. Huge understatement. Huge. The bones of the room are the same—wooden floor, exposed beam ceiling, low, multipaned windows—but the plastic surgery has rendered it a completely differ-

ent creature. Just as Kylie didn't know when to stop with
the lip injections, my aunt didn't know when to stop with
the florals. Floral wallpaper, floral drapes, floral bed-
spreads, a profusion of frilly floral pillows. It's like an
English country garden vomited all over the room. I like
girly girl. I *do* girly girl. But the frenzy of floral might be
too much frill even for me. Also, there are two twin
canopy beds instead of one large queen. Odd choice for a
master. So, I close the door and continue my exploration
of the second floor in search of the main bedroom. I find
a cozy sitting room with a flat-screen television hung over
a small fireplace and two more bedrooms, decorated with
the same amount of girly-girl enthusiasm, one in chintz,
the other in powdery-pink toile. All the bedrooms contain
twin beds. It's like a sorority house for shabby but seriously chic sisters. I wish I had a few sisters to share my
cottage. It's a little lonely—and spooky—up here all by
myself.

I head back downstairs, determined to start a fire that
will chase away the cold and make the empty house feel
more like home. Several minutes—and books of matches—
later and I've only managed to coax a wispy flame from the
mound of wadded up newspaper, kindling, and logs.

I stand up and brush the newsprint and ash from my
hands.

"Fires are highly overrated anyway," I say aloud, tossing the empty matchbook onto the ottoman. "What I need
is a good cup of tea."

The kitchen turns out to be one of the coziest, most
inviting rooms in the house, with a low, exposed-beam
ceiling and an old stone floor. There is a long rectangular
table and upholstered parson's chairs, and an antique cabinet filled with delicate bone china patterned with birds
perched on branches. The cabinets are painted robin's egg

blue and there's an iron stove, also painted robin's egg blue. If Martha Stewart bought a cottage in the Cotswolds, her kitchen would probably look like this one.

I pad over to the refrigerator and look at all the goodies Isabella left—a wedge of Somerset cheddar cheese, a bowl of pears that appear as if they were just plucked off their branches, a whole roasted chicken, a jar of clotted cream, all the fixings for a salad, a bag of artisan pasta, plump, juicy tomatoes . . . A cake plate sits on the counter beside the refrigerator, a tower of lemon-zested scones artfully arranged under the glass dome. There's a basket filled with a variety of teas, a jar of honey, a cellophane bag of lumpy demerara sugar cubes, a jar of Nutella, and a loaf of rustic bread.

I find a teakettle in a cabinet, fill it with water, and carry it to the stove. Only the stove isn't like any stove I've ever seen. There are no dials.

I set the kettle on top of the stove and pad back into the living room, pull my iPhone out of my purse, and snap a picture of the stove. My sister Tara is a chef. She knows how to make a gourmet meal on a campfire. True story: she made tender belly pork braised in sriracha and ale in the Memorial Stadium parking lot using only a camp stove. It was the best meal my sorority sisters and cheer squad ever had at a tailgate.

Text to Tara Maxwell:
OMG! Look at this stove. It's ancient. Isabella said Northam-on-the-Water dates to the Roman Age. I think this stove is from that era. What do I do to make it work? Pray to Vulcan, god of fire?

It's still early in Charleston, but Tara will be up. Her job as a food features reporter for WCSC, the Lowcountry's news leader, requires her to wake up before the crack of dawn. While I wait for her response, I send a group text to Kristin and Maddie. Kristin talked Maddie into joining her in a thirty-day squat challenge. Yesterday was day one.

Text from Madison Van Doren:
If my thighs are going to ache this bad, it should be from doing something more enjoyable, like . . . Liam Hemsworth.

Text from Kristin Carmichael:
Liam Hemsworth? Really?

Text to Kristin Carmichael, Madison Van Doren:
What's wrong with Liam?

Text from Kristin Carmichael:
I've heard Aussie guys aren't very big . . . you know . . . Down Under.

Text from Madison Van Doren:
Whatev. I'll take Liam.

Text from Kristin Carmichael:
. . . and I will take Orlando Bloom. Thank you very much.

Text to Kristin Carmichael, Madison Van Doren:
GTG. Happy squatting!

Text from Kristin Carmichael:
650 by the end of the month!

My phone rings. It's Tara. "Hello?"

"That's an Aga, you dork."

"What's an Aga?"

"The stove." She laughs. "It's an oil-operated stove and it is very expensive."

"So it's not a Roman relic?"

"No."

"There are no buttons or dial thingies. Do you know how to start it?"

"Yes, and I am pretty sure it doesn't involve praying to the god of fire."

I pad back into the kitchen. There are four square doors on the front of the stove. Tara tells me to open the top left door and then rattles off the instructions for lighting Aunt Patricia's Roman stove, six steps that involve opening oil pipe valves and lighting a wick with a match.

"Are you sure I'm supposed to use a match? I thought you weren't supposed to light a match around gas."

"It's oil, not gas."

"If this Roman stove explodes and I burn to death, I will not be waiting for you in the light. I mean it. Do not look for me in heaven."

"You'll be fine. Just follow my instructions."

I switch to speakerphone and stare skeptically at the stove.

"Do you remember what I told you about the Kappa Kappa Gamma charity barbecue, when Kristin put too much charcoal fluid on the coals and fried her eyelashes and eyebrows clean off her face? I'm not gonna lie, Tara, she looked freakish. Like an alien. It took months for them to grow back."

"Are there any open containers of charcoal fluid sitting around the cottage?"

I look around.

"No."

"Then you'll be fine."

With Tara listening on the line, I pretend to go through the steps for lighting the stove. I pretend to open the oil valves and flip a switch on the electrical control box. I pretend to turn a dial thingie and push a clickie button.

"Now, you have to wait for the oil to reach the burner," Tara says. "Give it about fifteen minutes, open the flap on the burner, and light the wick with a match."

"That's it?"

"That's it," Tara says.

"Easy-peasy."

"Lemon squeezy!" Tara chirps. "Gotta go. Text if you need the instructions again . . . or if you want me to order you an eyebrow pencil and some falsies from Sephora."

"Ha ha."

"Bye."

"Kisses."

I hang up and bend over, looking at the reflection of my eyebrows in the shiny copper teakettle. It has taken me years of dedicated plucking to achieve the perfect arch. Don't laugh. Brow shaping is a delicate art. Over-enthusiastic plucking at the ends results in stunted, comma-shaped brows, under the arches results in angry brow. Lord knows I love me some Michelle Obama, but the former FLOTUS was working some serious angry brows during the 2008 election season, harsh upside-down Vs that gave her a perpetual scowl.

"Sorry, Earl Grey, you might be hot, but you are not worth the risk," I say, carrying the teakettle to the sink and pouring out the water. "Brows over brews, baby."

I know! I will go to that cute little tea shop on High

Street. A brisk walk in the rain. A chance to shake off the jet lag and test out my new wellies. The perfect opportunity to mix and mingle with my neighbors, meet my future besties.

Half an hour later, I am standing in a long line outside Call Me Darjeeling. A popular tour bus company stops in Northam-on-the-Water for their midday break, and the teahouse is at the top of their must-visit list. I chat with the tour guide while waiting for my table, and she tells me the best place in the Cotswolds to get a trim and highlights (Llewelyn James in Cheltenham), who makes the tastiest curry takeout (Goopta Goopta in Moreton-on-Marsh), and where to spot celebs (the Swan in Southrop, a posh country pub that serves locally sourced delicacies like potted pheasant and mutton leg with Jerusalem artichokes).

Jamie Dornan lives in Charlford, near Stroud. Princess Anne and her daughter, Prince Harry's fab and fashionable cousin, Zara Phillips, live in Tetbury.

"I didn't realize the Cotswolds attracted celebrities."

"Loads of them," she says. "Liz Hurley. Richard E. Grant. Patrick Stewart. Hugh Grant. Kate Moss. Kate Winslet."

"Kate Winslet? Shut up!"

"Serious."

"The same Kate Winslet who played Rose DeWitt Bukater in *Titanic*? The same Kate Winslet who is BFFs with Leo DiCaprio? *That* Kate Winslet?"

"The one and only."

"Dying. Dy-ing." I wave my hand in front of my flushed cheeks. "If you say Queen Kate lives in Northam-on-the-Water, I am going to keel over. Dead. Just step over my body on your way to your table."

She laughs.

"Close," she says, laughing. "Her home is just up the road, in Church Westcote, but I've seen her here, in the sweet shop on High Street."

"Kate Winslet eats candy." I look over at the sweet shop. "Stars. They're just like us!"

I demolish a pot of Earl Grey and a cheddar and tomato chutney sandwich before heading over to Victoria's Candy Emporium. The teahouse was too busy for mixing with the locals, but I am confident I am going to meet my future BFF in the sweet shop. Maybe Kate Winslet will be there, arms loaded with candy. She will drop a bag of Lemon Sherbets. I will pick it up. She will thank me. She will notice my American accent and we will get to talking, you know, about the challenges of living a bicoastal life. She will invite me to her house for tea. We will hit it off, and the next thing you know, I will be chilling in Saint-Tropez with her and her bestie, Leo.

A woman with two rainbow-colored candy canes protruding from her messy topknot greets me as I walk through the door. She's wearing black-framed hipster eyeglasses, a short A-line skirt, a button-down blouse, and thick, dark tights embroidered with lollipops. Definitely not Kate Winslet.

"Welcome to Victoria's Candy Emporium." She smiles, and her glasses slide down her nose. "The queen of all candy stores, from the Cotswolds to Calcutta."

Knightley wasn't exaggerating when he described the owner of the sweet shop as irreverent and quirky.

"You must be Deidre," I say, smiling.

"Guilty."

"I'm Emma Lee Maxwell and I just moved into—"

She runs across the store and throws her arms around my shoulders.

"Emma Lee Maxwell! I cannot believe it! You are here. You are in Northam!" She stops hugging me, pushes her glasses up her nose, and grins. "We were supposed to meet tonight, at Welldon Abbey, but I think this is a more marvelous way to meet, don't you? Serendipitous encounters are the best, aren't they? So, what brings you into my shop? Of all the sweet shops in all the towns in all the world, you walk into mine. What are the odds?"

I don't bother pointing out Victoria's Candy Emporium is the only sweet shop in the village, and Northam-on-the-Water is the only village within walking distance from Wood House, because it would be like sticking a big old pin in her shiny happy balloon. Instead, I grab her hand and give it a squeeze.

"I had a feeling I was going to meet a forever friend today, and it looks as if I was right. I am so glad to meet you, Deidre."

"Do you mean it?" She looks at me through her glasses, wide-eyed and unblinking. "Do you really?"

I am a very good judge of character, and I judge Deidre Waites's character to be good, very good. She has a sweetness that rivals any of the treats in her shop.

"I mean it." I smile. "Now, what do you say you hook a sister up with a bag of Lemon Sherbets, the same Lemon Sherbets you sell to Kate Winslet."

I pay for the Lemon Sherbets and then Deidre and I chat. Actually, Deidre chats and I listen, and listen and listen. I learn she attended Cambridge with hopes of becoming a history professor but had to return to Northam-on-the-Water to run the candy shop after her father died of a sudden heart attack and her mother was diagnosed with macular degeneration. She has a complex love/hate relationship with Queen Victoria, is a walking encyclopedia on all things Victoriana, and has vehement opinions about the barbarism of colonialism. She enjoys music, gardening, and birdwatching, but taking care of the shop and her nearly blind mother leaves her little time to indulge those passions. She loves to read and is a member of Isabella's All Austen Book Club. She doesn't have a boyfriend, but "rather fancies a certain gentleman." She refuses to tell me his name.

I am sucking on a Lemon Sherbet and walking back to Wood House when it hits me: Serendipity didn't lead me to the sweet shop so I could buy a bag of overpriced lemon candy or claim Deidre Waites as my new BFF. Serendipity led me to Victoria's Candy Emporium so I could find Deidre Waites a man. A man who shares her passion for learning. Someone creative and colorful. Someone selfless.

I stick my hand in my coat pocket and feel a small, folded piece of paper.

Johnny Amor! Johnny Amor, the Oxford dropout who spends his days helping his best friend launch an indie book business, the would-be musician who spends his nights singing in pubs.

I unfold the paper, look at William Amor's tight, neat scrawl, and try not to squeal with giddy, triumphant delight. I pull my iPhone out of my pocket and dial Johnny Amor's number. It goes directly to voice mail. Should I leave a message? What do I say? *Hey there, Johnny! I met your granddaddy at JFK while waiting for a flight to London and he gave me your number. Give me a call so I can introduce you to your future wife. For reals.*

I hang up without leaving a message. Mental note: Call Johnny Amor as soon as possible. Johnny Amor, would-be musician, doesn't know it yet, but I am about to rock his world.

Chapter Ten

Emma Lee Maxwell's Facebook Update:
Single ladies shouldn't look for a prince; they should
look for the man who thinks they're a princess.

Knightley Nickerson arrives at the cottage as I am brushing a fifth shade of red lipstick onto my lips. Beauty bloggers often credit Kim Kardashian with developing the
technique for contouring lips, but the bloggers are wrong.
Kim K. did not invent lip contouring; Marilyn Monroe
did. The blonde bombshell made her lips look fuller by
using several shades of lipstick and gloss, applying darker
shades on the outer corners and lighter shades in the middle. I finish dabbing MAC Lipglass in Ruby Woo on my
bottom lip before answering Knightley's knock.

I open the door and have to clutch the doorknob to
keep from sinking to the ground in a flushed, flustered
heap. Knightley is standing on the stoop, hands clasped
behind his back, the amber light of the flickering gas
lamp reflected off his black hair. He looks so solemn, so
formal in his starched shirt and dark suit. So gallant!

Gallant?

Five chapters of *Emma* and my vernacular is sprinkled with words like *solemn* and *gallant*. When I returned from the sweet shop, I curled up on the couch with my iPad, intent on reading the first chapter of *Emma*. Would you believe I made it to chapter five before jet lag knocked me out? Jane Austen is good, y'all. I love Emma Woodhouse! Love! She is witty and clever. Now Knightley, Emma's *Mr.* Knightley, what an old fuddy-duddy. Always correcting Emma. He's throwing down some serious sexual chemistry with Emma, which is actually kind of pervy because he is thirty-eight and she is only twenty-one.

"Hey there, Knightley."

"Hello, Emma Lee." His gaze moves down my Draper James fit and flare LBD to my red-soled Louboutins and his lips curve in a smile. "Don't you look amazing."

"I don't know," I say, flipping my hair off my shoulder. "Do I?"

He chuckles, and I realize my response came off as confident, even coquettish, but I am not feeling confident or coquettish. I am feeling as jumpy as a long-tailed cat in a room full of rockers. Knightley makes me feel all jumpy inside. Maybe that's why I am nervous about making a good impression tonight.

"You do."

"Thank you."

Now what do I do? Shake his hand? Pat him on the back? Slug his shoulder? Kiss his cheeks? Give him a big old squeeze? I just feel gawky and gangly and all out of sorts.

"Right, then," he says, clearing his throat. "If you're ready? We should be going."

I grab my purse and a pashmina from the foyer table.

Knightley lifts my Burberry from the hook behind the door and holds it out for me to slide my arms in the sleeves. It's such a gentlemanly thing to do, such a *gallant* thing to do.

I lock the front door and we walk side by side down the path. The night air is cold and damp. Knightley opens the passenger door and I climb inside, shivering at the lingering warmth, the ghostly scent of his woodsy cologne. He climbs into the driver's seat and we are off, speeding down a dark, twisty country road.

"I should warn you," Knightley says, looking over at me. "Tonight might be something of a crush."

I look into his eyes and my heart skips a beat.

"A crush?"

"My mother has been talking about you for weeks. She invited most of the village, and they are all eager to meet the clever young American matchmaker. I expect it will be a rather taxing evening for you."

"Taxing is good."

"It is?"

"Sure," I say, smiling. "It's always better to have a full dance card than an empty one."

"I don't believe Emma Lee Maxwell has ever had an empty dance card."

My body feels warm all over, like Knightley turned all the vents toward me and dialed the car heater up to full blast. It's a girlish response, I know, but I can't help it. Knightley isn't a silly boy, hanging out his window, cat-calling as I walk by his fraternity. He's a man.

"You flatter me."

"Flattery, I am afraid, is not my forte." He looks at me briefly before returning his gaze to the road. "I meant it sincerely. There's something about you, Emma Lee, something charming and magnetic, something beyond your obvious physical beauty, that makes people want to be around you."

"Oh, pshaw."

He chuckles. "Pshaw?"

"You just met me. How can you possibly know that?"

We arrive at a crossroads and Knightley pulls to a stop.

"Because," he says, looking over at me. "I want to be around you and there aren't many people I want to be around."

"Well, thank you," I say, laughing. "That's quite an endorsement."

"I'm curious," he says, shifting the car into gear. "Have you always found it difficult to take a compliment?"

"My daddy used to say, *Never let a compliment go to your head or a criticism go to your heart.*"

"Sound advice, that."

An awkward silence stretches between us, and I regret not being more gracious, more receptive to Knightley's compliment. I wish I could be more like Manderley. Nothing flusters my big sister. Manderley is cool, calm, and collected, like the actresses in those old movies she loves. She is like the sophisticated heroine in that Grace Kelly-Cary Grant movie, the one set in the French Riviera about the notorious jewel thief.

The thing is, flirting is my forte. I am really good at it. *Emma Lee Maxwell, you're such a flirt!* You can't grow up in the South without learning how to bat your eyelashes and coo at a compliment. It's easy to flirt with someone when you're not interested in them—it's just being extrafriendly to someone you find mildly attractive. Not that I find Knightley attractive.

I mean, he is attractive, but I am not interested in him. Not in *that* way.

Not in a flirty, eyelash-batting, compliment-cooing kinda way. Totally not interested in him in that way.

Okay, so maybe I am a *little* interested in Knightley Nickerson. Why shouldn't I be? His momma appointed herself my honorary surrogate mother, which means he is practically my brother. He probably sees me as a kid sister, too. A kid sister who needs to be picked up from school and shuttled to ballet practice.

Then there is our age difference. Knightley is thirty-five years old. I turn twenty-five in November. I doubt Knightley Nickerson, the Oxford grad, the Saville-Row-suit-wearing, bigwig publisher would be interested in a recent Clemson grad who spent more time memorizing cheers than classic lit.

What is wrong with me? If Maddie uttered such a pitiful self-assessment, I would say, *You best hush your mouth and stop talking ugly about my friend.* I would tell her she was beautiful and precious, and any man would be lucky to score a girl like her.

Maybe I don't want Knightley to be interested in me because I don't want to be interested in him. I am nearly twenty-five, practically on the brink of spinsterhood, and I have never been in love. Not even once. By choice. I decided years ago that love was not for me. Not honor-and-obey, forsaking-all-others, till-death-do-us-part, for-ever-and-ever, amen love. I know what losing a love like that can do to a body. I grew up watching my daddy mourn the loss of his forever-and-ever, amen love. I don't know what my daddy was like before he lost my momma, but I know what he was like after he lost her. Sad. A little broken, with jagged edges that never smoothed out, never repaired. Aching for something he could never have. Daddy loved life, but I sensed a sadness, a longing in him, even when he was laughing.

I don't ever want to feel that kind of sadness, that sort of longing. No, thank you. Even if that means I will not know the joy that comes with a deep, abiding, forever-and-ever, amen kinda love. I believe in hearts-and-flowers, deep-sigh love; I just don't believe it is for me. That's the dichotomy of Emma Lee. I see cupids fluttering over everyone's head, but not my own.

I suddenly realize I have been zoning out, staring at a place somewhere on the dark, distant horizon. I realize I have forgotten my good Southern manners.

"It must be exciting to live and work in London," I say, picking up the lost thread of conversation. "Do you miss it when you are here, in the Cotswolds?"

"I would rather stay home, at Welldon Abbey, where it is quiet and cozy." He turns off the road onto a gravel drive. "Here we are."

There are many adjectives one might use to describe Welldon Abbey, but cozy is not one of them. Lavish. Stately. Grand. These are the adjectives I would use to describe the early Georgian manor house at the end of the drive. With expansive parkland surrounding it, and the skeletal remains of a medieval abbey perched on a hill behind it, Welldon Abbey could have been a filming location for *Pride and Prejudice*.

"This is your home?"

Knightley smiles.

"Welcome to Welldon Abbey, Emma Lee."

Chapter Eleven

Emma Lee Maxwell's Facebook Update:
Did you know a low serotonin level is a symptom of
OCD? When you fall in love with someone, your serotonin level drops. Guess that explains why you
obsessively doodled a certain guy's name on your
notebooks freshman year, **Madison Van Doren**. It
was the low serotonin levels!

"You look particularly pretty tonight, Emma Lee," Deidre says, turning to an elderly woman standing beside
her. "I said Emma Lee looks particularly pretty tonight,
Mother. Don't you agree?"

Mrs. Waites squints at me.

"Particularly?" she snaps. "How would I know if she
looks *particularly* pretty tonight? As we have only just
met, I have nothing to compare."

Deidre's face turns red, and I feel an immediate and over-
whelming desire to say something to blunt her mother's
sharp retort.

A tall, gangly man joins us. He has hollow cheeks and dark, deep-set eyes my literary sister would describe as penetrative.

"Ah, but here is William," Deidre says, smiling at the man hovering on the fringes of our conversation. "It's William Curtis, Mother." Deidre looks at me. "William is the proprietor of Curtis and Sons Apothecary, Emma Lee. If you get to feeling a bit peaky, he will sort you out. He's also your neighbor."

"Hello, Mr. Curtis," I say, holding out my hand. "It's a pleasure to meet you."

He stares at my hand, his lips pressing together in a thin, firm line, and I remember Isabella telling me about his fear of germs. I pull my hand back and pretend to smooth my hair.

"I was just saying Emma Lee looks pretty," Deidre repeats. "Don't you agree, William?"

He fixes his dark gaze on my face.

"You look lovely, Miss Maxwell, though I am worried about your rather liberal use of lipstick."

Mrs. Waites giggles.

Knightley clears his throat.

My cheeks flame with heat.

"William!" Deidre gasps. "That was rude."

"Was it?" William's brow furrows. "Forgive me, Miss Maxwell. My observation on your lipstick was meant as a caution, not a censure."

I wonder what danger the germophobe imagines exists in a tube of NARS Dragon Girl? Arsenic? Lead?

"Caution?"

"Carmine."

"Who is Carmine?"

"Carmine, an ingredient found in most lipsticks, is a

red dye extracted from female insects found in Central America." William stares at my lips as he speaks. "Beetles, to be precise."

"Is carmine toxic?"

"Carmine? Toxic? Don't be ridiculous," he snorts. "Carmine doesn't pose a health risk, but I can't imagine it is entirely hygienic for one to smear pulverized beetles onto their lips." He shudders, and it takes all my self-control not to laugh. I cannot help but feel Miss Belle would be proud of my restraint. "Seventy thousand beetles are killed to create one pound of dye. All that effort to manufacture lip rouge."

"Vanity run amok, if you ask me," sniffs Mrs. Waites.

Deidre looks mortified, and I suspect it is not the first time she has been embarrassed by her overbearing mother.

"Mrs. Waites, William," Knightley says. "I recently acquired a first edition of Emily Brontë's *Wuthering Heights*. Would you care to see it?"

"Emily Brontë." William clucks his tongue and shakes his head. "Such a talent. Such a waste. A simple cold, unattended, developed into tuberculosis. Emily was frightfully mistrusting of doctors. She rejected medical attention and the disease ate away at her until she was a skeleton of her former self. Her coffin measured only sixteen inches wide. Can you imagine?"

"I cannot," Knightley says.

"Thank you," William says. "I would like to see your acquisition."

"As would I," Mrs. Waites concurs.

Knightley holds out his arm, but Mrs. Waites begins walking unassisted.

"Emily Brontë was not the only author to die of tuberculosis," William says, walking beside Knightley. "Orwell, Thoreau, Keats, Maupassant, Molière . . ."

Knightley looks over his shoulder and smiles.

"I am sorry about my mother," Deidre whispers. "Macular degeneration has blunted her vision but not her tongue."

"No worries," I say. "I love your blouse. Are those flowers?"

"Violets." Deidre beams. "Violets are my favorite flower. They were also Queen Victoria's favorite flower, though I don't hold that against them."

I laugh. "Good of you. There's no room for floral prejudice in today's progressive climate."

Deidre giggles.

Isabella strides into the library, her head held at a regal angle, a smile lifting the corners of her mouth. She sees me and hurries over.

"Emma Lee," she says, pulling me into her arms. "I am sorry I wasn't here to greet you properly. The Cornish game hens required a bit of my attention, I am afraid. Basting is a time-consuming business, you know." She squeezes me before letting me go. "Have you met everyone?"

I look around the room at the people gathered in clusters in front of the fireplace, beside the grand piano, around a massive antique globe, and shake my head.

"Well, then," she says, linking her arm through mine, "shall we?"

Half an hour later, Isabella introduces me to the last guest, Vicar Parsons, an affable man with kind eyes, though not as cute as the actor who plays Sidney Chambers in *Grantchester*. Besides William Curtis, Deidre, and Mrs. Waites, the eclectic group includes Hayley Bartlett, the pretty though tomboyish owner of the only fresh, organically grown produce market in Northam-on-the-Water; John Barrington, an intensely quiet farmer who bears a striking resemblance to the actor Michael Fassbender; Harriet Cole, a middle-aged widow and the owner of Call Me Darjeeling; Annalise Whittaker-Smith, a striking brunette who happens to be Hayley's half sister, though I sense little sisterly affection between the pair; and assorted members of Isabella's book and women's clubs.

Bingley and Brandon Nickerson arrive as Vicar Parsons is trying to convince me to join the church choir, despite my confession of being practically tone-deaf. Isabella's younger sons kiss their mother's cheeks and offer me warm welcomes. All Isabella's sons are handsome, though Knightley is the hottie of the trio.

Bingley, the baby, is cheerful, clever, and quick with a quip. He has a thatch of artfully messy curls, bright, sparkling blue eyes, and what my sister Manderley calls *designer stubble*. He wears his stylish blue-checked suit with nonchalance, like a male model posing at the end of a runway. Yet, when I compliment his fashion-forward wing-tip boots, he beams with obvious pleasure.

Brandon, the middle son, is tall and muscular, with close-cropped dark hair and a wired-up-tight military bearing. Isabella told me Brandon attended Royal Military Academy Sandhurst and served with Prince Harry before joining Nickerson Publishing as director of marketing and promotions. Frankly, I am surprised Bingley, with his outgoing, jovial personality, doesn't work in marketing and promotions. Isabella told me Brandon is an adventure junkie, always pushing himself to learn and excel at some extreme sport.

I'm not gonna lie, y'all, looking at Knightley, Brandon, and Bingley Nickerson, I am stunned, I mean flat-out floored, they're still single. Handsome heterosexual men with good breeding and superior education. It defies logic. While Bingley tells his momma about an article he is writing for the men's magazine *The Rake*, I build a mental dossier for each of the Nickerson men. Brandon, with his serious demeanor and athletic bent, might be perfect for Kristen, my overachieving, hypercompetitive sorority sister. Too bad she is squatting her little heart out three thousand miles away.

In my heart, I just know Bingley will be the easiest to match. Who wouldn't want to date a young, stylish free-lancer with a wickedly great sense of humor and loads of fashion sense? Maddie would die. Keel over, kick out her legs, and gasp her last breath die to date someone like Bingley, someone smart and irreverent.

A maid in a starched black dress and apron enters the library, clears her throat, and announces, "Dinner is served."

Knightley is seated at the head of the table, while I am seated in the chair of honor beside Isabella, at the opposite end. Happily, Bingley is seated to my right. The hypochondriac pharmacist and tea-hocking widow are across from me.

"Our first course is parsnip and potato soup"—Isabella gestures toward the maid holding a tureen—"made with vegetables from Hayley's farm. Bon appétit." Isabella looks at William and lowers her voice. "William, you will be happy to know Mariah used arrowroot powder to thicken the soup."

"Splendid."

Isabella looks at me.

"Arrowroot powder is gluten-free, grain-free, and paleo-friendly," Isabella says, smiling. "Isn't that right, William?"

"Arrowroot is excellent for digestive disorders. Most people think of it as an alternative to cornstarch, but its applications and medicinal benefits are considerable."

I imagine Miss Belle's spirit, flitting around us unseen,

having an apoplectic fit when William uttered the words *digestive disorder*. I reckon she would classify his casual reference to GERD and IBS as a grievous infraction of the rules of etiquette.

Bingley entertains me with scathingly witty stories about life in sleepy old Northam-on-the-Water, projected trends in fashion, and biting social commentary. He is a charming dinner companion. He is the kind of guy a girl wants to meet for coffee and gossip, the superfun, super-snarky BMF—best male friend—in every rom-com made since *Bridget Jones's Diary*.

During a lull in the conversation, William Curtis makes a random declaration that captures everyone's attention.

"Nutella will kill you," he says.

Harriet smiles. "Nutella?"

"That's right."

"The hazelnut spread?"

"I noticed you offer Nutella-toasted muffins on the menu at Call Me Darjeeling."

"I do."

"You realize palm oil is a key ingredient in Nutella?"

"Don't tell me," Deidre quips. "Palm oil is made from the pulverized carcasses of the extremely rare South African cabbage palm caterpillar, right?"

Bingley snickers. Isabella presses her lips together, as if restraining a laugh. William rolls his eyes.

"Palm oil is carcinogenic."

"Carcinogenic?" Harriet looks from Deidre to the pharmacist. "Ferrero is a major corporation. I simply can't believe they would purchase carcinogenic palm oil."

William sighs. "Palm oil isn't carcinogenic."

"You just said palm oil was carcinogenic." Harriet looks at me. "He just said palm oil is carcinogenic, didn't he?"

"When the palm oil is refined at a high temperature, as

it is during the processing of Nutella, glycidyl fatty acid esters, or GE, form." William talks in the slow, measured voice one uses when explaining simple concepts to intellectually challenged children. "GEs occur in nearly all refined edible oils, but despite that fact, they are potentially carcinogenic."

"Potentially?" Harriet sniffs. "My Nutella muffins are my most popular item. I refuse to stop making them simply because they might contain a *potentially* carcinogenic oil."

"Suit yourself"—William shrugs—"but I would remove Nutella from the name; think of a different name."

"What do you suggest?"

"Malignant Muffins?" Bingley quips.

"Benign Biscuits?" Deidre adds.

Later, after the Cornish game hens and garlic mash, after the baked apples and Brie, we gather in the library to drink digestifs and engage in pleasant chitchat that does not include carcinogens, wasting diseases, or pulverized insects.

Hayley Bartlett reminds me of Judy Greer, the actress who played the wisecracking best friend in *27 Dresses* and *13 Going on 30*. Only Hayley is prettier, much prettier, if a bit challenged in the style department—hmmm, maybe Bingley could help her with that? With a riotous mane of ashy blond curls and a strawberries-and-cream complexion, she looks like a rom-com leading lady, not a sidekick. More than once, I catch her eyeing John Barrington, which confuses me. Hayley is beautiful and lively. John Barrington, in his rumpled khaki pants and workman's Henley, is just . . . well . . . I don't mean to be uncharitable, y'all, but John Barrington is as bland as a bowl of Cream of Wheat: plain, without the butter or brown sugar heaped on top.

By the time Knightley is helping me on with my coat, I have made plans to meet Hayley for lunch, join Bingley on a trip to scout out a new boutique in Marylebone, and become a member of Isabella's All Austen Book Club. I have concisely written dossiers for Bingley, Brandon, Hayley, Deidre, and even William, though finding the germophobe, medical-trivia-obsessed pharmacist a mate would challenge Patti Stanger's impressive matchmaking skills.

Chapter Twelve

Emma Lee Maxwell's Facebook Update:
The greatest relationships are the ones you never expected to be in.

I am sitting in Call Me Darjeeling, listening to Miss Cole and William engage in the Great Nutella Debate Part II, when my phone chimes.

Text from Alexandria Armistead:
Cash has been acting strange.

Text to Alexandria Armistead:
Cash is strange. Don't tell me you're just noticing it.

Several minutes go by without a response from Lexi. I sip my tea, a house blend called Chai Love You, made with white chai tea, fresh strawberries, and a "loving dose of sugar," and wait for Hayley Bartlett.

A stylish little British birdie named Miss Isabella

whispered a few biographical details about Miss Hayley. Apparently, Hayley was raised by her grandparents and grew up working on their farm. She won a prize from the National Federation of Young Farmers' Club when she was a teenager and used the money to open a small produce market on the edge of the village. She was born a month after Bingley Nickerson, though their social circles rarely intersected, what with Bingley having attended a posh boarding school and Hayley up to her elbows in soil.

I study William Curtis, in his buttoned-up navy peacoat, a heavy scarf wound several times around his neck. Would he be a good match for Isabella Nickerson? With messy, finger-combed brown hair, sunken cheeks, and a piercing gaze, he reminds me of the actor David Tennant. He's handsome-*ish*. Stable. Local. He obviously cares deeply about the well-being of his friends and neighbors. Miss Isabella is a caretaker, too. So, they would have that in common. William appears younger than Miss Isabella by at least ten years, but hang-ups over age disparity are *so* last decade. Hollywood has made the May-December romance superhot. Look at Kate Beckinsale, caught smooching a steamy actor half her age. J.Lo bust a sexy move with her significantly younger backup dancer. Aaron Taylor-Johnson, the hottie who played Count Vronsky, Keira Knightley's lover in *Anna Karenina*, married a woman old enough to be his mother.

William has a thick, hardback book tucked under his arm. *Germs: The Biological Weapons Outside Your Front Door, Stay Inside, Stay Alive.*

Then again, I reckon he might be too much of a homebody for a woman as worldly and sophisticated as Isabella Nickerson.

My phone chimes again.

Text from Alexandria Armistead:

I'm serious. Cash been distant ever since our engagement party. Maybe he's changed his mind. Maybe he doesn't want to marry me.

Text to Alexandria Armistead:

Cash talks slow, but that doesn't mean he's stupid, darlin'. He's lucky to have a girl as smart, kind, and beautiful as you. If he forgets it, I'll sure enough remind him. Chill, girl.

I read Lexi's text again. Should I be more concerned about Cash? He was a major player in high school. Major. I always thought he just needed the right coach, a strong, confident woman who could whup his crazy ass into shape. Sure enough, Cash went to college, dated a few strong, confident women, and gave up his major player ways. Hmmm. I should send him a text just to be sure he hasn't suited up and hit the playing field again.

I open my photos application and scroll through the pictures of the engagement party. Lexi, looking prettier than any old Disney Princess, leaning her head against Cash's broad shoulder. Cash laughing with his best friends. Cash and Lexi dancing too close for Jesus; whenever we had dances with our brother school, Miss Belle would thrust her hands between dancing couples and say, *Leave room for Jesus.*

Instead of texting Cash, I write a second, more supportive message to Lexi, including a link to an article on theknot.com, "How to Deal with Pre-Wedding Jitters." I sip my tea and think about the reasons Lexi Armistead and Cash Aiken make a mighty fine pairing.

I love my best friend something fierce. She is beautiful, compassionate, and generous. She has great taste in designer handbags *and* Disney heroes. She can be loads of fun—nobody brings the *High School Musical* heat to Kappa Kappa Karaoke Night better than Lex—but she also has this super*saaad* side to her. Occasionally, she gets real blue and seems to disappear inside herself. She looks as fragile as the pale purple petals that used to tremble on the branches of the old crape myrtle outside my bedroom window, like the slightest breeze might sweep her away.

Lexi's daddy was diagnosed with leukemia when she was nine-years-old, and it affected her something fierce. Most people die within months of being diagnosed with that terrible-awful disease, but Lexi's daddy laid up in his bed for two years. Two long, agonizing years. Lexi said watching him suffer made her feel small and helpless. I think it's why she decided to study nursing, because a part of her still feels small and helpless.

I thought Cash, with his sturdy, corn-bread-fed physique, and Southern boy sense of fun, would be a good match for my fragile friend. He has the body of a Clemson Tiger and the heart of a pussycat, big and strong, but gentle as all get-out. He graduated two years before us with a business degree and returned to help manage MeeMaw Creek, his family's corporation. I know what you're thinking. MeeMaw Creek sounds like a sparse patch of land with some tin-roofed shanties selling moonshine out of recycled Mason jars, but don't let the name fool you. MeeMaw Creek happens to be the largest pastured pig farm in the South. When he was still a teenager, Cash's daddy used his trust fund to purchase MeeMaw Creek Farm and every farm within a twenty-mile radius. MeeMaw Creek has the finest heritage hogs in the country, and Cash Aiken Senior is considered an expert on humane pig husbandry.

Cash worships Lexi. When they aren't together, he

sends her a wake-up text each morning: *Have a good day, babydoll. I love you.* When they *are* together, he gets up early, drives to the closest Starbucks, and returns with Lexi's favorite: venti skinny vanilla latte with soy and an almond croissant. Lexi brings out Cash's softer, sweeter side, and that big, old brawny boy makes my girl feel safe.

Isn't it romantic when two halves come together to form a whole? *You complete me.* Remember that scene in *Jerry Maguire*? Tom Cruise barges into Renée Zellweger's living room and declares, *You complete me.* Two halves coming together to form a whole.

"That was a deep sigh." I look up to find Hayley standing on the other side of the table. She pulls a slouchy cap off her head, and her riotous blond curls fall around her shoulders. "Homesick already?"

"Hayley!" I jump up and give my new friend a hug. "I'm so glad you're here."

Hayley stands with her arms at her sides. I give her a quick squeeze and sit back down.

"Sorry," she says, shrugging out of her coat. "I am complete rubbish at greetings. I become awkward and gangly. I don't know what to do with my hands. Should I hug, shake hands, offer a solid fist bump?"

"I'm a hugger!"

"Yes, you are." Hayley chuckles. "I will take a quick, enthusiastic American hug over the strangely cold, but too intimate French cheek kiss. Annalise is fond of the French greeting. Three bloody kisses every time I see her."

Annalise Whittaker-Smith. Hayley's beautiful half sister, who spent most of the dinner party flirting with Knightley and Brandon Nickerson. I thought I picked up some bad vibrations between the sisters.

"My sister is in the south of France. I can't imagine Manderley greeting people with cheek kisses, though. She's sweet but crazy shy."

"Are you close to your sister?"

"Manderley? She is the best big sister ever. My momma died when I was a baby, so Manderley practically raised me." I open my photos app, find the picture Manderley sent me last week of her standing on the red carpet at the Cannes Film Festival, and show it to Hayley. "What about Annalise? Are you two close?"

"Not at all."

With her thick British accent, *not at all* sounds like one word, *notall*. Harriet stops arguing with William long enough to greet Hayley and take her tea order.

"I'll have a cup of We're a Perfect Matcha," Hayley says.

"Sorry, love," Harriet says. "We are out of matcha. I used the last of it to make matcha sugar cookies. How about a nice pot of I Love You Oolong Time and a matcha sugar cookie?"

"Lovely," Hayley says.

Harriet returns with Hayley's tea and cookies. She refreshes my teapot before resuming her debate with William.

"Ferrero lost more than three million dollars in class-action lawsuits in America," William says.

"The Americans!" Harriet waves her hands. "The Americans are the most litigious people in the world, after the Germans."

"Oi!" Hayley shouts. "American here."

Harriet looks at me and her cheeks flush.

"Sorry, love. No offense."

"None taken." I smile. "For the record, I have never sued Starbucks for putting too much ice in my iced coffee or Subway for serving me an eleven-inch *footlong*"—I raise three fingers on my right hand as if making the Girl Scout promise—"and I promise I won't bring a lawsuit against the tea shop if you serve me a Nutella muffin." William frowns at me. "Though, as a rule, I prefer good old American peanut butter over carcinogenic hazelnut spread."

"Well done, you," Hayley whispers. "Being drawn into the Nutella Crisis could be disastrous. Neutrality is your best course."

"The line has been drawn in the sand"—I lower my voice to a whisper—"but I shall not choose sides."

Hayley laughs. My Aunt Patricia once said, *Laughter is an elixir of beauty. It has the power to transform a plain girl into a pretty girl, and a pretty girl into a remarkable beauty.* Hayley is one of those pretty girls who becomes beautiful when she laughs.

William tucks his book farther up under his arm and strides out of the tea shop, nodding as he passes our table. Harriet arrives to take our lunch order—bowls of pea soup made with organic veg from Hayley's farm and grilled cheese sandwiches on fresh-baked brown bread. Hayley's eyes shine with pride when Harriet tells me the bit about the vegetables being sourced from her farm. I wonder if she always wanted to be a farmer? Did she ever think about choosing an easier career, one not dominated by men? Does she always wear jeans and tees, even when she is working in her market? I wait until Harriet leaves before hitting Hayley with questions.

"Have you always wanted to be a farmer?"

"Farming is all I have ever known."

"Is it your passion, though?"

"I know it's not sexy"—she wraps her slender fingers around her teacup and smiles at me in a sweet, self-conscious sort of way, her bottom lip pulled tight over her straight white teeth—"but farming is in my blood. It is satisfying to spend my day engaged in work that is truly meaningful, work that sustains life. My sister and her lot spend their days selling a concept—and a vapid one at that—posing in designer clothes, beside luxury automobiles, holding overpriced handbags. They *work* at creating images of a lifestyle that is unobtainable for most people."

Yikes! As Taylor Swift might say, *We got some bad blood up in here, y'all.*

"My sister Manderley works as an assistant to a playwright," I say, keeping my tone light and upbeat so I don't come off judgmental. "My other sister, Tara, is a trained chef but works as a reporter for a television station. She films segments about food and the hottest restaurants in Charleston. Some might say their work is meaningless and even a little vapid, but wouldn't the world be a boring place without movie-script writers and handbag-hocking models? I think creating art, in any form or format, is meaningful work for some people, don't you?"

"Bloody hell! First, I cock up the greeting and then I carry on about my sister like some mad, jealous cow. Maybe I should just bugger off."

"Get out of here."

Hayley gasps. She pushes to a stand and is about to snatch her hat off the table when I realize she thinks I want her to leave.

"I didn't mean that literally, Hayley," I say, reaching for her wrist. "*Get out of here* is American slang for *you have to be kidding.* I don't really want you to bugger off."

She sits back down, her back ramrod straight, her lips pressed together in a tense, tight slash.

"And you didn't sound like a mad cow. A little judgy

maybe, but not mad. Not crazy-eyes, foaming-at-the-mouth, tongue-lolling-out, stomping-hoof mad, anyway."

I laugh, and she relaxes her posture.

"Sorry," she says, brushing a curl out of her face. "I get a little defensive about my job."

"Really?" I grin. "I hadn't noticed."

She laughs.

"What's that about?"

"You mean you haven't heard *The Tragic Tale of Hayley Bartlett*?"

"Nope."

"Not even the *Reader's Digest* version?"

"Not even the *Reader's Digest* version."

She draws a deep breath, wraps her hands around her teacup as if it is a talisman for summoning strength, then begins telling me her tale—the unabridged version. I wouldn't call it a tragic tale, but it is *saaad*.

Annabelle, Hayley's momma, got pregnant when she was a teenager and refused to name the baby daddy, which caused a bit of a scandal in Northam-on-the-Water. A few months after Hayley's birth, Annabelle packed a bag and moved to London, leaving her baby, and the baby daddy gossip, behind. She worked as a successful model until she met and married Robin Whittaker-Smith III, heir of Whittaker-Smith Bespoke, a luxury tailor specializing in country clothing. Apparently, Whittaker-Smith Bespoke has been supplying made-to-order tweed garments for Britain's blue bloods since 1873. Annabelle stopped modeling and started designing superchic tweed ware for a younger, hipper demographic. Today, Annabelle Whittaker-Smith's brand, Cavalier, is popular with young aristocrats, socialites, and heiresses hoping to pull a Kate (marry way, way up the social ladder). Hayley calls them the Chestertons, because she says the people who buy Annabelle's clothes always attend a champagne-fueled, fascinator-free social event called Chestertons Polo in the Park.

"Toffs who sip chilled Moët at four hundred pounds per glass and whinge about how much it costs to maintain their piles."

"Whinge?"

"Moan," she says, rolling her eyes.

"Piles?"

"Massive country estates."

"Ah."

"Polo and piles," Hayley says, her tone tinged with bitterness. "Vapid toffs, the lot of them."

Should I tell Hayley how I used to be part of the Charleston polo and piles set, how I faithfully attended the Whitney Turn Up, how I used to sip overpriced champagne and *whinge* about the challenges of living in a two-hundred-year-old plantation? I like Hayley. I don't want her to think I am a vapid *toff*, but my daddy used to say, *A true friend sees your rickety old fence but pays it no mind because she would rather admire the flowers you got growing in your garden.* How will I know if Hayley is a true friend if I bring her around the back way, if I hide my rickety old fence?

"If you had known me in Charleston, you would have called me a toff."

Hayley looks surprised by my admission.

"I lived a vapid life," I say. "Designer bags and debutante balls."

"Lived. Past tense. What made you change?"

"For reals?"

Hayley nods.

"I didn't have a choice," I say, looking her dead in the

eye. "My daddy died owing a mess of back taxes, so the IRS yanked my silver spoon right out of my mouth. They froze Daddy's accounts and seized his assets. They even repossessed my car! A humbling and humiliating experience."

"I can imagine."

"The thing is"—I tip my teacup to the side and pretend to study the soggy grounds clinging to the sides and bottom of the cup because what I am about to say is embarrassing—"that humbling, humiliating experience was the best thing my daddy could have left me, more valuable than some old plantation or luxury car, because it forced me to grow up, to take charge of my life. Suddenly, I couldn't afford to treat my life like it was a big old pool party and I was just lounging on an inflatable pink flamingo, waiting for a breeze to push me from one side to the other." I take a deep breath and look at Hayley. "I miss my daddy something fierce, Hayley, so I hope you don't think I am cold or selfish when I say this, but I don't think I would have had the compulsion to grow up if he hadn't died."

I said I was moving to Northam-on-the-Water so I could live rent-free in my aunt's cottage, but I realize that was a whole lotta hogwash. I moved to Northam because it was the only way I could get off my pink flamingo pool float. Staying in Charleston and living with my sister would have been like floating on that flamingo and letting the breeze take me from one side of the pool to the other.

"I don't think you sound cold or selfish." She lets go of her teacup, and for a second I think she might reach over and pat my arm, but she shoves her hands in her pockets instead. "You might have run with a posh set, but you could not have been vapid, not truly, terminally vapid anyway. A vapid person would have used her loss and humiliation as an excuse to garner sympathy; you used it as an impetus for change and growth. Good on you."

"Thank you!"

Harriet brings our soup and cheese sandwiches and we chat about slightly less serious matters, like the new Harry Styles album (love), our favorite Netflix binge-worthy programs (*Peaky Blinders*), the latest celeb scandals (looking at you, Kendall Jenner), and our predictions for the Prince Harry and Meghan Markle mash-up (Hayley thinks they will end up like Prince Andrew and Fergie, with Meghan caught by the paparazzi in a toe-sucking peccadillo, while I feel they will follow the Disney route, remaining faithfully and happily wed till death do they part). Harriet clears away our empty dishes and refills our teacups.

"Did you spend a lot of time in London when you were growing up?"

"Not at all."

"Didn't you visit your momma?"

Hayley's face hardens. "Annabelle hid my existence from her husband and her new family. She sent money to my grandparents so they could buy birthday and Boxing Day gifts, but that was the extent of her involvement in my childhood. When I was fourteen, she suffered a pang of conscience and confessed her dirty little secret to Robin."

"How did he react?"

She fiddles with the handle of the tiny silver spoon sticking out of the sugar bowl, toying with the brown lumps of demerara.

"He invited me to live with them, said he would buy me a car, send me to the best schools, but I didn't want to leave my grandparents. The farm is my home. Robin asked me to be involved in Annalise's life, but I was a moody, sullen teenager by then. The last thing I wanted was to play big sister to my mum's beloved brat."

Hayley looks as bruised as she sounds, just a big, old emotional sore, and I can't stop myself from reaching out and grabbing her hand.

"Annabelle didn't even name me. My grandparents named me after Hayley Mills, the actress."

I think about my momma and try to imagine how I would have felt if she had up and left me. I only know my momma through memories—other people's memories. Still, I take comfort in knowing my momma wanted me and only left me 'cuz the good Lord needed another angel in heaven. I reckon it hurts Hayley something fierce to know her momma couldn't be bothered to give her first-born a name, but she sure enough gave her secondborn a name. Annabelle. Annalise. Ouch. Annabelle was a model. Annalise is a model. Now I see why Hayley seems to reject anything associated with the fashion industry—from modeling to tinted moisturizer.

"I grew up with the stigma of being the unwanted child of Hester Prynne of Northam-on-the-Water."

"Hester Prynne?"

"*The Scarlet Letter*?"

Sweet lawd have mercy! Another book I only pretended to read in freshman lit. I skimmed it. Honest I did. I remember it had a whole mess of Mensa vocabulary words like *ignominious*, *physiognomies*, and *contumaciously*. For real, y'all. Who—besides Neil deGrasse Tyson and Manderley Maxwell—uses the word *contumaciously* in everyday speech? Brainiacs, that's who. *Note to self: download* The Scarlet Letter. *Unabridged version, not CliffsNotes.*

"Um, Literature has never really been my thing, so

you're going to have to explain the Hester Price reference."

"Prynne," Hayley says, smiling. "Hester Prynne, the protagonist of *The Scarlet Letter*, lives in a village in New England. She has an affair with a puritan minister and gets up the duff."

"Up the duff?"

"Pregnant."

Hayley tells me the rest of Hester's sad, sordid story, peppering it with British slang and snarky editorial asides.

"Lawdy! I wish you would have been my freshman lit study buddy," I say, laughing. "I might have enjoyed Orwell."

"I have just had the most brilliant idea!"

"Ooo! Goody!" I clap my hands. "I love brilliant ideas."

"I will entertain you with a Hayley Bartlett original retelling of any classic novel, if you teach me how to make my eyeliner flick up at the ends like yours." She thrusts her hand at me. "Do we have a bargain?"

Hayley has this whole jeans-and-tee, I-don't-care vibe going on, with her fresh-scrubbed face and unmanaged curls, but with a little help, a little of *my* help, she could be beautiful, as beautiful as her half sister. Her passion for her vocation and her commitment to excel in her field—pun accidental—reminds me of Kristen. Focused, driven women are so inspiring (and intimidating), aren't they? They make me want to be more focused and more driven.

"It's a deal," I say, shaking Hayley's hand. "When do you want to start?"

"Are you busy next Saturday night?"

"Nope."

"Brilliant! I planted a mango tree in my greenhouse and the first fruit is ripe. Nigella has a mango margarita recipe that sounds scrummy. I will bring the fruit—"

"—and I will supply the tequila!"

I want to jump up and cheer, but I am afraid my American enthusiasm might be too much for my new friend, so I settle for softly clapping my hands and letting out a restrained and dignified squeal.

Chapter Thirteen

Emma Lee Maxwell's Facebook Update:
I saw the sweetest thing this morning, y'all. I was walking in the village when I noticed an elderly couple strolling arm-in-arm ahead of me. The woman stopped, looked in a shop window, frowned, and began fussing with her hair, patting the sides, twisting her curly bangs in place. This went on for a while. Finally, her husband bent down and kissed her cheek. She stopped fussing and smiled up at him. Isn't that what we all want—someone who has the ability to make us stop our fussing with a simple touch?

It was his overcoat that caught my attention. Single-breasted, expertly tailored wool in Prince of Wales check. The sort of coat found in European fashion magazines or old-time movies. The sort of coat created by an Italian fashion designer and sold exclusively in Bergdorf's *Goodman's Guide*. The sort of coat I would expect to see on—

"Knightley!"

"Hello, Emma Lee." He smiles and tiny, happy crinkles appear around his eyes. "You've been exploring the village, I see. How do you find Northam-on-the-Water?"

Sweet lawd! The skies are leaden, the air cold and wet, but I suddenly feel flushed all over, like the time I ate dodgy oysters and got food poisoning. I wonder if it was Harriet's pea soup? Or the sandwich? The cheese smelled off.

"Hey there, Knightley," I say, casually untying the belt around my trench coat to let in a blast of cool air. "I love Northam! I feel as if I have stepped into the pages of a fairy tale."

Knightley turns around and we walk along the river in the direction of the cottage.

"I am curious; which of our neighbors is to be the first to benefit from your matchmaking expertise?"

I assume he is teasing me, because, well, everyone has teased me about my desire to become a matchmaker—everyone, that is, except Knightley's momma, Miss Isabella.

"Well," I say, peeking at him out of the corner of my eye. "I was fixin' to start with you."

The happy crinkles around his eyes deepen and his lips lift in a smile. His laughter, warm and comforting, wraps around me like a familiar hug.

"Is that so? And what makes you think I want to be matched?"

"Everybody wants to find their perfect match."

He suddenly stops walking. "Everybody?"

I turn back, see his slow, smoldering smile, and my heart skips an entire beat, like the needle of my daddy's old vinyl player when it hit the scratch in his favorite Otis Redding record. Lawd, Knightley is a beautiful man!

"Sure."

"Even you?"

Skip. Skip. I can't tell if Knightly Nickerson is flirting with me or just teasing me back, and it's got me feeling all flustered. Manderley would respond with something deeply wise and poetic. Tara would twist her hair around her slender finger and say something so witty, so brazen, Knightley would make like her hair and twist himself around her little old finger.

I am not as wise as Manderley.

And I am not as brazen—read: sexually confident—as Tara.

So, I opt for unvarnished candor.

"No, I reckon I don't want to find my soul mate."

He stops smiling, and the happy crinkles disappear.

"You don't? Why not?"

It's probably the same reason I never pressed my daddy to get me a pet. Growing up, my best friend in the whole, wide world was Ginger May Harrison, on account of she could play basketball like a boy and still look mighty pretty in a dress and Mary Janes. I remember Ginger May begging her momma and daddy to let her have a silky-haired Boykin Spaniel pup from a litter of pups we saw at the pet store near Citadel Mall. They said no, but Ginger May kept on them. They finally gave in. Ginger May named her sweet little pup Baby Dumpling and fastened a big old floppy pink polka-dot bow to her collar. For three years, Baby Dumpling followed Ginger May everywhere, faithfully trotting behind her with that bow still fastened to her collar. Then, one day, Baby Dumpling up and stopped eating. Her stomach bloated, and she died. Ginger May was devastated. And I was devastated for her. That's why I never pressed my daddy for my own Baby Dumpling, and that's why I am not pressing for a soul mate.

"Love is a risky game"—I look down at my feet, nudge a toadstool growing alongside the path with the toe of my boot, and pray this flushed-all-over, heartbeat-skippy feeling isn't food poisoning—"and I am not an intrepid player."

"Perhaps you didn't know it, but there is a game far riskier than love."

I look up. "Russian Roulette?"

"No."

"Playing chicken?"

"No."

"Poker?"

He shakes his head.

"Eating muffins made with Nutella?"

"Riskier."

"I know, ordering an iced beverage from Caffè Nero?"

He laughs. The happy crinkles around his eyes reappear. My heart skips another beat.

"You dangled the bait, madam, and I am taking it. I must know, why is it risky to order an iced beverage from a Caffè Nero?"

Obviously, I didn't think this one through. I overheard William telling Harriet the European coffeehouse chain failed recent health inspections after fecal bacteria was found in their ice makers. I can't say the word *fecal* to a man as educated and polished as Knightley Nickerson, y'all. *I just can't!*

"Apparently, an undercover investigation determined their stores to be less than hygienic, and their iced beverages to be the riskiest of their products. All I am saying is, don't order the iced tea."

"That should not be a problem," he says, grinning. "I am British. I take my tea with cream and without ice."

"Don't be a tea snob!"

"I make no apologies for my tea snobbery," he says, laughing. "There are only a few things in life that demand thoughtful discrimination, and tea is most definitely one of those things."

"Is that so?" I laugh. "What else brings out your inner snob, Knightley Nickerson?"

"Hmmm." He looks at me, narrowing his gaze, and I get that weightless tummy feeling I get whenever I am at the top of a rollercoaster ride, just about to plunge down. "Literature and whiskey, definitely. I am also rather particular when it comes to choosing tailors, best mates, and women."

Lawdy Miss Clawdy! Harriet's pea soup isn't making me feel flushed all over and out of sorts; it's Knightly Nickerson in his fine-fitting bespoke coat, staring at me with his sexy, slow-smolder eyes, and teasing me with his flirty banter. Women! Knightley said women, as in plural. Lawdy! I need a spritz of Evian Facial Spray to cool my cheeks. Why didn't I slip a travel-sized can in my pocket before leaving the cottage?

Knightley clears his throat and looks away, as if suddenly embarrassed, and I feel a compulsion to put him at his ease.

"All right, Knightley Nickerson," I say, crossing my arms over my chest. "Are you going to tell me which game is riskier than love or do I have to whip out my iPhone and Google the answer?"

"Life, my dear Miss Maxwell." He leans closer, and I catch a whiff of his woodsy cologne, notice the droplets of rain sparkling like Swarovski beads in his dark hair. He lowers his voice. "Life is the riskiest game you will ever play. The moment you are born, you enter a massively dangerous arena, a place that incessantly challenges your wits and your stamina. You can hide in the shadows, play it safe, but even then, you aren't assured survival. You are too bold, too bright, to live in the shadows, Emma Lee."

Right now, standing in the shadow of this very sophisticated, very handsome Englishman, I don't feel very bold or very bright. *I feel . . . I feel . . .* I feel like I am in a big old canoe, trying to get across a big old lake with just one paddle. I'll bet Knightley Nickerson would be surprised if I admitted that to him. I know how I come off, like I'm the Second Coming of the excessively cheerful, optimistic orphan girl in that old Disney movie Manderley used to make me watch. What was her name? Pauline? Prudence? Penelope? Whatever. The point is, even pervasively plucky girls like Pippa (Paisley?) experience moments of doubt.

"Maybe I'm not as bold as you think."

"You are."

He is so close, his breath fanning warmly over my cheeks, smelling of peppermint.

"I saw what happened at the Clemson–South Carolina game."

"What? *How*?"

It was my junior year at Clemson and it was the biggest game of the season. There are many rivalries in the world of sports, but none as heated and contentious as the one between the Tigers and the Gamecocks. We had just finished the second quarter and were leading by twenty points (Go Tigers!). We decided to get the crowd fired up by doing a basket toss we had practiced a thousand times, a slick move that involves tossing a squad member straight up in the air so she can flip around and assume a swanlike position. If it's done right, the cheerleader lands in a nest of hands, like a bird, head up, back arched, arms outstretched. Only, something went wrong.

One minute I was flying straight up in the air, and the next minute I was flat on my back on a stretcher, being wheeled out of the stadium by two paramedics.

"YouTube."

"How did you even know to look on YouTube?"

"I Googled you."

"You Googled me?"

"Guilty." Two spots of color appear on Knightley's cheeks, as bright as the toes of my military-red rain boots. "They wheeled you out on a stretcher, Emma Lee, but you came back, under your own steam, and cheered your team to victory. Well done, you."

"Oh, pshaw!" I wave my hands at him. "It wasn't as serious as it seemed, not like that basketball player who collapsed and had to have his heart restarted with defibrillators, with his poor momma looking on, pleading with the Lord Jesus not to take her son."

"It looked rather serious," he argues. "The people who were supposed to catch you—"

"—the base."

"Right," he says. "Your base royally cocked up!"

"*Cock up* sounds harsh. It was an accident."

"An accident? They let you fall on your head! I am *gobsmacked* you didn't suffer traumatic brain injury or permanent paralysis."

His concern, his proximity, his yummy *cologne*. It's too much. I am tempted to press a hand to my forehead and fake an old-time Southern girl swoon, but I don't really do fake, and I've never even attempted a swoon. So I do what I always do when I need to wedge a little space between me and an uncomfortable situation.

"Who says I didn't suffer brain damage?"

I look at him with crossed eyes and smile crazylike. I

hold the face until my eyes ache from the strain, but Knightley doesn't laugh.

"Sorry," I say, uncrossing my eyes. "Bad joke."

"You make me laugh, Emma Lee," Knightley says. "Though I fear you use humor to keep me at a distance. Am I right? Do you wish to keep me at a distance?"

"No!" A breeze lifts the end of his scarf, slapping it against my face. Soft, cologne-scented cashmere brushes my cheeks, my nose, my lips. I imagine Knightley's lips brushing against me in the same soft, silky manner, and I shiver. "Why would I want to keep you at a distance?"

"Hmmm," he says, grabbing his scarf and tucking it inside his jacket. "Why would you, indeed?"

He doesn't say it, but I hear the implication, like one of those movie trailer voice-overs: *Emma Lee Maxwell, the impassioned matchmaker, the seeker of soul mates, has intimacy issues. She is a hopeless romantic who doesn't want romance.* Knightley is staring at me like he expects an answer to his question, so I try to think of something to say, something true and heartfelt, something that isn't too cheesy. In my head, I see Julia Roberts standing in a shabby used bookstore in *Notting Hill*, saying, *I'm also just a girl, standing in front of a boy, asking him to love her.*

Way, way too cheesy.

"You showed tremendous courage and fidelity in returning to the field, just as you have shown tremendous courage by beginning a new life in a place wholly unfamiliar to you," he says, his voice low. "Falling in love, risking your heart, requires the same courage."

"Does it?"

"Absolutely."

"Have you ever been in love?"

"Absolutely."

My stomach roils, the taste of tea-soaked cheese bread burbles at the back of my throat, and a thought occurs to me, sudden and shocking: a pea *is* responsible for this flushed-all-over, sick-and-queasy feeling. Pea-green envy. That's it! Harriet's soup isn't making me feel sick. I have nausea-inducing envy. Right now, on some swank street, in a swank part of London, there is a woman who was the object of Knightley Nickerson's affection, a swank woman with a closet full of Burberry trenches, who sprinkles her conversations with obscure literary references. A woman who doesn't have intimacy issues.

Ew! Do you smell that? I stink to holy heaven with self-doubt and negativity. I am so gross right now. I can't even stand it. I need to just stop. Stop stinking up the air with my rancid pea-green envy and icky self-doubt.

"Thank you, Knightley." I belt my trench, nice and tight, and look him in the eye. "Thank you for watching the video of my accident and reminding me of the strength it took to get back out on that field. I am glad we are becoming . . . friends."

Friends? I hear Maddie's chiding voice in my head. *Slick, Emma Lee. You just banished Prince Charming to Friendship Forest, the place where budding romances and boners go to die.*

"I was hoping we—"

"There you are!"

Knightley clears his throat and takes a step back, clasping his hands in front of him. His lips press together in a polite, enigmatic smile.

I turn around and discover Bingley strolling toward us looking like he just walked off the pages of a fashion magazine for young jet-setters, a thick leather-bound book tucked under his arm. He is dressed in a stylishly frayed tweed vest and dark jeans rolled up at the ankles to show off leather brogue boots, boots that are so on-trend, they're practically pre-trend. His mop of sun-kissed dirty dish-water blond curls have been artfully styled to flop to one side and his sparkling blue eyes are hidden behind a pair of Cartier aviators, the golden mirrored lenses adorned with two tiny gold and black lacquer panther heads. Bin-gley Nickerson is the only man I have ever met who could wear thousand-dollar golden sunglasses on a rainy day and make it look completely natural. He is a walking glam squad. Head-to-toe fabulous.

He strolls up to us, devil-may-care grin on his boy-ishly handsome face, sun-kissed curls glowing as if he is being illuminated by a heavenly shaft of light. He glows like an old-time bronzed Hollywood matinee idol, like Leonardo DiCaprio glowed when he played Jay Gatsby in *The Great Gatsby*. I half-expect him to lower his sun-glasses, wink, and say, "Hiya, doll!"

Instead, he hands Knightley the book, and then he presses a kiss to each of my cheeks.

"Emma Lee Maxwell!"

"As I live and breathe," I say, bobbing a curtsy.

He pushes his sunglasses on top of his head and squints at me through red-rimmed eyes. "Spare me the Southern belle routine. You just cost me ten pounds, I'll have you know."

"I did? How?"

"I made a bet with old bean that you looked out your window this morning, saw our drab little village bathed in the light of a typically drab Cotswolds morning, and decided to return from whence you came. I was certain we would find you trudging down the road to Cheltenham, dragging your suitcases behind you, desperate to make it to the station in time to catch the three twenty-six to Paddington."

"Old bean?"

Knightley clears his throat.

"Old bean is the moniker I affectionately crafted for Knightley many years ago, just after our dear papa passed." Bingley grins and slaps his brother on the back. "Isn't that right, old bean?"

I want to ask Bingley why he would refer to his brother—a man who was neither old nor beanlike—by such a ridiculous name, but something else he said has piqued my curiosity. I look at Knightley.

"You really made a bet I wouldn't last more than a night in Wood House?"

"I did not," he says softly, fixing me with a serious stare. "I *would not* bet against you, Emma Lee. Not ever."

My pulse quickens. *Easy, Em. There is no reason for your sweaty palms and red cheeks. He promised not to bet against you. He did not promise eternal devotion and a platinum two-carat Cartier Destinée engagement ring.*

Bingley chuckles, and I am struck by just how different he is from his older brothers—as different as I am from my older sisters. Bingley, the golden-haired imp with the razor-sharp wit who commands the attention of any room he inhabits, is Knightley's opposite in physique and personality. Knightley, with his wavy dark hair and conservative suits, seems to be the standard bearer for all that is proper and polite, while Bingley appears eager to set a match to that standard, to torch all expectation that he behave like a British blue blood.

"Mum will be pleased to learn William hasn't frightened you off with all his talk of flesh-eating bacteria," Bingley says. "She is so looking forward to you joining the Blue-Haired Book Lovers Club, another person to knit tea cozies and rhapsodize over Jane Austen's idiosyncratic punctuation, stylistic innovations, and delightfully modern characters."

"I knew we would be discussing Jane Austen's novels, but nobody told me about the knitting." I laugh. "Tea cozies, you say?"

Bingley grins. "Loads of them, chunky sweaters for squat little pots. I believe they are working on floral-themed cozies at present. How are you with knitting roses?"

"Golly," I say, widening my eyes. "I don't know how to knit, but I have always wanted to learn! Think your mum would be willing to teach me?"

Knightley chuckles—like I am joking.

Bingley narrows his gaze.

"Funny," he says. "I didn't have you pegged as a Janeite."

"What is a Janeite?"

"A devotee of all things Austen."

"And what makes a Janeite?"

The sky has turned as dark and flat as a slate tile roof, and each breeze brings with it the random raindrops. We should hurry to Wood House before the heavens let loose, but I am having too much fun talking to Bingley (and standing on a supersweet lover's bridge, still close enough to Knightley to catch the occasional whiff of his cologne).

"Besides the aforementioned blue hair and requisite knitting needles?" He strokes his chin as if he is a professor pondering an intriguing question posed by a student. "A cultlike worship of Jane Austen and a compulsion to memorize and regurgitate the minutiae of her novels. A Janeite has an ardent passion for costume balls, tea parties, and campy Anglophilia. She will tittle over a man in uniform, mourn the passing of the fine art of letter writing, and moan with ecstasy whenever she shoves her nose between the pages of a musty old book. Plain of face and physique, she reeks of desperation, pining for a love that does not exist beyond the pages of her beloved romance novels. Her wardrobe is filled with sensible loafers, matching sweater sets, and thick-rimmed glasses. Her home is filled with chintz, cats, and a frighteningly large collection of tea cozies."

Bingley's bright blue eyes are twinkling with mischief behind his golden lenses, and I wonder if he disdains Austen and her ardent Janeists half as much as he would have me believe.

"I don't know what campy Anglophilia is, but the woman you described is the polar opposite of your mother."

"Bollocks!" Bingley laughs. "Don't let her fool you with her posh airs and dowager countess of the Abbey routine. Next time you're at Welldon, venture beyond the great hall and grand library. You'll see. Her private quarters are jammers with cozies and cats."

I laugh so hard I nearly snort. What would Miss Belle say? "Shut up!"

"Yes, Bingley." Knightley smirks. "Do shut up!"

"Consider yourself warned," Bingley says, sniffing. "She will woo you with her lemon zest scones and talk of Mr. Darcy's haughty reserve, his ten thousand per annum, and before you know it, you will be sitting in some hair salon, instructing a stylist to fashion your fabulous blond tresses into a sensible, chin-sweeping bob with wispy bangs."

"Never," I gasp, seizing the ends of my hair as if to protect them from invisible shears. "I am a Southern woman, Bingley Nickerson, which means I like my hair long and my lashes false, and anyone who tries to alter that will be kicked to the curb. I sure don't need that kind of negativity in my life."

Bingley and Knightley laugh—like I am joking.

A terrific crash of thunder, like brass cymbals in a marching band, has us finally moving, headed over the bridge and down the path to my Wood House. Knightley puts his hand on the small of my back, guiding me around potholes and puddles. Fat, icy raindrops begin to fall, plopping on my cheeks and forehead. Bingley runs ahead, but Knightley shrugs out of his coat and holds it over my head as a makeshift umbrella.

"That's awfully kind of you."

"It's nothing," he says, looking surprised.

Nothing? I suppose using his expensive cashmere coat as an umbrella to keep a relative stranger from getting drenched is nothing to a man as wonderfully well-bred as Knightley Nickerson, but to a Southern girl who has only casually dated unsophisticated jocks or smarmy frat boys, it is chivalrous and romantic.

"You're going to be soaked to the bone," I say, moving close to him, pressing my shoulder against his surprisingly warm, surprisingly muscular side. "If we huddle together, we might-could share."

Knightley looks offended, as if my offer to share the space under his coat is an affront to his masculinity, but then he wraps his arm around my shoulders and pulls me closer. We press our heads together and race back to the cottage. I am breathless by the time we join Bingley under the narrow, vine-covered awning hanging over the back door of Wood House. I reckon Knightley has more to do with my breathlessness than the dash through the raindrops. I'm not gonna lie, y'all, the man does things to me, dangerously delicious things.

Chapter Fourteen

Emma Lee Maxwell's Facebook Update:
Y'all know I am a sucker for a Nicholas Sparks movie. Today, I was thinking about a line from *The Lucky One. She was struck by the simple truth that sometimes the most ordinary things could be made extraordinary, simply by doing them with the right people . . .* Like a walk in the rain.

"Do you know what I fancy?"

Our sodden coats are hanging from hooks affixed to the foyer wall. Bingley is in the bathroom, blow-drying his golden curls, and Knightley has just finished building a fire in the fireplace. He has finger-combed his wet hair in place, but my hands itch to mess it up, to ruffle it until he looks less serious, until he looks a little dangerous. His damp white button-down is clinging to his chest, revealing chiseled pecs and a sprinkling of dark hairs. He is staring at me with those smoldering hazel eyes and—*sweet lawd!*—he doesn't need ruffled hair to be dangerous.

"What do you fancy?"

He smiles, and my breath catches.

"A proper cup of tea."

"Of course," I say, my cheeks flushing with embarrassed heat. "You must think I am a rude American, not offering you a drink. I promise my daddy raised me right. Only . . ."

"Only?"

"The electric kettle stopped working this morning, and I don't know how to light that bl—"

"Blasted stove?"

"I was going to say *bleeping* stove, but blasted works, too."

"Come on." He laughs, grabbing my hand. "I will show you how to light your bleeping stove."

"You will?"

"Absolutely," he says, leading me into the kitchen. "What sort of chap would I be if I allowed my favorite American to begin her new life in England without the means to make a proper cuppa?"

He shows me how to light the stove, taking me through the procedure step-by-step. I half pay attention, because in my head a clip of him calling me his favorite American is playing on loop. *My favorite American. My favorite American.* Knightley Nickerson is the first man who has made me feel like . . . like . . . like I don't know what. Just all distracted and self-conscious.

"Your turn," he says, extinguishing the stove and handing me a match. "Think you can manage it?"

I want to muster up some of my sister's fierceness and audacity. Tara would slant a seriously sassy, seriously sexy look at him and say, *Can I manage? A Southern woman is only helpless when her nails are wet, darlin'.*

Of course I can manage! Now, step your sexy self back because I am fixing to light me a stove.

I am not Tara.

I am tempted to do what I always do when faced with a daunting task: pout my bottom lip, bat my eyelashes, and ask a big, strong man for help. Instead, I take the match and, even though I fumble a step or two, I light that blasted, bleeping stove. I light it like nobody's business!

"Well done, you!" Knightley cries.

I am so stinking proud of myself I can practically taste it! And you know what? It tastes as fine as a bag of bourbon balls from the Candy Kitchen, as a slice of Tara's fresh-out-of-the-oven pecan pie. Shoot! It tastes as fine as the salty-sweet golden breading on a piece of Cane's fried chicken.

I assemble the accoutrements necessary for a proper English tea tray and Knightley carries the tray into the living room.

"Bloody hell!" Bingley emerges from the bathroom, his curls artfully styled again, and collapses on the couch. "Why must I live in a climate that is not conducive to my coiffure? It is only half three and I am knackered from wrestling my curls—twice!" He notices the tea tray and leans forward. "Are these ginger crisps? Mind if I have one?"

I pour tea into three cups and offer the first cup to Knightley, trying not to react as his fingers touch mine. I hand Bingley the second cup and then settle myself in a chair across from the Nickerson men, balancing the delicate saucer on my hand.

"Thanks for the tea, Emma Lee," Bingley says.

"Don't thank me," I say, smiling. "You would be dunking your ginger crisps in tepid tap water if your brother hadn't shown me how to light that blasted stove."

"What's this?" He looks at his brother, eyes twinkling. "I didn't know you possessed domestic skills, old bean."

"This might astonish, Dear Brother, but there are things you don't know about me."

"Interesting," Bingley says, stroking his chin. "I thought I was the only one with secrets."

The brothers exchange an unreadable look—volumes of unspoken words passing between them in a single glance. Is it my imagination, or did Bingley's comment seem to carry a deeper message? What secrets are Knightley hiding? I wonder.

"Bingley?"

"Yes, darling?"

"Why do you call your brother old bean?"

Bingley grins. "Well now"—he brushes ginger crumbs from his fingers and leans back, wriggling himself between two down pillows—"that is a story I would be happy to share."

"Naturally," Knightley says, rolling his eyes.

"Come now, old bean, you would not deny me the pleasure of sharing an embarrassing story, would you? After all, sharing a revealing story is the best way for people to become better acquainted, and we want to become better acquainted with Emma Lee, don't we?"

"I would prefer if the story you shared revealed your humiliations."

"Very well," Bingley says, crossing his arms. "I will tell Emma Lee the reason I call you old bean, and then you tell her what happened the first time I flew on an airplane, the year we flew to Gstaad for Christmas."

Knightley clears his throat.

"On second thought"—he shifts in his seat—"perhaps we should limit the stories to one per day. We don't want to overwhelm the poor girl."

"Ooo!" I clap my hand on my knee, causing my teacup to rattle against the saucer. A drop of tea splashes onto my knee. "Tell me what happened on your way to Gstaad! Something tells me it is a far more interesting story than the old bean one."

Truth, y'all? They both sound like interesting stories, but Knightley's palpable discomfort is rousing my protective, momma hen instincts.

"Right, then," Bingley says, rubbing his hands together. "It was Knightley's winter break during his first year at Oxford. This was when he was running with the Devonshire set."

"Devonshire? As in the Duke and Duchess of Devonshire?"

"Yes." Bingley looks at me quizzically. "Are you acquainted with the Duke of Devonshire?"

"I have no desire to be acquainted with him. I saw *The Duchess*."

Knightley chuckles.

"The Duchess of Devonshire?"

"*The Duchess* was a movie, starring Keira Knightley and Ralph Fiennes," Knightley explains. "A biographical drama about Georgiana Cavendish, the fifth Duchess of Devonshire. I believe that is the duchess to which Emma Lee was referring."

"Did you know the screenplay was an adaptation of a book?"

"*Georgiana, Duchess of Devonshire,* by Amanda Foreman. Brilliant book," Knightley says. "Did you read it?"

Oh, yes, I did! World History 101. My midterm assignment was to write an essay on a notable person from the eighteenth century. I watched *The Duchess* because I thought I could glean enough pertinent facts to bluff my way through a thousand words, but I was so moved by

Georgiana's loveless marriage and tragic affair with Charles Grey that I went straight to the library and checked out a copy of Amanda Foreman's book.

"Why, yes," I say, smiling proudly. "The Duchess of Devonshire's influence on eighteenth-century British politics and fashion was the subject of one of my college papers. I idolize her. Georgiana is BAE!"

"Ugh," Bingley says, wrinkling his nose. "For the sake of our rapidly developing friendship, I am going to pretend you did not just utter that wretched slang word. It's *sooo* two thousand sixteen."

I roll my eyes and mouth the word *whatever*.

Knightley chuckles.

The first notes of Ed Sheeran's latest love ballad begin playing. I jump up, run over to the foyer, and fish my iPhone out of the pocket of my Burberry. I look at the screen. It's Lexi. I excuse myself and step into the kitchen.

"Hey, girl," I say. "What's up?"

Lexi sniffles.

"Lex?"

"C-C-Cash said he needs a b-b-break," she sobs.

I sink down onto a kitchen chair, feeling as if the wind has been violently knocked from my lungs.

"A break-break?" I say. "A Ross-and-Rachel break?"

Ross and Rachel, two characters from the television show *Friends*, took a break from dating each other, with Ross immediately engaging in a drunken hookup with a skank he met in a bar.

"No," Lexi sniffs. "Not a Ross-and-Rachel break."

"What kind of a break?"

"He wants to go on a boys only weekend to Pigeon Forge."

"Pigeon Forge? Where in God's creation is Pigeon Forge?"

"Tennessee."

"Tennessee?"

"Right."

"What is there to do in Pigeon Forge, Tennessee?"

"That's what I asked!" Lexi does a sad little laugh-cry. "He said he just wants to blow off a little steam with his boys. Do a little fishing, maybe hit a water park."

"Is that all?" I laugh. "Girl, let the boy have his break."

"You think?"

"Cash loves you or he wouldn't have gotten down on one knee and asked you to marry him in front of his momma, your momma, and half of Charleston!"

"You think?"

"Alexandria Armistead!" I adopt my best scolding, Manderleylike voice. "It doesn't matter what I *think*. What matters is that you *know* the man you are about to promise to love, honor, and obey forever and ever, amen, loves you as much as you love him!"

"You're right."

"No doubts?"

"No doubts." She takes a deep, jagged breath. "You're the best, Ems."

"Yes, I am!"

We laugh.

"How are things there?"

"Great!"

"Are you making friends?"

I lean forward and crane my neck so I can look out into the living room. Knightley and Bingley are chatting quietly.

"I *am* making friends," I say, lowering my voice. "In fact, I am entertaining now. A proper afternoon tea party."

"Who are the girls?"

I cup my hand around my mouth.

"They're not girls."

"Boys?" she squeals. "You're having an afternoon tea party with boys?"

"Proper English boys."

"Are they cute?"

I look at the back of Knightley's head, the rectangle of exposed skin between his white shirt collar and dark hairline, and feel that flushed-all-over feeling again.

"One of them is very cute."

"How cute?"

"Lexi! They're right here."

"I don't care! I need a reading, please. Where does the cute English boy fall on the Disney hero hotness scale?"

Flynn Rider!

"I don't know, Lexi," I say, still whispering behind my hand. "I have to go."

"Uh-uh. Where, Ems? Prince Phillip? Shang? Eric?"

"Eric? Ugh! That chauvinist?"

"Okay, which hero?"

"You're a nag."

"Oh my god! He's a Flynn Rider. Isn't he?"

"Yes," I hiss. "Now hush."

"Try to snap a selfie with him. I want to see."

"I am not snapping a selfie with him."

"You love selfies."

"I really do have to go now," I say, raising my voice again. "Listen, Lex, stop worrying about Cash. Let him go on his little weekend. While he's whooping it up in Pigeon Gorge—"

"—Forge."

"Grab your girls and hit the spa."

"Ooo, that sounds like fun, but it would be way more fun if you were here. I miss you, Emma Lee."

"I miss you, too."

We say good-bye and disconnect. I walk back into the living room, misty-eyed, a tiny bit homesick, and concerned about Lexi's insecurity. I sit across from Knightley and force a bright smile.

"Sorry about the interruption."

"Is there something wrong?" Knightley asks.

"My best friend needed me to talk her down from an emotional ledge." I retrieve my cup from where I left it on the tray and take a sip of the lukewarm tea. I am not thirsty, but Knightley is staring at me with such concern, like he knows my smile is as fake as Kylie Jenner's lips, that I want to avert my gaze. A Southern woman doesn't burden others with her concerns. "Now, where were we? Oh, yes! Bingley, you were about to tell me what Knightley did to earn the nickname old bean."

"Yes, I was!" Bingley grins like a gargoyle and rubs his hands together. "Knightley went off to Oxford wearing jeans, a Swansea football jersey, and trainers. He returned that first winter break looking like a character from *Jeeves and Wooster*—"

"*Jeeves and Wooster?*"

"An old British comedy series starring Hugh Laurie," Knightley explains. "It was based on the works of P. G. Wodehouse."

"P. G. Wodehouse," I repeat. "Of course."

Of course, I have not heard of P. G. Wodehouse and I have not read her (*his?*) works. I can only hope Bingley will describe how a Wodehouse character might dress.

"Knightley strolled into the library wearing a Savile Row tweed jacket, a silk ascot tucked into his button-down, and a pipe clenched between his teeth."

"I have never smoked a pipe," Knightley protests.

"I remember a pipe." Bingley sniffs.

"There was no pipe." Knightley rolls his eyes, and I laugh.

"It pains me to admit this now, but I was obsessed with *Assassin's Creed* and spent an inordinate amount of time with a PlayStation controller in my hand, fighting off Crusader attacks on the home base."

I have a difficult time imagining someone as stylish and energetic as Bingley Nickerson loafing around paying video games.

"Knightley strolled into the library, pipe clenched between his teeth, and declared in a nasal voice, *Video games will bloody well rot your brain, Bingley. Reading is a far healthier pursuit for a lad, develops the intellect, and all that.*" Bingley is practically snorting with laughter. "Then he thrust a copy of *The Inimitable Jeeves* in my hands and strolled out of the room."

"I have never affected a nasally tone," Knightley says.

"I remember a nasally tone." Bingley wraps his arm around his middle and leans forward, hooting with laughter. "I borrowed a line from *The Inimitable Jeeves* and began greeting Knightley by saying, *I say, Old Bean, frightfully good to see you.* That is how he became old bean."

I laugh until I remember Isabella telling me her husband passed away the year Knightley went to university. I glance at Knightley. He is smiling at Bingley the same way Manderley smiles at me when I needle her for being too serious. I suddenly wonder if Knightley's old bean routine was an attempt at being the man of the house, the same way Manderley assumed a maternal role after our momma died. Knightley notices me looking at him. I expect him to be self-conscious, but he shows no signs that he is embarrassed.

"I would be crazy rich if someone had given me a dollar every time my sister Manderley said, *Read a book, Emma Lee. Read a book! Read a book!* Lawd! It annoyed me something fierce."

"Right?" Bingley asks.

"Right," I say. "Only . . ."

"Only?"

"Only, I wish I would have listened to her and read a few of those books. Manderley is the smartest person I know. She is creative and clever, a brilliant conversationalist. She can talk to practically anyone about practically anything." I look at my teacup. "I imagine you feel the same way about Knightley, don't you, Bingley?"

"Abso-bloody-lutely," he says, sarcastically blowing a kiss at his brother. "I am afraid that's the best you are going to get from me, old bean. Mum said we were to treat Emma Lee like a sister; she did not say we had to adopt her sickeningly sentimental American ways. So, do not expect me to leap up and throw my arms around you."

"Thank God!" Knightley says, chuckling.

We all laugh.

"Speaking of books." Knightley snaps his fingers, then walks over to the foyer and retrieves the book he had tucked under his arm from the table near the door. "My mother asked us to bring you this with her compliments."

Knightley presents the book with a slight bow.

"Thank you." I accept the heavy volume and trace a finger over the roses and vines embossed in gold and silver on the Tiffany-blue leather cover. *Seven Novels of Jane Austen* is also embossed on the cover. "Seven novels? *Sweet literate lawd have mercy!* How long does it take someone to write seven novels? Jane Austen must have died a very old woman, quill in hand, scratching away until her last breath."

Knightley chuckles.

"Would you believe she was only forty-one when she passed?"

"How *saaad*." I open the cover, turn the gilt-edged pages until I arrive at the table of contents, and read the titles. "Should I read them in order, starting with *Sense and Sensibility*?"

"Mum recommends you begin with *Emma*."

"Ugh!" Bingley groans.

"I am curious." I focus on Bingley, who looks as if he just swallowed the bitter dregs at the bottom of his teacup. "Why don't you like Jane Austen novels?"

My iPhone chimes, alerting me to a new text, but I ignore it and wait for Bingley's response.

"I do not find them to be revolutionary masterpieces of literature. When it comes right down to it, they are snarky little romance novels, aren't they? Don't get me wrong. I adore snark and romance"—he chuckles and points at his brother—"there's a name for your next modern retelling of a Jane Austen novel, *Snark and Romance*. I can see the opening line now: *It is a truth universally acknowledged that a man in possession of a wife must be in want of an unjaded heart, free of bitter disillusionment and the accompanying snark.* What do you say, old bean? The makings of another best seller?"

Knightley whistles. "You *are* jaded."

"I will tell you what I envision"—Bingley continues speaking, as if completely unfazed by Knightley's criticism—"yet another *Sense and Sensibility* with zombies, but the creatures only devour married women, thereby liberating men from their marital shackles. I see a whole series. *Peevishness and Perversity*."

"*Snide and Separation*?" Knightley suggests.

"Brilliant!" Bingley laughs. "Followed by *Acrimonious Abbey* and *Misanthropic Park*."

I sit quietly, observing the exchange with a growing sense of sadness and unease. Does Bingley truly equate matrimony with slavery? If so, I am going to have a difficult time finding him his perfect match. What would Patti Stanger do? On second thought, Patti Stanger doesn't really do forever and ever, amen, love matches, now does she? She does speed dating that results in high-priced booty calls and reality-television-worthy breakups.

I want to raise my hand and say, *Um, excuse me. Hopeless romantic and incurable matchmaker here. Would you mind keeping your jaded views hidden, because they look super ugly through my rose-tinted glasses?*

"Have you always been this jaded about love, Bingley Nickerson, or did you meet a Juliette Van Der Beck? Did she rip your heart out of your chest and stomp all over it with her red-heeled Louboutins?"

Bingley laughs so hard a single golden curl breaks free from its pomade prison and flops against his forehead.

"Love the obscure reference to a French rom-com and love, love, love the scrummy visual of a woman walking over my heart with a pair of heels designed by the most fabulous shoe designer ever"—he tosses his head back—"and I would love to titillate you with a tragic little tell-all, but, alas, I have no Louboutin-wearing, heart-stomping ghost rattling around in my closet of girlfriends past."

I stare at him, wide-eyed with disbelief.

"Zero. Zilch. Zippo."

"I don't believe you."

"*Zhere* does not exist"—he sniffs and affects a comical French accent—"*zhis* girl who, how you say, walk in my heart!"

"Despite the atrocious accent, he is telling the truth," Knightley says. "My little brother has been far too busy playing the bon vivant to fall in love."

"*Moi*?" Bingley gasps. "A bon vivant?"

"Yes, you."

"I don't deny I enjoy the sociable and luxurious lifestyle to which I was born and have so fervently endeavored to maintain, but I am not the only Nickerson to live the life of a bon vivant, *mon frere*. There is a wonderful little psychological theory called projection. Have you heard of it, old bean?" Bingley does not wait for his brother to answer. "What am I asking? Dr. Malcolm Dühring is one of your authors, isn't he? Your modern-day Freud, on a mission to help the masses unravel the mysteries of their minds, might suggest you practice classic projection in calling me a bon vivant. You, Monsieur *Town and Country*, are the most bon of the Nickerson vivants."

"Monsieur *Town and Country*? Is this another of Knightley's nicknames?" I ask.

Knightley clears his throat and shoots Bingley a withering, hush-your-mouth look, the sort of look Manderley has shot Tara hundreds of times.

"*Town and Country* is a lifestyle magazine for the Georgian country house set and the glossy arbiter of London high society, fashion, and culture. It is positively brimmers with articles like, 'What to Wear to Meet the Queen,' 'The Delish Sex Secrets of Britain's New Establishment,' and 'Why You Should Covet Sir Ian and Lady Tildy's Sublime Art Collection.'" Bingley grins, and again I am reminded of a gargoyle, a devilishly handsome, wickedly smart gargoyle. "If *People* and *Vogue* had a baby, it would resemble *Town and Country*. Tidbits of juicy gossip and splashy pieces about what it means to live the luxe life."

"Ooo, fun." I clap my hands. "Where can I get a copy?"

"I wonder!" Bingley cocks his head to one side, slaps his cheek, and fixes Knightley with a wide-eyed, inno-cent-as-baby-Jesus expression. "Do you know where Emma Lee might score a copy of *Town and Country*, per-haps the last winter edition?"

"Bingley writes for *Town and Country*," Knightley says, looking at me. "I believe his last piece was some-thing terribly weighty and terribly clever, like 'Caviar and Cocaine: European Restaurants That Define Deca-dence,' or was it 'How to Shag like a Thoroughly Modern Aristo'?"

Bingley gasps and presses a hand to his heart.

"Gutted, old bean. Mortally, massively wounded. You make it sound as if I penned a penny-dreadful piece." Bingley looks at me. "I wrote a retrospective on royal fashion, how the monarchy has wielded fashion to further their personal, political, and philanthropic causes. Kate loved it."

I sit up so fast I practically lift off my chair.

"Kate Middleton?"

Bingley closes his eyes and shrugs.

"The Duchess of Cambridge reads *your* articles?"

"We are practically best mates." Bingley sniffs.

"Shut up!"

Knightley groans and rolls his eyes.

"You are not best mates, not even close."

"I party with her brother, James," Bingley says, ignor-ing his brother. "He might have come up with the idea for Boomf, his marshmallow company, when we were doing shots of Smirnoff Fluffed Marshmallow at Bunga Bunga."

"What is Bunga Bunga?"

"A pizzeria-cum-karaoke bar in Battersea. Utterly kitsch.

Loads of fun. Prince Harry used to hang there, when he was still on the pull. Jennifer Lawrence, Margot Robbie, Harry Styles—"

"Harry Styles?" I squeal again. "I love, love Harry Styles."

"Me too," Bingley says. "I will take you to Bunga Bunga. We will eat pizza, do Smirnoff shots, and sing 'Kiwi' at the top of our lungs."

"Are you serious?"

"Abso-bloody-lutely!"

I look at Knightley, beaming, because this, *this,* is the life I imagined when I pictured myself moving to England. Hobnobbing with British blue bloods. Dinner parties at historic country houses. Popping to London to visit swanky shops and eateries. Sipping tea and chatting about classic literature. Okay, not the chatting about literature bit, but the rest of it. Definitely.

"You will come with us, won't you?"

"Old bean at Bunga Bunga? Have you completely lost the plot?" Bingley's explosive laughter startles me, and I nearly drop my teacup. "Can you envision Knightley getting pissed on flavored vodka and belting out 'It's Raining Men'?"

"I'll bet you have a great voice," I say, smiling a Knightley. "Though I can't imagine you singing that song."

"I will take that as a compliment."

"I meant it as a compliment."

Knightley smiles, and I imagine him pulling me into his arms and holding me real tight while he softly sings "I've Been Loving You Too Long" in my ear. On sultry summer nights, my daddy used to sit in one of the rocking chairs on the veranda at Black Ash, a glass of brandy sweating in his hand, a cigar clenched between his teeth, listening to *Otis Redding's Greatest Hits*. I sensed those were the times he was missing my momma something fierce. So, in my young mind, Otis Redding became the soundtrack of lovers, and the mournful "I've Been Loving You Too Long" the quintessential love ballad.

"You should join us, old bean," Bingley says, capturing our attention. "Invite Annalise. The editors of *Town and Country*'s Society pages are right-wing nutters. Wouldn't they just lose the plot if they were able to snag pictures of publishing titan Knightley Nickerson and supermodel Annalise Whittaker-Smith belting out a duet in some campy club miles from Marylebone?"

My heart suddenly aches, as if someone ripped it out of my chest and impaled it with their six-inch stiletto heel.

"Annalise?" I try to keep my tone casual-like. "Oh, I didn't know you had a thing going with Hayley's sister."

"I don't."

"He did." Bingley looks like the Cheshire cat, all mischievous, glowing eyes and broad, toothy smile. "And I have the back issues of *Town and Country* to prove it. My brother and Annalise were one of the couples featured in a four-part article entitled 'London's Bright Young Things,' an utterly splashy, slightly trashy piece about the lovely ones that comprise the new aristocracy."

Knightley glances at his wrist, and I notice he is wearing an antique Cartier watch, the sort that might be passed down from father to son.

"Come, Bingley," he says, standing. "It is growing late, and we have imposed on Emma Lee enough for today."

"You haven't imposed."

"You heard her," Bingley says. "We haven't imposed."

Knightley gathers our empty teacups and carries the tray back into the kitchen, returning seconds later.

"Mum is expecting us for dinner and it is after six already." He walks to the foyer and removes his coat from its hook. "That reminds me, my mother wants to know if you fancy joining her for a proper tour of Welldon Abbey tomorrow afternoon, followed by a casual dinner."

I look at him from beneath an arched brow, remembering the last time Isabella Nickerson invited me to a casual dinner at Welldon Abbey.

"How casual? Little black dress and five-course-meal casual, or jeans, tee, and pop-a-squat-on-the-grass-while-you-eat-leftovers-off-a-paper-plate casual?"

"Good God!" Bingley cries. "Our mum has never popped a squat in her life."

"Somewhere between caviar and cold cuts." Knightley laughs. "A humble home-cooked meal shared with Isabella Nickerson and her three charming sons."

"Well, when you put it that way . . ."

"I will be back to pick you up tomorrow afternoon, say around half two?"

"Sounds great."

"What are leftovers?" Bingley asks, putting a space between the words *left* and *overs*.

"Good night, Bingley."

"Good night, Janeite."

I wait until Knightley's car disappears, his headlights fading in the darkness, before grabbing my iPhone and opening my text application.

Text to Hayley Bartlett:
Hey girl! I had loads of fun with you today. Can't wait for our mango margs and makeup mash-up. What do you say we make it a sleepover and invite Deidre to join us?

Text from Hayley Bartlett:
Deidre Waites?

Text to Hayley Bartlett:
Yes. Miss Isabella told me she spends most of her free time looking after her mother, and I got the feeling she could really go for some girl time.

Text from Hayley Bartlett:
Um. Why not?

Text to Hayley Bartlett:
Yay! This is going to be so much fun. Don't forget: BYOJ.

Text from Hayley Bartlett:
Bring Your Own Jameson?

Text to Hayley Bartlett:
Jammies, silly!

Next, I text Bingley and ask for Deidre's cell phone number. His response hits my phone faster than greased lightning.

Text from Bingley Nickerson:
The more relevant question would be: Does Deidre Waites own a mobile?

Text to Bingley Nickerson:
I am serious!

Text from Bingley Nickerson:
So am I. In case it escaped your notice, No Date Waites is a spinster. Do I look like the sort of chap who surrounds himself with plain-faced, verbally incontinent spinsters? (Rhetorical question)

Text to Bingley Nickerson:
Harshness looks ugly on you, Bingley Nickerson. It clashes with your fierce Cartier Panthère specs.

Text from Bingley Nickerson:
LOL. Well played, Miss Thing. HOAS.

HOAS. Hold on a second. I grab a nail file out of my purse and file my nails while I wait for Bingley's next text. I wonder if Bingley Nickerson is as jaded and harsh as he presents himself to be, or if it is merely a shtick he has adopted for his career as a lifestyle writer. People have shticks. Olivia Tate, Manderley's bestie, adopted a Botox and *Breakfast at Tiffany's*, dahling, shtick after she moved to Hollywood. Don't get me wrong, Olivia was always a character, but she upped the volume on her *I'm ready for my close-up, Mr. DeMille* routine once she was surrounded by the plastic fantastic, Manderley's term for people in the moviemaking industry. Strip away her chakra-clearing sessions, oxygen treatments, caviar hair packs, and twenty-four-karat gold facial masks, and Olivia is just a sweet-hearted, poor girl from Poughkeepsie, trying to make a name for herself in an industry that binges and purges names like a supermodel before Paris Fashion Week. I hope Bingley has a kind heart under his sharp-dressed, sharp-witted, party boy façade.

My iPhone blings. I look at the screen. Bingley has located Deidre's contact information and texted it, along with a GIF of Taylor Swift in a pair of thick black hipster glasses, sitting in a room *brimmers* with cats. I thank him for Deidre's number but ignore the mean GIF.

Text from Bingley Nickerson:
Beware! The rapid descent into spinsterhood begins

with an invitation to join a Jane Austen book club and ends with Thursday night text sessions with a cat-loving, cozy-knitting, candy-selling virgin. Consider yourself warned.

Text to Bingley Nickerson:
   Charitable acts are the finest accessory a lady can add to her wardrobe. I have no intention of descending into cat-cuddling, cozy-knitting spinsterhood. I intend to lift Deidre up.

Sororities have this thing called Big/Little. It's when an older, more experienced sister (a Big) is paired with a younger new recruit (a Little). The Big acts as a role model to the Little, guiding her through campus and sorority life; guiding her through life, really. Sometimes, a Big has a rush crush. She sees a pledge—a sorority sister wannabe—with the cutest Lily Pulitzer dress, like, *ever*, or the Little says something superclever about the Kardashians or global warming, and the Big is gone, crushing harder than a preteen. Now, let's say a Big meets the pledges but doesn't develop a rush crush. In that case, the Big will interview several Littles. Inevitably, a Big and Little will bond over a shared passion, whether it be Netflix binging, planning theme parties, scrapbooking, or saving the whales one orca at a time. When a Big finds her perfect Little, the rush crush develops into an enduring, lifelong bestie-ship. Roberta Hearst was my Big, and I love her as much as I love my blood sisters. When it came time for me to be a Big, I rush crushed *hard*. I mean superhard, y'all. I was ready to lock it down, put a Kappa Kappa Gamma ring on it, within minutes of meeting Gemma Duncan, communications major and former all-state dance squad member. I thought Gemma was a mini-me, my perfect sorority sister match. A petite, blond people lover who wanted to make the world a happier place one friendship at a time. The Emma-Gemma union was ill-fated, tragically doomed, because Gemma turned out to be a faithless Little (fill in the blank). I am too much of a lady to go into the details. Last I heard, Gemma Duncan is living in Goose Creek, South Carolina, working as a manager at the Piggly Wiggly on Saint James Avenue. A mutual acquaintance spotted her stumbling out of a bar in the middle of the damn day with some Air Force pilot hot on her heels. Enough said.

Long story short, Gemma Duncan taught me a thing or two about how to choose a Little. The first flush of a rush crush fades mighty fast, so if you don't pick your partner for the right reasons, you're going to find yourself half of a miserably unsatisfying union. When choosing a Little, I found it is more important to share values than Netflix watching habits. Hobbies change; character is forever.

What do I know about Deidre Waites? She dropped out of college when her dad died so she could help her mom run the family business, which means she is self-less, a trait I totally admire. She takes care of her invalid mother, which means she is compassionate and nurturing. She wears tights patterned with lollipops, Heidi braids, and iridescent eye shadow, which means she is unafraid of being unique (and in a world of pouty-lipped Kardashian copycats, unique is priceless). She is warm, talkative, creative, clever, and totally puts the quirk in quirky. I don't know what Deidre binges when she signs in to her Netflix account, or if she even has a Netflix account. I don't know which One Directioner she favors (naughty Harry, with sweet Niall coming in a photo-finish close second). I don't know much about Deidre, but I know she has a good heart. That's why I am confident in my choice of Deidre Waites as my second Little.

Text from Bingley Nickerson:
   And how, pray tell, do you intend to lift No Mates Waites?

Text to Bingley Nickerson:
   Easy-peasy! Deidre Waites is going to be the first person from Northam to benefit from my God-given skills as a matchmaker.

Text from Bingley Nickerson:
   ROFL

Text to Bingley Nickerson:
   Just you watch. By this time next year, you will have to call her Many Dates and Found Her Soul Mate Waites.

Text from Bingley Nickerson:
   Doesn't exactly trip off the tongue.

Chapter Fifteen

Emma Lee Maxwell's Facebook Status Update:
Everybody wants to live happily ever after! Those
words might have been uttered by the beautiful Amy
Adams as Giselle in *Enchanted*, but that doesn't make
them less true!

I am staring at my MacBook screen, waiting for Deidre to
answer my FaceTime call, and daydreaming about the
sleepover, envisioning fun bonding activities and staying
up all night talking with my new girls, when someone in
a terrifying mask and frilly white mobcap suddenly appears on my screen.

"Deidre?"

"Emma Lee!"

"Lawd have mercy!" I cry. "What are you wearing?"

"This?" She plucks at the ruffle of her frilly white
apron. "It's a Victorian bib apron. I made it using a pat-
tern I discovered in an old manual written for nineteenth-
century domestics."

"Your face, Deidre!" I laugh. "What are you wearing

on your face? You look like the psychotic creeper in *Halloween*."

"Blimey! I forgot I was wearing my mask."

She pulls the cap off her head and removes the mask. A thick green paste is smeared over her cheeks and forehead.

"Why were you wearing a *Halloween* mask? You weren't thinking of stalking and killing Northam's teenage babysitters, were you?"

"What?" She reaches for her phone. The picture tilts and blurs, and then her paste-covered face fills my entire screen. "Stalk? Kill? Why would you think such a thing?"

"I was making a lame reference to a horror flick." Something tells me Deidre doesn't watch horror flicks. "A serial killer named Michael Myers escapes from an asylum and stalks the babysitters in his hometown wearing a supercreep white mask, like the one you were wearing."

"He wore a Victorian toilet mask?"

Ew! Toilet mask? Ew! What could possibly be happening with Deidre's digestive system that requires her to wear a full-face mask when she visits the toilet? Even though I don't think I want to know the answer to my question, I ask it anyway.

"What is a toilet mask?"

"Madame Rowley's Toilet Mask, also called a face glove, was worn by Victorian ladies of refinement to aid in the beautification and preservation of their skin. When used in concert with certain potions and lotions, it promised to give even the oldest, most tired flesh the resiliency and freshness of youth. Would you believe some women applied thin slices of raw meat to their faces before donning the mask?"

I think I might be sick. Y'all, Deidre is wearing some

old Victorian woman's meat mask. That is so nay-nay. What if she gets E. coli or Ebola? I am pretty sure you can get one of those diseases from handling raw meat.

"You're not afraid you might catch a disease from wearing someone's discarded beauty implement?"

I don't even want to know what William Curtis, village germophobe, would say if he knew one of his neighbors spent her evenings with her face strapped into a nay-nay old mask she picked up in some flea market.

"I wasn't wearing an actual Victorian-era beauty mask." She snorts. "That would be mad!"

That would be mad? Because answering a FaceTime call in a Mary Poppins apron and Michael Myers face mask isn't mad enough?

"I assume your toilet glove—"

"—face glove."

"Right, face glove," I say, wondering if all my conversations with Deidre Waites will leave me feeling like I tumbled down a rabbit hole. "Listen, Deidre. I invited Hayley Bartlett over Saturday night for a little glam session, and I wondered if you would like to join us?"

Deidre squeals. The picture blurs, there is a loud thud, and the next thing I see is Deidre's lollipop-patterned legs.

"Bloody hell!" The picture blurs again before Deidre's white-paste-covered face appears on my screen. "Sorry about that! I would be delighted to join your glam session, Emma Lee. What would you like me to bring? Zinc oxide and lotus flour extract paste guaranteed to whiten, brighten, and correct complexional imperfections? Victorian toilet masks for everyone?"

My heart lurches. Sweet Miss Watling and her precious pearls, too! What is the polite response when your guest offers to bring you a meat mask as a hostess gift?

Deidre snort-laughs.

"I am just taking the piss out of you, Emma Lee," she snorts. "I bought this mask on Etsy from an artist who specializes in Victorian reproductions. He lives in Piscataway, New Jersey. There is no way he could send two masks by Saturday. Besides"—she props up her phone and steps back, affording me a wider view of her room and the creepy mask lying on the dresser behind her—"I am having serious doubts about the efficacy of Madame Rowley's Toilet Mask. It makes my face perspire and itch."

"It's totally worth it. You have beautiful skin."

No lie. One of the first things I noticed about Deidre— after her creative use of candy canes as hair pins—was her smooth, translucent skin.

"Thank you," she says, swiping her finger across her cheek. She holds her finger up to the camera. A glob of paste is stuck to the tip. "It's the zinc oxide, lotus flower paste. Zinc oxide is good for whitening the skin. Queen Victoria used a similar formula. I have been testing out various nineteenth-century beauty rituals for a piece I am writing."

"You're a writer?"

I noticed an iron sign near the church designating Northam-on-the-Water as the winner of the "Best-Kept Small Village in Gloucestershire." If Her Majesty the Queen handed out awards for Most Literate Small Village in the United Kingdom, I reckon there would be two iron signs standing in the churchyard. Everyone I have met participates in book clubs, writes articles, publishes books, or quotes bloody Shakespeare.

"Writer? Me? Hardly." Deidre snorts and looks away. This time, the snort is more of a snort-scoff than a snort-laugh. "I have a blog. I post bits about Queen Victoria."

"That's impressive."

"My mum doesn't think so." She begins speaking in a warbly voice. "*Who do you think you are, John bloody Keegan, standing behind a lectern at Cambridge? Lucy bloody Worsley, narrating Victoriana for BBC Four? You manage a village candy shop, miss. Chocolate buttons. Wine gums. Jelly bears. Licorice allsorts. Leave the history to the historians.*"

Ouch. That's harsh.

"I would love to read your blog."

"You would?"

"Abso—" I almost mimic Bingley by ending with bloody-lutely "—lutely."

"I'll send you the link as soon as we ring off." She smiles so broadly, two giant cracks appear in her face paste. "By the way, how did you get my number?"

"Bingley gave it to me."

She moves the phone closer.

"Bingley?" Her voice rises, and she grabs her phone, holding it so her face fills my entire screen. "Ha! Ha! Very funny. Bingley Nickerson."

Is it me or does Deidre sound excitable when she talks about Bingley—more excitable than her already elevated baseline of excitability?

"Deidre?"

"Yes?"

"Do you like Bingley Nickerson?"

"What?" She snorts. "You mean like-like?"

"Yes!" I laugh. Isn't it nice to know like-like is a universal phrase for when a girl feels more than friendship for a boy? "Do you like-like Bingley Nickerson?"

She flushes, and it look as if someone drew big, bold circles on her cheeks using a stick of tarte Cheek Stain in True Love. One April Fool's, Maddie swapped my tube

of tarte Cheek Stain in Blushing Bride and I walked
around looking like Wendy, the mascot for the hamburger
fast-food chain.

"I don't like-like Bingley."

"Yes, you do!"

"No, I don't!" She reaches for something offscreen, and
a second later she is wiping the paste from her face with a
disposable makeup cloth. "Besides, Bingley is . . ."

"What?" I wait for Deidre to finish her sentence, but
an awkward pause stretches between us—the first awkward pause of our easy, free-flowing new friendship.
"Bingley is what, Deidre?"

"Bingley is . . . clever."

"You're clever."

"Me? Clever?"

Deidre seems surprised by my compliment—genuinely surprised. When you spend your life surrounded
by girls (especially sorority girls), you learn how to spot a
faux-surprised reaction to a compliment—you know, the
faux-surprised reactions that are bait meant to snag bigger, fatter, juicier compliments? *You think I look pretty?
Really? I just spent six hours at the hair salon having my
brows waxed, lashes tinted, hair highlighted and trimmed,
and another hour at MAC getting a full face, but I wasn't
sure I looked good.*

"Sure!" I smile. "Victoria's Candy Emporium: First in
Candy and Colonialism? That is wicked clever."

"Thank you," she says, brushing away my compliment
like gingersnap crumbs on a tea tray. "Bingley is a different sort of clever, though. He is like a flame, a bright,
dazzling flame, drawing people like moths with his witty
commentary and interesting stories."

Deidre might say she doesn't like-like Bingley, but her

tarte-y cheeks are telling me a different story. The cheeks don't lie, y'all.

"Deidre?"

"Yes?"

"What do you know about Knightley Nickerson?"

"What do you want to know?"

Does he always smell like a pine forest? Does he have a reputation for being a player? How long did he date Annalise Whittaker-Smith? Is he in *love* with her?

"I don't know," I say, shrugging. "Whatever."

"Emma Lee?"

"Yes?"

"Do you like Knightley Nickerson?" She leans in so her face fills the screen and waggles her eyebrows. "Do you like-like him?"

"Don't be ridiculous!"

"What's ridiculous?"

"He's old."

"He's not *that* old." She's right. He's not *that* old. "How old are you, Emma Lee?"

"Twenty-five in February."

"It's May."

"Next February."

"Well, there you go."

I shake my head, confused.

"Where am I?"

"Knightley was four years ahead of Bingley in school. Bingley is the same age as me, twenty-six, which means Knightley is thirty."

"OK?"

"Knightley's age passes the dating equation test."

"Dating equation?"

"You can date anyone who is at least half your age

plus seven; any younger and you are a pedophile." She pronounces *pedophile* with a long A instead of short E— *pay-duh-file*. "Knightley is thirty years old. Half that plus seven would be twenty-two. You are twenty-four going on twenty-five, which means he would not be a pedophile if he dated you."

"Whew." I pretend to wipe my forehead and flick perspiration from my fingertips. "I was worried Knightley might be a pedophile. Thank you for putting my mind at rest."

"Does Knightley know you fancy him?"

"I don't fancy Knightley."

"Why not?"

"Well, for starters, he's Miss Isabella's son."

"So?"

"Miss Isabella has been like a fairy godmother, breezing into my life and changing things for the wonderful."

"*Bibbidi-Bobbidi-Boo, I think you like-like you know who*!" Deidre sings, waving a tube of mascara like a wand. "*Scallama do methink a boo, Emma Lee and Knightley-poo. Put 'em together and what have you got? Bibbidi-Bobbidi-Boo.*"

"And you think you aren't clever," I say, laughing. "I doubt Bingley Nickerson could compose a Disney tune on the fly."

"It's hard to kick free from the current when you are swimming in the river Denial, isn't it, Miss Bibbidi?"

I laugh. "It sure enough is, boo."

The door behind Deidre opens. Mrs. Waites shuffles into the room, squinting behind a pair of Coke bottle–thick eyeglasses. Her cardigan is misbuttoned. She looks directly into the camera lens and a smile flickers at the corners of her mouth, but then she starts moving her head

all around like one of those bobblehead dolls and blink-
ing her eyes.

"Deidre?" She flails her hands through the air. "Is that
you, Deidre?"

"I am here, Mum."

"Deidre," Mrs. Waites says, still groping at nothing.
"Are you there? Is anybody there?"

I feel like the worst kind of sinner for thinking this,
y'all, and I swear, one hand on my heart and the other on
the Bible, swear, the good Lord can strike me dead if I am
lying, but I wonder if Mrs. Waites might be exaggerating
her level of dependency to keep Deidre at her disposal.
Last night, at Miss Isabella's dinner party, Mrs. Waites
appeared needier when Deidre was chatting with guests
closest to her age.

"Hello, Mrs. Waites," I say, raising my voice. "It is
nice to see you. I hope you are having a good evening."

"Who is there?" Mrs. Waites opens her mouth and
squints her eyes so tight she looks like Mickey Rooney
when he played Mr. Yunioshi in *Breakfast at Tiffany's*,
one of the most cringeworthy performances ever because
of the offensively stereotypical way Rooney portrayed an
Asian man. "You didn't tell me you were inviting a guest
home, Deidre."

"Be right back, Emma Lee," Deidre says, before grabbing one of her mother's arms and leading her out of the
room. "It's Emma Lee, Mum. We are talking on the Face-
Time . . ."

She returns a minute later, flushed and out of breath. I
tell her my little margarita-and-makeup-themed soirée is
a sleepover. She squeals. I ask if she will be able to find
someone to stay with her mother, but she says her mother
is fine on her own, that she only needs help when she is

moving about the village. I remind her to bring her jammies and we disconnect.

Poor Deidre! She is on the losing side of the toss whichever way the coin lands. Either Mrs. Waites is optically challenged and requires as much care as a toddler, or she is a talented actress with serious attachment issues. It is quite a burden for someone so young.

I grab my MacBook, walk over to the couch, and flop down, nestling into the down-filled cushions and resting my feet on the edge of the ottoman Bingley style. I balance my MacBook on my stomach and formulate an action plan to transform my Little's life from drab to fab.

First, I will help her become the fierce, empowered woman she is meant to be by encouraging her to turn her blog into a book. That will help her gain financial independence and allow her an outlet for her stifled creativity.

Second, I will be her Big. I will give her the support and encouragement she craves, the support and encouragement her mother seems incapable of giving her. And I will ease her caretaking burdens by helping care for her mother.

Finally, I will find my Little a man. No, not a man. I will find her *the* man—*the* man created by God Almighty, delivered to this earth by a host of heavenly angels, and divinely selected to be Deidre's soul mate. It is my moral obligation, my sacred duty as a Big.

Chapter Sixteen

Emma Lee Maxwell's Facebook Update:
Did you know Queen Victoria set the white bridal gown trend? She wore a white satin gown for her big day because she thought the fabric showed off her lace trim and veil. Just like Meghan Trainor, old Vic was all 'bout that lace, 'bout that lace. The train of her gown was ten feet long and made entirely of Devonshire lace. Her shoes were white-satin ballerina slippers with laces that wrapped around her ankles—proving Audrey Hepburn wasn't the first style icon to opt for flats, ladies. Victoria's wedding slippers are on display in the Northampton Museum and Art Gallery in Northampton, England. My friend, **Deidre Waites**, writes a superinteresting, superhilarious blog about Queen Victoria. Check out We Are Not Amused, y'all.

I have mixed feelings for Queen Victoria. On the one hand, I dig that she was so hopelessly in love with Prince Albert of Saxe-Coburg-Gotha that she defied convention, as well as parliamentary and public opinion, and asked him to marry her. You go, royal girl! Forget the haters, get down on one little knee and ask Albert for his hand in marriage. She was also interested in technology, encouraging advances in transportation, medicine, communication, and photography. If she were alive today, I think she would be a social media sensation, snapping selfies at her many palaces and starting trending topics, #MonarchyMonday. Victoria was also a romantic who tried her hand at matchmaking. What's not to love about a romance-addicted queen with talent for making marvelous matches?

On the other hand, she was short-tempered, stubborn, spoiled, and downright callous about the Irish Situation. A nasty potato blight ravaged the potato crops throughout Europe. Potatoes were a staple of the Irish diet. Do you know what Queen Victoria did when she found out tens of thousands of Irish were starving to death? She sent two thousand pounds. Two thousand measly pounds! Her satin wedding dress with the ten-foot lace train probably cost more than two thousand pounds! Shame.

Then, when Prince Albert died, she went nuttier than a heaping helping of Tara's pecan pie. She turned his rooms into a mausoleum and forced the servants to continue their morning ritual of delivering hot water to the prince's bathroom. Pecan pie nutty, y'all.

And the way she treated her children, especially her oldest son, poor Bertie, I can't even . . .

I have spent the evening reading Deidre's blog and learning loads more about nineteenth-century history than I ever did in my World History classes. We Are Not Amused is written from Queen Victoria's perspective, with snarky asides and hilarious advice on marriage, motherhood, and how to masterfully manipulate a prime minister.

It's nearly nine thirty, or half nine as they say here in England, when I click out of Deidre's blog. It's probably too late to text a friend who isn't a bona-fide bestie, but I can't help myself.

Text to Deidre Waites:
I was right. You are wicked clever. Your blog is sooo smart and sooo funny. I can't remember when I enjoyed reading about history.

Text from Deidre Waites:
You are too kind.

Text to Deidre Waites:
Girl, I am not being kind. You are a good writer. Have you considered turning your blog pieces into a book?

Text from Deidre Waites:
Thank you, but I doubt anyone would want to read it.

Oh, Deidre. Deidre! Ye of little faith and many doubts! *This*. This is why God has chosen me to be your Big, my dearly, doubting Little. He wants me to infect you with a bit of my highly contagious confidence.

Text to Deidre Waites:
I saw your comments section. It was jam-packed with comments from readers all over the globe. You have a serious following, Sister. Capitalize on it. Write a book from Queen Victoria's perspective.

Text from Deidre Waites:
I would not know where to begin.

Text to Deidre Waites:
You begin with a title.

Text from Deidre Waites:
Ha. Ha.

Text to Deidre Waites:
What if you wrote a manual on how to raise children, like one of those *What to Expect* books, but in the queen's voice? You could call it *A Very Nasty Object* because that is what Queen Victoria called her baby.

Text from Deidre Waites:
I love that idea! You are bloody brilliant.

Text to Deidre Waites:
Yes, I am. You're welcome.

Text from Deidre Waites:
Good night, Emma Lee.

Text to Deidre Waites:
Good night, Your Majesty.

I click out of my text screen, enter the words *monetize* and *blog* into my search bar, and scroll though the hits until I find a Forbes article about ten wildly successful blogs that earn outlandish incomes. I send a copy of the article to Deidre, urging her to monetize her blog.

My daddy always said, *Your head will rest squarely on your pillow, and you'll sleep a whole lot easier, Emma darlin', if the balance of your daily deeds includes more positive than negative.* Tonight, my balance sheet is in the black, and it feels fab!

I wish I could call Daddy to tell him about my day. I know he would be mighty proud to hear I talked Lexi down from her emotional ledge *and* conquered my fear of death by AGA explosion. I know he would approve of my plan to befriend and empower Miss Deidre Waites. Still, it would be nice to tell Daddy about my day, to hear the reassuring *puh-puh* sound of him sucking on his pipe while he listened to my prattling.

I reckon I could tell Miss Isabella when I see her to-morrow. Miss Isabella! Shoot! I lift the massive leather book off the ottoman and flip to the table of contents. I got so caught up in Deidre's blog, I plum forgot about my reading assignment.

I look at the clock: 9:42.

I might-could knock it out tonight. How long could it take to read one little old Jane Austen novel? An hour or two? Three, tops.

Let's see. *Emma* starts on page 657 and ends on page 915. Sweet lawd! That's over two hundred and fifty pages! Two hundred and fifty *hardback* pages, not teensy paperback pages. Two hundred and fifty hardback pages of teensy-tiny print.

I groan and close the book. I have a flashback to sophomore year statistics class, to reading the textbook (over and over) and feeling hopelessly lost in the gob-bledygook terminology and theories of inferential statistics. Efficient estimators, root mean square errors, transposed conditional fallacy. *Mwah-mwah-mwah.* Charlie Brown teacher-speak. That's what I hear in my head whenever I attempt sustained reading. *Mwah-mwah-mwah.*

I stare at the cover, at Jane Austen's name stamped in swirly silver font, and feel a pang of guilt. My momma loved reading so much, she named her babies after her fa-vorite novels. Manderley was named after the hero's home

in Daphne du Maurier's *Rebecca*, Tara was named after
Scarlett O'Hara's plantation in *Gone with the Wind*, and I
was named after the heroine of Jane Austen's *Emma*.

Manderley can recite huge passages from *Rebecca*.

Tara has watched *Gone with the Wind* so many times,
she knows the entire movie word-for-word.

Me? I haven't read *Emma*. Not one word.

Manderley would say my refusal to read *Emma* is a
manifestation of the deep psychological distress I suffered from losing my momma while I was still in Pam-
pers. Invisible wounds to the psyche and all. Sure. That.

Or—

Maybe it doesn't go that deep. Maybe I don't have the
attention span to sit through 157,887 words (just Googled
it, y'all)! Maybe I have attention deficit hyperactivity disorder, or dyslexia, or maybe I am just flighty.

Or—

I might-could have a few teensy-tiny blemishes on my
psyche. Teensy. Tiny. Maybe I haven't read my momma's
favorite books because it would be like giving her a
voice. Right now, Momma is this mute ghost of a woman
who inhabits a small room in the attic of my mind. She is
a picture in the family photo album, a distant relative we
remember on holidays. I know she existed because people tell me she did.

I have kept my momma at a distance because letting
her in, gathering precious memories of her, and holding
them close, would only remind me of what I lost, what I
never really had.

Maybe I keep myself busy with a dizzying swirl of activity and fill my life with a dizzying number of friends because I am trying to keep my momma's ghost in the attic.
Ghosts do not haunt busy houses, do they? They haunt
quiet houses, houses inhabited by sad, solitary people.

Chapter Seventeen

Emma Lee Maxwell's Status Update:
I am in love, y'all! I started reading Jane Austen's *Emma* last night and now I have a major lady crush on Emma Woodhouse. Talk about #goals. She is so sweet and generous to everyone she meets. She befriends Harriet Smith, even though Harriet is fashionably challenged and dumb as a packet of Pop Rocks. I got to the part where Emma wisely advises Harriet against marrying Mr. Martin (the uneducated farmer) and suggests, instead, she consider Mr. Elton (the sociable village vicar). Clever girl, Emma! I like Mr. Elton!

I am applying my fourth shade of red lipstick and daydreaming about Knightley—Mr. George Knightley, Emma Woodhouse's old and intimate friend—when the sound of the iron knocker pounding against the wood door echoes down the hall.

I blot my lips with a Kleenex, brush some illuminator on the apples of my cheeks, then spritz Viva La Juicy into the air and walk through the vanilla-berry scented cloud.

I open the front door and find Knightley standing on the steps—Knightley Nickerson, my new and not-quite-intimate friend. Bingley is striding up the path, dressed in charcoal utility pants rolled up at the ankles, a gray cashmere hoodie, high-top leather trainers, and a slouchy checked coat. He has a scowl on his handsome face and is patting his errant curls.

"Hello, Emma Lee." Knightley smiles, and my tummy feels the same way it did when the squad would toss me up in the air—a momentary tensing and then a sense of weightlessness and joy. "You look awfully happy today."

"Do I?"

"Your smile could chase the darkest clouds away."

My teeth ache the same way they ache when I drink too many glasses of sweet tea. *My smile chases away the clouds.*

"That is the sweetest thing anyone has ever said to me," I say, smiling even bigger, even brighter. "Like, ever."

Bingley climbs the steps.

"Hello, Emma Lee."

"Hello, Bing—"

"Are you seeing what is happening up here?" He waves his hand around his head. "This humidity is wreaking havoc with my hair. My curls won't behave. They look positively barking. Would you mind if I borrowed a spritz of that Morrocanoil Frizz Control Mist you have in your bathroom, the one I used yesterday?"

I step back into the foyer. Knightley and Bingley follow.

"I might-could let you have a spritz or two."

"Ouch!" Bingley presses his hands to his ears. "What was that?"

"What was what?"

"The offensive sound that came out of your mouth?"

Offensive sound? Did I make an offensive sound? Confused, I look from Bingley to Knightley. Knightley rolls his eyes and shrugs.

"Look at you"—Bingley gestures toward me—"in your Burberry trench and statement red lips, working this foyer like Gigi working the runway in Milan. Love the trench, love the lips. I even love the military red Hunters, despite the brand-suffering massive prole drift ever since Kate was photographed in those French-made wellies."

"What is *prole drift*?"

"*Prole drift* is a fabulously snooty term to describe when posh items become popular with the middle or lower classes," Bingley says, nudging the toe of my boot with the toe of his trainers. "Hunter wellies, Molton Brown soap, embroidered slippers, signet rings. Prole drift, love. Prole drift."

I look down at my beloved and long-coveted wellies, freshly polished and gleaming in the subdued foyer light.

"What's wrong with my wellies?"

"Nothing," Knightley says.

"Bingley says they're not posh."

"Sorry, love. Hunters are not posh," Bingley says. "They're just plain naff."

"Naff?"

"Common, drab," Knightley explains.

"Drab?" I cry, resting my hands on my hips and giving him a serious face. "Darlin', I am a Southern woman. There's nothing drab about me!"

"You're missing the point," Bingley says. "You're a picture, darling, a veritable masterpiece, until you open your mouth. Don't do that."

"Bloody hell, Bingley!" Knightley growls. "You venture too far."

"Sorry-not sorry." Bingley grins at me. "Mum told me to treat you as a sister, Emma Lee. Do you think I, Bingley Nickerson, would let my sister say anything as uncouth as *might-could*?" He links his arm through mine and pulls me with him toward the bathroom. "Have you been to the Louvre?"

"No."

"So, you haven't seen the *Mona Lisa*?"

"No, I haven't."

"I have"—he sniffs—"and it was one of the most anticlimactic moments of my life, a crushing disappointment. First, the canvas is only about this big"—he makes a small frame with his fingers—"and it hangs on a wall behind a wooden railing, too far for proper observation. It's offensive, really."

"Your point?" Knightley calls after us.

"*Mona Lisa* is a beauty, a work of genius. Now, imagine if by magic or miracle, she was animated and given voice—"

"Like the portraits in the *Harry Potter* movies, the ones hanging in the gallery at Hogwarts?"

"Exactly." Bingley strides into the bathroom, seizes my bottle of Moroccanoil hair mist, and begins spritzing his curls. "You are standing in the Louvre, marveling at her sphinxlike beauty, when she opens her mouth and lets out a massive belch."

Knightley groans, the sound carrying down the hallway. Bingley continues to spritz his hair with the oil until the curls are slick.

"You are the *Mona Lisa*, Emma Lee"—he stops spraying and points the bottle at me—"and your *might-could* is a massive belch."

"I will make you a deal." I wrest the Moroccanoil mist from Bingley's hand and put it back on the counter, then grab my can of dry shampoo and spray his overly misted curls, fluffing them until they look normal again. "I promise not to say *might-could* if you promise not to say *prole drift*. Deal?"

Bingley looks in the mirror and grins.

"Deal!"

We are driving to Welldon Abbey when my Ed Sheeran love ballad/ringtone begins playing. Hearing the happy computerized xylophone beats makes me want to tap my feet. Then Ed makes the same throaty moan I make when I eat Cane's chicken, *mmm-mmm-mmm*, and sings about putting his hands on someone's body, and Knightley looks over at me, eyebrow raised, lips curved in a half smile, and the song suddenly sounds nasty, something a naughty girl would choose as her ringtone.

I pull my phone from my purse and push the Mute button. The car is quiet again, a loud quiet. I look at the screen. Oooo! It's Johnny Amor calling me back! I look over at Knightley.

"Do you mind if I answer this call?"

"By all means."

I tap the screen and press the phone to my ear.

"Hello?"

"'ello. Emma Lee?"

Johnny Amor has a gravelly, rock-star voice, as if he has spent his life gargling whiskey and singing Stones tunes. I imagine him in his pink velvet suit, sprawled out on a black-leather couch, a cigarette dangling from his bottom lip.

"Yes!" I sound girlish, giddy. "Is this Johnny Amor?"

"The one and only, love."

"I am so glad you called!"

Did my voice just squeak? I think my voice squeaked.

"Of course I called, love," he says in his growly, gravelly voice. "Grand has been banging on about the pretty American girl he met at the airport. He is gone mad for you, barking mad, love."

Bingley leans forward from the backseat, resting his arm on the back of my seat and staring at me with unabashed curiosity.

"Aw!" I stare out the windshield, ignoring Bingley. "Thank you for saying that, Johnny Amor! I am gone, too. Totally gone. I was supernervous about traveling alone to a foreign country and—"

"—and Grand granded you, right?"

"Right!"

"He has adopted grandchildren from Chelsea to Changzhou."

"Seriously?"

"There is a sous chef slaving his little fingers to the bone in the kitchens of Traders Fudu Hotel so he can earn the money to send Grand a Boxing Day gift." He chuckles. "True story."

"How great is that?" I laugh, because Johnny Amor and his grand Grand make me feel happier than computerized xylophone beats in a naughty Ed Sheeran song. "Goal: I want to be William Amor when I am older."

"You want to be a tweed-wearing septuagenarian ornithologist? Groovy, love. Groovy."

"Orin-what?" I laugh.

"Ornithologist."

Bingley taps my shoulder. I look at him, and he mouths the word *bird-watcher*. I shift my phone to my other ear and glare at Bingley. He sits back.

"Oh," I say. "You mean bird-watcher?"

Johnny Amor laughs.

"Did you just Google ornithologist?"

"No." I laugh. "My extremely nosy, extremely literate friend is creeping on this call. He told me what it means."

"*He*? This just got infinitely more interesting." Johnny lowers his voice. "Did the pretty American take a British boy as her new lover? Grand will be devastated."

"Lover?" Did my voice just squeak again? "Oh my sweet heavenly *lawwwdd*! Bingley Nickerson is *not* my lover!" I laugh, a squeaky, high-pitched laugh that makes me sound as if I just sucked helium from a balloon. "No. Bingley Nickerson is not my lover. What is the opposite of lover?"

"Hater?"

"That's a tad too strong. Do you have a little brother, Johnny Amor?"

"Yes."

"Is he annoying?"

"Abso-bloody-lutely."

"There you are," I say. "You have an annoying little brother, and I . . . well, I have a Bingley."

"Are you hearing this, old bean?" Bingley leans forward, sticking his head between the front seats. "Should I be offended? I am feeling offended."

I put my hand over the phone mic and tell Bingley to hush, then say a silent prayer that Johnny Amor doesn't ask me about old bean. *Old Bean? Who is Old Bean? Is he your lover?* Knightley Nickerson might not be my lover, but he might-could be. Sweet lawd! I did not just say that (in my head), did I?

"I have a confession to make," Johnny says.

"Already?" Thank you, Jesus! Johnny Amor did not ask me if I was bumping uglies with Old Bean Nickerson. "I am not sure I am ready to hear your confession, Johnny Amor. We just met."

"Don't worry, love," he growls. "I only confess my dark deeds to someone who can offer absolution, like my vicar. I was just going to admit that I did a little creeping myself."

"Creeping?"

"I internet-stalked you before calling you back. Had to make sure you weren't a nutter." He takes a deep breath. I hear ice clinking against glass and imagine him mixing an old-fashioned, splashing bitters over a sugar cube, squeezing an orange, pouring whiskey over the ice. "Love your Facebook profile. Supersexy pic, love."

"Thanks," I say. "So, you could tell I wasn't a nutter from my profile photo?"

"Profile photo, Insta feed, and some great snappies on a sorority blog."

"You found the Kappa Kappa Gamma blog?" I whistle. "Wow! You went deep."

"That is the only way to go, love. The only way."

Bingley groans and leans back. A bubble of nervous laughter rises in my throat, pops out of my mouth. Is Johnny Amor flirting with me? Or is this part of his shtick, his rock-star-on-the-rise, yeah, baby, yeah shtick?

"This is so not fair! You went deep into me"—Knightley clears his throat and my cheeks flush with humiliating, mortifying, please Lawd, let-me-die-right-here, right-now heat—"Yikes! That came out wrong. I meant, you internet-stalked me and probably found a bunch of embarrassing photos from my Kappa days."

"Like the one of you in that hilarious bunny costume at the Reading Is Fundamental fund-raiser?" Johnny Amor must be swirling his old-fashioned because I can hear the rhythmic clink-clink-clink of ice hitting glass. "Who were you supposed to be, Peter Rabbit?"

"Bridget Jones."

"Bridget bloody Jones?" He laughs. "In a flannel onesie?"

I remember the costume. Red flannel penguin pajamas, high heels, tall satin bunny ears, and puffy white tail. Thank God Knightley didn't fall down the internet rabbit hole when he was searching for my Clemson cheer vids and land on those tragic photos!

"We were supposed to dress as our favorite literary character."

"And you went as Bridget Jones?"

"Bridget Jones happens to be one of my favorite literary characters." I lift my chin and raise my attitude. "Ain't no shame."

"Chick lit?" Johnny Amor asks.

"Chick lit?" Bingley cries.

"What's wrong with chick lit?" I glance at Knightley, but he is staring straight ahead, his fingers wrapped around the leather steering wheel. "Chick lit is about the four Fs: friendship, fabulous shoes, funny moments, and finding yourself."

"I thought it was about fat girls who lose the stones, find the man, and score the rock," Bingley says. "Who knew?"

Johnny Amor laughs.

"Honestly, Bingley Nickerson," I sniff. "I don't know what I find more appalling: your blatantly sizeist attitude or your ill-informed, warped view of one of the finest subgenres of literature."

"Give it to him, love," Johnny Amor says.

"I could even argue that *Emma* is a chick-lit novel."

"*Emma*?" Bingley laughs. "Chick lit?"

"At the risk of sounding absurdly reductive," Knightley says, keeping his gaze fixed on the road, "*Emma* is a witty tale featuring a female protagonist and themes of friendship, romance, self-discovery, and, ultimately, personal growth. If it were published today it would be categorized as chick lit, or farm lit, because the story takes place in a rural setting."

"If Jane Austen were alive today, she would be writing about Manolos and martinis instead of kid slippers and Madeira," I say, resisting the urge to stick out my tongue at Bingley. "Say what you will about the vacuousness of Bridget Jones, but Emma Woodhouse spends an inordinate amount of time talking about ribbons. Hair ribbons. Basket ribbons. Ribbons for her gown. Ribbons for her bonnets. How many ribbons does one girl need?"

Knightley chuckles.

"Listen, love," Johnny Amor says. "As much as I am enjoying this convo, I must ring off."

I feel a flush of shame and I know, deep down in my bones *know*, Miss Belle's ghost is hovering nearby, pursing her pale, ghostly lips and shaking her pale, ghostly head, because I conducted a conversation with one person while being on the phone with another. Then again, Miss Belle never met Bingley bleeping Nickerson!

"I'm sorry," I say. "The next time you call, I promise I will give you my undivided attention."

Next time, I will make sure Bingley isn't buzzing around in the background, like some pesky old gnat. Buzz, buzz, buzzing. I hear Miss Belle's voice in my head. *Your mood should not dictate your manners, Emma Lee Maxwell; best not blame your rudeness on young Mr. Nickerson.*

"Are you joking?" Johnny says. "I loved our tête-à-tête. Fancy meeting me for drinks sometime?"

"I would love to meet you for drinks, Johnny Amor! Would you mind if I brought a friend?"

"The highly literate friend?"

"A girlfriend."

"I'm easy!" Clink. Clink. "I have a massive gig in a few weeks. Loads of bands. Fancy watching me prance around a stage in a velvet suit?"

"Are you kidding? I would love to watch you perform!"

Bingley groans.

"Brilliant! I'll text you the address. It's a late slot, so leave the glass slippers at home and plan on staying out past midnight, Cinderella."

"Ooo, fun."

"I'm chuffed to meet you and your girlfriend," he says. "If something comes up, give me a bell. Cheerio."

"Bye."

Text from Johnny Amor:
Saturday, June 16 @ 7. The Lucky Pig. 5 Clipstone Street, Fitzrovia. Oxford Circus is the closest Tube station.

I have barely finished slipping my phone back into my purse when Bingley leans forward and drapes his arm over the back of my seat. He pushes his sunglasses on top of his head and pierces me with his sharp, green-eyed stare.

"Who is Johnny Amor?"

"A boy."

"A boy!" He rolls his eyes. "Where did you meet this boy?"

"I haven't met him. I am meeting him in London next month."

"Are you off your trolley?" Bingley nudges his brother. "Did you hear that, old bean? Emma Lee has a date to meet some wanker in London."

"I heard," Knightley says.

"Johnny Amor is *not* a wanker!"

"There's another thing," Bingley cries. "Stop calling him bloody *Johnny Amor*."

"That's his name."

"Is it?" Bingley reaches into his coat and whips his mobile phone out of his pocket. "Is it really? Are you quite certain? Have you Googled him?"

"Why would I Google him?"

"He Googled you, didn't he?" Bingley lowers his voice, his words rumbling in his chest. "*I stalked you, love, stalked you harder than a lad searching for spank shots of Adriana Lima. Did you feel it, love?*"

"Ew!"

"Too far, Bingley," Knightley snaps. "Apologize to Emma Lee."

"Apologize? Have you completely lost the plot?" Bingley exhales so hard his breath flutters his curls. "What would Mum say if she knew Emma Lee planned to meet a strange man in London? A strange man named *Johnny Amor*?"

"What's wrong with his name?" I ask.

"Johnny Amor? Honey, please." Bingley rolls his eyes. "I'll wager that is not his real name. Johnny Amor! Johnny Amor! It sounds fictitious."

"Says the man named after a character in a Jane Austen novel," I say, grinning. Knightley laughs, and I suddenly remember he was also named after a character in one of Jane Austen's novels. "No offense, Knightley."

"None taken," Knightley says. "Seeing as you are also named after a character from the same novel."

"Johnny Amor sounds like a right tosser," Bingley says.

"You don't know anything about him."

"What do you know about him?"

"I know he has the sweetest granddaddy in the world

and I know he studied English language and literature at Oxford."

"Studied?" Bingley asks, eyebrow raised.

"Yes, studied. What's your point?"

"*Studied*, not graduated?"

"He dropped out to pursue his passion."

"Internet stalking?" Bingley scoffs. "No, don't tell me, he's a gigolo. His passion is meeting innocent women and bilking them of their fortunes."

"He is *not* a gigolo."

"Are you sure? Johnny Amor sounds like the name of a gigolo." Bingley nudges his brother. "What do you think, old bean? Is Johnny Amor a dodgy sort who will diddle Emma Lee the moment he has the chance? Is he a gigolo?"

"Ew!" I slap Bingley's arm. "You're nasty. Nobody is diddling Emma Lee."

"Diddle means rob," Knightley explains, his lips quirking.

"Oh." My cheeks flush with heat. "Well, he's not a dodgy diddler and he's not a gigolo."

At least, I don't think Johnny Amor is a gigolo. Then again, Mr. Amor did mention something about Johnny wearing velvet suits and engaging in a concerning number of Tinder hookups.

"Aha!" Bingley points at my face. "See there?"

"What?"

"Your forehead is furrowed."

I slap my hand over my forehead, feeling for wrinkles.

"My forehead isn't furrowed." I look at Knightley. "Is it?"

"It was slightly furrowed," he says.

"I definitely saw furrowing"—Bingley leans forward until he is practically sitting on the armrest—"which means you have misgivings about Johnny Amor, international man of mystery and gigolo extraordinaire."

"I am not about *that* life."

"What life?"

"That life of doubting people and being skeptical of everyone I meet," I say. "I trust people until they give me a reason to distrust them." I look at Knightley, frowning. "Distrust or mistrust?"

"They are roughly the same," Knightley answers. The sunlight is slanting through the driver's window, illuminating his handsome face. "Though, when you distrust someone it is usually based in a negative experience. Mistrusting someone means you have a general feeling of unease, even if it is not based in a negative experience."

"Thank you."

"Yes," Bingley says. "I am sure Emma Lee is grateful for the grammar lesson, Professor Nickerson, but I am more concerned about her safety. She is about to go on the pull with a gigolo."

"On the pull?" I ask.

"Slang for hookup," Bingley explains.

"I am not hooking up with Johnny Amor."

"You're not?"

Knightley exhales. Loudly. Is it my imagination or does he look relieved, has his posture relaxed a little?

"I am meeting Johnny Am"—I stop myself before saying Johnny's last name—"to see if he would be a good match for Deidre."

"Deidre? *Waites*?" Bingley laughs. "What makes you think a flamboyant lounge singer would be a good match for a shy village sweetshop owner?"

"Johnny's granddaddy said one of the reasons Johnny dropped out of Oxford was to help his best friend start an indie book publishing company. Deidre left Oxford to take care of her mother and tend to the family sweet-shop." Knightley looks at me and smiles, and my heart feels weightless again. "That tells me they are both compassionate and self-sacrificing. It doesn't matter if Johnny lives in London and dresses in velvet suits—"

"Hang on!" Bingley hoots with laughter. "You didn't say anything about velvet suits. I think we have the answer to our most provocative question. Johnny Amor is certainly a gigolo."

"—just as it does not matter if Deidre lives in a village and wears quirky hipster clothes," I say, continuing as if Bingley had not interrupted me. "Those things don't matter. What matters is character. Fashion is transient, Bingley; an ugly soul is forever."

"Hear, hear," Knightley says, turning the car off the road and onto the long drive leading to Welldon Abbey. "Jane Austen couldn't have said it better herself. Though, surely she would have mentioned something about ribbons."

I grin, pleased as pineapple punch by Knightley's compliment, and rest my head against the plush leather headrest, staring out the window at the rolling hills dotted with wooly sheep. The Johnny Amor–Deidre Waites match is going to be a tremendous success. I can feel it, deep down in my bones, the same way I felt Lexi and Cash would make a great match, the same way I felt Zac Efron would be the breakout star of *High School Musical*. Lexi and Cash are engaged to be married and Zac is the only member of the *HSM* cast to make a name for himself in Hollywood, a real name. What has Ashley Tisdale been in since *HSM*, *Scary Movie XVII*? I am not hating on Ashley. I swear I'm not. Snaps to her for sticking in there and acting her little heart out in a string of B movies, voice-over gigs, and Disney shows, but she is no Zac Efron.

"Emma Lee?" Knightley's deep voice startles me.

"Yes."

"Bingley is concerned about you, even if he has expressed his concern in a childish and offensive manner," Knightley says, staring at me with an intensity that takes my breath away. "We are both concerned about you traveling to London to meet a stranger. It is a big city and we would feel personally responsible if something bad happened to you."

"You would?"

I look at Knightley, see the concern reflected in his brown-green eyes, and my tummy tenses again.

"Yes," he says. "I would."

"Where are you meeting Johnny Velvet Amor?" Bingley asks.

"A place called The Lucky Pig."

"In Fitzrovia? I will go with you," Bingley says.

"That's not necessary."

"It is," Bingley says, leaning forward again.

"Seriously?"

"I believe it is my solemn duty as your foster brother to keep you from making atrocious errors in your speech and to safeguard you from velvet-wearing gigolos. You wouldn't deny me the right to complete my duties, would you?"

"Bingley," Knightley growls. "What gives?"

"What?"

"Why the sudden interest in chaperoning Emma Lee?"

"What?" Bingley cries. "What are you implying? That I have an ulterior motive?"

"Don't you always have an ulterior motive for the things you do?"

"Ouch." Bingley presses a hand to his heart. "That hurt, old bean."

"You will survive," Knightley says.

"I have an idea," Bingley says. "Why don't *you* go with Emma Lee to meet Johnny the Velvet Gigolo, Knightley?"

Knightley remains silent, gaze fixed on the drive, a muscle working in his jaw.

"Ha!" Bingley laughs. "What am I saying? Knightley Nickerson, publisher and CEO of Nickerson Publishing, would not be seen in Fitzrovia."

"What's wrong with Fitzrovia?" I look over at Bingley. "Is it the dodgy part of London?"

"Dodgy?" Bingley chuckles. "I wouldn't call Fitzrovia dodgy. A lot of celebs live there, even though it ranks as one of the worst places to live in the country because of crap housing, air quality, and traffic. It attracts a bohemian crowd—the boujie bohemians, the sort that order pomegranate martinis and spend their Friday nights touring art galleries. Loads of camp pubs, lively bistros, and indie publishing companies have moved into the area. The Lucky Pig is popular with the posh set because it is bloody brutal to make it past the door attendant and has this speakeasy vibe—dark corners and overpriced gin cocktails."

"Gee, Bingley. It almost sounds as if you want to go to The Lucky Pig."

"Are you serious? I would love to go with you to meet Johnny Amor!" Bingley says, grinning. "Thanks for asking."

I laugh.

"Did I just ask you?"

"Yes, you did!"

"What about you, Knightley?"

"What about me?"

"Fancy spending a night drinking overpriced gin cocktails in a dimly lit speakeasy?"

Knightley pauses so long I am afraid he is going to say no. He pulls to a stop outside a long, honey-hued brick building with arched doorways that remind me of the doorways on the carriage house at Black Ash. He kills the engine and looks at me.

"With you?"

"Yes."

"I would love to go with you, Emma Lee."

"You would?" I clap my hands. "Yay! This is going to be so much fun."

"Are you serious?" Bingley says, narrowing his gaze at his brother. "Knightley Nickerson swilling giggle water in a pub in Fitz, rubbing elbows with boujies. This *is* going to be fun."

Chapter Eighteen

Emma Lee Maxwell's Facebook Update:
My daddy used to say, *If you want to know why the
South has a reputation for hospitality, just look at our
architecture. We build our homes with deep front
porches, wide verandas, and multiple French doors,
welcoming features that beckon passersby to stop
and say, Hey.* Approach life in a similar way: remain
open to new experiences, be welcoming of strangers,
and grateful for those who sit and stay awhile.

Miss Isabella strides over to the car and grabs my hands,
kissing my cheeks and laughing. She has a lovely laugh
and smells like sunshine and lilacs and the hint of expensive French perfume. She smells like happiness, if you
could distill and bottle happiness. An image flickers in
my brain of the silver-framed photograph Manderley always kept beside her bed, a hazy shot of our momma
reaching out a window to snatch a pale purple blossom
off a wisteria branch. Silly, unexpected tears fill my eyes.

Miss Isabella steps back but keeps hold of my hand. She notices the tears in my eyes and frowns.

"What happened?" She spins around, facing her sons. "Bingley? Emma Lee looks as if she is about to burst into tears. What did you say? Were you thoughtless?" She turns back to me. "Was Bingley thoughtless? Did he say something unkind? Was it about your matchmaking scheme?"

"Why do you assume I said something unkind?" Bingley looks aghast. "Knightley was also in the car."

"Knightley is never unkind," she says. "It is not in his constitution."

"Bingley demonstrated his usual level of unpleasantness. Nothing unusual or extraordinary, I assure you." Knightley slaps his brother on the back before walking around the car. He reaches into his coat pocket and pulls out a cotton handkerchief. "Besides, I would not allow Bingley to be unkind to Emma Lee, not ever."

"Whatever." Bingley snorts, striding toward the main house.

"Are you all right, Emma Lee?" Knightley asks, handing me his handkerchief. "Was it something I said?"

Miss Isabella looks from me to her son. Her brow knits together, as if she is trying to work a difficult puzzle; then a smile spreads across her lovely face.

I take the handkerchief and dab under my eyes. *Please Lawd Jesus, please let my Too Faced Better Than Sex mascara be waterproof.* What good are intense, thick, dramatic lashes if they melt with the first tear? I stop dabbing my eyes and look in horror at the faint, watery black mark my tears have made on Knightley's crisp, white monogrammed handkerchief. Monogrammed! Oh Lawd Jesus!

"You didn't make me cry, Knightley."

I try to give him a big, bright, reassuring smile but am

acutely aware of my nose. I am afraid it is going to drip right here, right now, with Knightley Nickerson and his glam momma staring at me. I swear, y'all, if that happens, I'll forget all about becoming Britain's next millionaire (and middle-income) matchmaker. I'll be on the next plane back to Charleston. I'll get a job at Raising Cane's Chicken working the fryolater and spend the rest of my God-given days wondering what could have been if I hadn't snotted on Knightley Nickerson's expensive shoes.

"I knew it!" Miss Isabella says. "Bingley made you cry."

"It wasn't Bingley." I pretend to dab my cheeks and discreetly press the handkerchief against my nose. "I swear it wasn't Bingley. It is silly, really. When you hugged me, Miss Isabella, you smelled so good, like the gardens at Black Ash, all floral and sunny, and it reminded me of my momma. Well, not really my momma, but a picture of her, reaching out the window to snatch a flower."

"I know the picture you are talking about, my dear," Miss Isabella says, squeezing my hand. "It was taken just before you were born. I have a copy. It arrived with the last letter your mother sent to me, just before she passed away."

Knightley clears his throat. He is such a curious man. Kind and thoughtful, but noticeably uncomfortable with displays of emotion.

"I am sorry for carrying on," I say, folding his handkerchief into a neat square and handing it back to him. "Miss Belle would have a conniption if she could see me weeping big old crocodile tears and staining your beautiful handkerchief."

"Who is Miss Belle?" Miss Isabella asks.

"Miss Belle Watling taught Emma Lee comportment

and etiquette at Rutledge Hall Academy"—Knightley doesn't look at his momma when he speaks, he looks at me, and his forest-green eyes sparkle like a Tyra Banks *How to Smize* video—"and she did a wonderful job."

He turns and begins strolling toward the main house, one hand thrust in his coat pocket. I clutch his handkerchief in my fist and watch him, his easy, long-legged stride, the confident tilt of his head, until he disappears around a corner. I look at Miss Isabella. She is grinning at me like I am one of those Sudoku puzzles and she just figured out which digit to put in my last box.

"He forgot his handkerchief," I say.

"Don't worry about the handkerchief," she says, linking her arm through mine. "I see you are wearing your new wellies. Shall we give them a proper workout?"

"Sure," I say, tucking Knightley's handkerchief into my pocket. "What do you have in mind?"

"Fancy a hike to the ruins?"

"Lead the way."

We follow the drive to a gravel path.

"This building"—Miss Isabella gestures to the brick building with the arched doorways—"is the old stables, built in the mid-eighteenth century, when Charlotte Welldon married Archibald Nickerson. Sir Archibald was an enthusiastic equestrian, so Charlotte had the stables rebuilt and expanded as a wedding gift. Their son, Archie, was a brilliant rider, known throughout Europe for his daring exploits. He was close with the Chevalier Saint-Georges."

"I am not familiar with the chevalier."

We follow the gravel path around the stables and wend our way through an English flower garden, through clusters of blue delphinium, purple freesia, white roses, and pale pink peonies, until we arrive at a tree-lined stream.

We follow the path along the stream, crossing a series of stone footbridges.

"Ah, the Chevalier Saint-Georges." Miss Isabella sighs. "Now there is a man worth remembering: deadly swordsman, skilled equestrian, gifted musician, and unmatched lover. He was an intimate friend of Marie Antoinette, the Duc d'Orleans, Choderlos de Laclos."

"Choderlos de Laclos?"

"The author of *Dangerous Liaisons*," Miss Isabella says.

"Ooo, I loved that movie," I say. "Beautiful costumes, romantic intrigue, and young Keanu Reeves brandishing a sword. Sigh."

Miss Isabella chuckles.

"You should read the book." She stops to pick a jagged-edged peony petal off the gravel path, gently bruising the pink blossom between her thumb and forefinger. She lifts the petal to her nose, inhaling. "I have a copy I could lend you."

"I will add it to my list."

"Your list?"

She hands me the petal and I lift it to my nose, breathing in the perfumed scent.

"It turns out"—I stick the peony blossom in my pocket with Knightley's handkerchief—"I am not a well-read young woman."

"I don't believe it!"

"I swear." I press my left hand to my heart and raise my right like I am about to swear the Kappa Kappa Gamma oath. "You should see my list, longer than my Amazon and Sephora Wish Lists. Who knew?"

She laughs.

"What are some of the books on your list?"

My brain aches just thinking about all the books I have

downloaded to my Kindle in the last few days. Thank God Manderley gave me an Amazon gift card for Christmas last year.

"Hmm, let me see," I say, rubbing my forehead. "*The Scarlet Letter, The Inimitable Jeeves, The Grantchester Mysteries*, the novels of the Brontë sisters . . ."

"*The Inimitable Jeeves*?" There is a smile in Miss Isabella's voice. "I say, old girl, splendid choice. The adventures of thick-headed Bertie Wooster and his clever valet, Jeeves, are jolly good reads, filled with elegantly turned phrases and hilarious scenes. Knightley adores P. G. Wodehouse."

"He does?"

I meant to agree with Miss Isabella, but my voice goes up at the end, which makes my statement sound like a question. *He does? He does?* I hear my voice in my head and inwardly cringe. I should just tell Miss Isabella the truth, that I know Knightley favors P. G. Wodehouse, that I decided to read *The Inimitable Jeeves* after learning it was one of his favorites, but I am afraid it will make me sound like a Lisa. Lisa was the psychotic temp worker in the movie *Obsessed* who developed an unnatural crush on her boss, even though he was happily married to a strong, beautiful woman (as played by Beyoncé: *yaaas, queen!*). You don't want to be a Lisa. Ever.

"Oh!" I say, changing the subject. "Where are my manners? I plum forgot to thank you for the book. I started reading *Emma* and I love, love it! I love Emma, with her philanthropic efforts and social swirling. She's an original SG."

"SG?"

"Sorority girl."

Miss Isabella laughs.

"I love her hypochondriac father and all his fretting

over puddings. I love poor Harriet Smith, the orphan who is so desperate for affection she believes she is in love with that yawn fest of a farmer, Mr. Martin. I love Mr. Knightley"—I sigh—"do not even get me started on my affections for Mr. Knightley. I even love Mr. Elton."

"Oh, dear." Miss Isabella sniffs. "You might want to reserve judgment in that quarter."

"Seriously." I laugh. "Thank you for giving me such a lovely gift."

"You sent me a thank-you text, love. Remember?"

"I know. Some things should be practiced in moderation—like, applying iridescent cosmetics, consuming alcoholic beverages, and practicing self-recrimination—but not gratitude. Gratitude should be practiced in excess and free of expiration dates, especially if you really appreciate the gift." I smile at Miss Isabella. "Once, I sent Daddy a second thank-you card years after he gave me a particular gift just because I loved it so much."

"Your mum was the same way."

"She was?"

"Absolutely."

I stop walking. Miss Isabella stops walking. I stare at her, wondering how many more tidbits she knows about my momma, and why it took her so long to make an appearance in my life.

"Miss Isabella?"

"Yes, love?"

"Can I ask you a question?"

"Absolutely."

"What happened between you and my momma? It sounds as if you were good friends, BFFs."

"We were BFFs, yes."

"So, what happened?"

"What do you mean, what happened?"

I get a sense Miss Isabella understands my question but is stalling, as if she needs time to find the words in her brain before speaking them. The story is there, written on the pages of her memory. Miss Isabella just doesn't know how to translate it.

"You know I love you, Miss Isabella?"

"Yes."

"So, I swear I mean this with all due respect." I press my hand to my heart like I am making a solemn promise to one of my KKG sisters. "If Lexi passed away after having a baby, God forbid, I would be so involved in that child's life she would grow up thinking I was her momma—or, at the very least, a crazy auntie who liked to take her shoe shopping and tell the same tired old stories about how her momma sang the 'Kappa Kappa Gamma' song in the sweetest voice and once made a quilt out of Greek shirts for a sister diagnosed with cancer."

A breeze causes the tree branches over our heads to bend and sway, sends pastel-colored flower petals skittering over the gravel path, over the toes of my rain boots. Miss Isabella takes a deep breath through her nose, looks up at the leaves, and slowly exhales through her mouth.

"I wanted to be a part of your life, but my relationship with Malcolm was complicated."

"Daddy? Complicated?"

My daddy was an easygoing man. Easy as a Carolina morning. Easy as a rumpled linen suit, as falling asleep to the sound of cicadas singing in the trees outside your bedroom window, as floating on an inflatable raft in your swimming pool and watching the clouds drift by. He was up at sunrise, biscuits and peach jam for breakfast, haircut and shave once a week at the barber on Broad Street, doze on the veranda listening to Otis Redding. That was Daddy. There wasn't a complicated bone in his body.

"Your daddy was . . ."

Clever? Generous? Kind? More in love with my momma than a man has a heart to be? The best daddy ever?

"Go on."

She squares her shoulders, lifts her chin, and looks me in the eyes. I suddenly hear Winston Churchill's baritone, lisping voice in my head: *We shall defend our island, whatever the cost may be, we shall fight on the beaches, we shall fight on the landing grounds* . . . Miss Isabella, with her upturned nose and steely gaze, is the personification of the saying *British stiff upper lip*.

"Your father and I were involved before he met and married your mother," Miss Isabella says, smiling softly, as soft as the peony petal in my pocket. "He was, in fact, my first love."

"*You're* Izzy-B?!"

My father told me his first love was a gangly, knock-kneed brunette named Izzy-B, a brilliant girl who graduated at the top of her class from the finest boarding school in Europe. An exasperating girl who wore a leather bustier under her sensible cashmere cardigan, numerous strands of vintage Chanel pearls, and danced barefoot to Madonna's "Like a Virgin." Looking at the serene English-woman standing before me, her silver hair cut in a sensible though stylish, chin-sweeping bob, her magnificent ancestral estate in the background, it is difficult to imagine her as the champagne-guzzling, Material Girl–worshipping Izzy-B.

Two spots of color, as vibrant as the red Burberry scarf tied around her neck, appear on Miss Isabella's cheeks. She pushes her bangs off her forehead in a girlish gesture practiced by self-conscious women since Eve noticed Adam checking out her strategically placed fig leaves.

"I haven't heard that name in almost forty years. Izzy-

B! How my mum loathed that name." She giggles, links her arm through mine, and we continue our stroll to the ruins. "I have no wish to give this story more importance than it deserves, because the events occurred without drama. We were young. We fell in love, ran around like a pair of bloody fools. Drank too much, danced too much, spent too much. What can I say? It was the eighties." She sighs. "We talked about doing something completely mad, like eloping to Gstaad, but then your mother and Aunt Patricia came for a visit and . . . well, Malcolm fell head over Sperry Top-siders in love with your mum."

"Daddy left you at the altar?"

"Nothing that Harlequin-esque, love." She chuckles, patting my arm. "Your daddy was a kindhearted, genteel man, the quintessential Southern gentleman, holding doors, pulling chairs, taking other men to task if they used foul language in the presence of a lady. He lived in the 1980s, but he behaved as if he had been born in the 1780s. I always said he was born two centuries too late."

"Manderley says that, too."

Lost in the fog of memory, unhearing, unseeing, compelled to find her way through the mist, Miss Isabella continues her story.

"Your daddy was honest. He held my hand, looked me in the eye, and told me he was developing feelings for your mum, one of my best friends. . . ." Her voice trails off and we walk on in silence, arm in arm. "My heart broke a little, but what could I do? The man I loved fancied my best friend. I loved them both and didn't want to risk losing either of them. So, I wished them well and soldiered on. In the end, your father married the love of his life and I married mine."

In my head, I let out a whistle. Miss Isabella sure didn't lie when she described her history with my momma and daddy as complicated. Isabella Nickerson, the chic, worldly woman who befriended me at *the* Charleston social event of the year, is Izzy-B, my daddy's first love.

"I am sorry Daddy broke your heart, Miss Isabella." I squeeze her arm and rest my head on her shoulder for just a second. "Thank you for not holding it against him, for being my momma's BFF and my fairy godmother."

"Fairy godmother? I am your *real* godmother."

"*What*?" I stop walking so fast I nearly trip over my wellies. I am still holding Miss Isabella's arm, so she is forced to stop and look at me. "What do you mean, you're my godmother?"

"Your mum found out she was sick a few months into her pregnancy, so she planned your baptism for the day after you were born. I flew over and we had a little ceremony in the garden at Black Ash, beneath the branches of a magnificent oak tree dripping in moss." Tears fall from Miss Isabella's eyes, slide down her cheeks, but she dashes them away with the flick of her finger. "I made two visits to Black Ash in the year following your mum's death, to spend time with you and your sisters, but my presence only exacerbated your daddy's grief. It was as if the fun, easy relationship we had formed died when your mum took her last breath. Eventually . . ."

She takes a deep, jagged breath. I don't prod her to finish her sentence. What would be the point? Eventually, she stopped visiting, stopped calling, because she knew she reminded my daddy of my momma, and she loved my daddy too much to cause him pain.

"Thank God for Patricia. We were always close, but our friendship deepened in the years after your mum's death. She became the sister I never had, and I became . . ."

". . . the sister she lost," I say, finishing her thought.

"It was a wretched way to gain a sister."

Another freesia- and peony-scented breeze rustles the leaves, so it sounds as if the trees are murmuring their condolences. I want to say something to express my sympathy, but Miss Isabella starts talking again.

"I kept a diary," Miss Isabella says. "I wrote in it every year on your birthday and on the anniversary of your mum's death. I intended to give you the diary the night we met at the polo match, but your grief over the loss of your father was too fresh. Perhaps it is still too fresh."

In my head, I hear the song from *Winnie the Pooh and the Blustery Day*—*the one about the rain coming down, down, down and rushing over Piglet*. I am Piglet, trapped in a honeypot, swirling around and around, as the waters rise, rise, rise, transforming the world around me into an unrecognizable place. Daddy and Miss Isabella were in love? Miss Isabella is my real godmother? *Helllooo? Is anybody there? It's me, Piglet.*

"I know this all must come as quite a shock." Miss Isabella unhooks her arm from mine and gives me a quick, one-armed shoulder hug, as if she fears she might violate my personal boundaries. "I hope what I shared with you, about my relationship with your father, hasn't upset you terribly. I want to be a part of your life ever so much, but I want to be an honest party of your life. Secrets can so toxic."

"Are you kidding?" I stop walking and throw my arms around Miss Isabella's shoulders. "I am not upset! I mean . . . I am not gonna lie, Miss Izzy-B . . . it is going to take a little time for me to wrap my head around the idea of you and my daddy dirty dancing to 'Like a Virgin' . . ." I break the hug and give her a sassy, mm-hmm, Miss Thang face. She laughs. "I am superhappy and feeling all kinds of blessed."

"Blessed?"

"Sure," I say, linking our arms. "Today, I learned that my momma had a loyal, selfless bestie and that my god-mother is not a figment of my wishful imagination, but an actually flesh-and-bone person. I would call that blessed."

"Thank you, love, that was a beautifully worded senti-ment." She squeezes my arm. "I feel blessed to have you here, living in Northam. You are the daughter I never had and the goddaughter I always wanted."

I swear, my heart is so jam-packed full of love and grat-itude, it feels as if it is going to explode out of my chest. We continue following the path, ahead the skeletal remains of the Abbey loom on the top of a hill.

"Miss Isabella?"

"Yes, love?"

"What happened to Archie, the dashing horseman who was besties with the chevalier?"

"Poor, miserable Archie," Miss Isabella says, shaking her head. "Sir Archibald forced him to marry Lady Henri-etta Swinbrook, the daughter of an impoverished noble-man."

"Would it have been less tragic if Lady Henrietta had been the daughter of a wealthy nobleman?"

"Henrietta could have been the daughter of King Midas and it would not have mattered to Archie, because he was in love with Sophie DeMille, his former gov-erness, a sweet-natured woman reputed for her beauty, who also happened to be fifteen years his senior. Archie wanted to marry her, but Sir Archibald threatened to cut him off and ruin Sophie's reputation."

"So, he married Lady Henrietta?"

"He married Lady Henrietta, a loathsome creature with deeply pitted skin, a pug-like underbite, and squinty eyes. Her portrait hangs in the gallery. Nightmarish, really. Used to make Bingley cry. Contemporary accounts describe

Lady Henrietta as cruel, condemning, and utterly obsessed with morality."

"Poor Archie."

"Yes, poor Archie."

"Whatever happened to the governess?"

"Now *that* is a romantic story," Miss Isabella says, pulling the edges of her scarf closer. "Archie and Sophie maintained a secret correspondence for over twenty years. The archive at Welldon contains hundreds of letters: beautiful, heartfelt prose that spoke of their undying passion for each other. Archie, it would seem, was a gifted poet."

"How romantic!"

"Quite," Miss Isabella agrees. "Many of the letters detail fervid trysts in the ruins."

"Seriously?"

"Seriously."

"I can't even." I sigh. "That is so romantic."

"In one letter, Archie promises to meet her where the earth touches the sky and to make love to her with such ardor even the moon will turn his silvery face in modesty."

"Yes, please!"

Miss Isabella laughs.

"So that's it?" I ask. "Archie and Sophie spent the rest of their days writing sexy letters to each other about their stolen moments in the ruins?"

"Not exactly."

"Ooo!" I rub my hands together. "This is about to get juicy, isn't it?"

"Yes."

"How juicy?"

"Fairly juicy." Isabella says, chuckling. "Juicier than a properly cooked Sunday roast."

"Ooo, dish."

"All of those passionate love letters and moonlight trysts and the next thing you know, old Sophie is in the pudding club."

"In the pudding club?"

"Pregnant, love."

"Archie and Sophie had a love child?"

"Twins."

"No way!"

"Way!" Isabella says. "Honora and Hartley DeMille were born in a cottage Archie had built on the edge of the estate."

Isabella steps off the path and begins walking up a gently rolling hill toward the Abbey ruins.

"Does it still stand?"

"It does, though it stands empty at present," Isabella says. "It is a charming, snug little place, with a thatched roof, exposed beams, and windows that look out onto the ruins. The wooden beams over the windows are carved with Sophie and Archie's interlocking initials."

"The house that love built!"

"Indeed," Miss Isabella says. "Would you care to hear another story?"

"Abso-bloody-lutely!" I toss my hair back and attempt my best Bingley impersonation. "I say, these are cracking good stories, Izzy-B! Cracking good."

"Well done, you." Miss Isabella laughs. "You sounded like Bingley attempting to sound like a P. G. Wodehouse character."

We arrive at the top of the hill and pause to take in the magnificent sandstone ruins, glowing in the late afternoon sunshine. From a distance, the ruins reminded me of those ceramic castles you see in home aquariums, a tumbledown pile of bricks but up close it is breathtaking, with pillars towering into the clouds. Miss Isabella leads me on a

tour, pointing out what would have been the nave, clois-
ter court, and refectory. She tells me the Abbey was first
established in the twelfth century.

"The ruins are not as large nor as well preserved as
Fountains Abbey, but they are still quite dramatic, and
they have a wonderful history," Miss Isabella says, taking
a seat on the ledge of an arched window and patting the
space beside her. I sit beside her, leaning my back against
the cool, damp stone and turning my face up to the sun.
"William the Conqueror awarded this land to Sir Robert
Welldon in recognition of the bravery he demonstrated at
the Battle of Hastings in 1066. Having survived a bloody
battle, most men would have built a large home and spent
the rest of their days living off their spoils, but not Sir
Robert. He vowed to give thanks to God. Proper thanks.
Sir Robert polished his armor, mounted his horse, said
farewell to his betrothed, and rode off to the Holy Land.
Something must have happened to Sir Robert on his way
there, though, because eight long years passed without
word as to his well-being. Believing Sir Robert dead,
Helewise became a bride of Christ."

"What? Are you kidding me?"

"She became a nun."

"That's *saaaad*."

"Wait," Miss Isabella says, raising a finger. "The story
is not over. Sir Robert finally returned from the Holy
Land, thinner, wiser, holier, ready to settle down to married life, only to find Helewise gone. He searched every
abbey, chapel, and convent in England but did not find
his beloved. Sir Robert spent the next twenty-four years
crusading in the Holy Land, amassing enormous wealth,
which he donated to the Church with the stipulation it be
used to erect an Abbey here, in Helewise de Morville's
honor."

"Oh my lawd," I gasp. "Sir Robert's tribute to Hele-wise is the sweetest thing I have ever heard, sweeter than Mark Darcy telling Bridget Jones he liked her just as she was, sweeter than the real Mr. Darcy risking scorn and ridicule to court Elizabeth Bennett."

"Careful there, love." She wags her finger at me. "Not Darcy. He's sacrosanct."

"Ugh!" I wrinkle my nose. "I don't get the whole Darcy thing. Personally, I think he was reaching with Elizabeth. Did you see his bushy sideburns? I don't care if manscaping wasn't popular in the nineteenth century, someone needed to tell him to weed whack that mess. And don't even get me started on his broody-moody moods! I heard Katy Perry's 'Hot N Cold' playing in my head every time he came on the screen. Hot and cold. Yes and no. In and out. Up and down."

She pats my hand.

"We will have to agree to disagree there, love."

I let it go, but deep down I reckon Miss Isabella must agree with me or she would have named her sons Bingley, Brandon, and Darcy, not Bingley, Brandon, and *Knightley*.

"Where was I?" She frowns, staring off. "Ah, yes. When Sir Robert was an old man, too broken to crusade, blind in both eyes, without family or fortune, he returned to his home at the bottom of this hill to die."

"No!" I hold my face in my hands, pressing my palms against my closed eyes to erase the image of poor, broken-down Sir Robert dying alone on some sad straw pallet. "I thought you said this was a *good* story? You lied! This is definitely not a good story."

"Do you want me to finish?"

"You are killing me, Miss Isabella. Kill-ling!"

"As if by divine intervention, Sister Helewise suddenly

returned. She took care of Sir Robert in his final days and was by his side when he drew his last breath."

Miss Isabella stands and walks out of the nave. I follow her to a small graveyard.

"It is believed Sir Robert Welldon is buried here"—she points to a worn stone slab set into the ground and then takes a step to her right and points to a small cross-shaped headstone freckled with lichen—"and Sister Helewise de Morville is buried here."

I look at the graves, worn by time and forgotten by most of the world, and a wave of emotion washes over me. I pluck a wildflower from the ground and place it over Sir Robert's grave, my tribute to a man who showed undying devotion to the woman he loved. Sigh. Sir Robert and Sister Helewise are relationship goals! Such undying devotion.

The sun has settled low in the sky and the ruins cast long shadows down the side of the hill as we begin our hike back to Welldon House.

"You are unusually quiet," Miss Isabella says.

"I am thinking about Sir Robert and Sister Helewise."

"What about them?"

"Their graves make me *saaaad*." I stick my hands in my pockets, rubbing the monogram on Knightley's handkerchief between my thumb and forefinger, feeling the silken threads. "The writing on the stones has been worn away. Why hasn't more been done to preserve them?"

"It costs an enormous amount of money to run an estate the size of Welldon Abbey." She exhales, and her shoulders roll forward, as if she suddenly slipped on a backpack filled with Jane Austen novels. "We considered expanding the gardens and adding extravagant water features to draw summer tourists, but the liability would be extraordinary. Longleat has a safari park. Goodwood has a racetrack. Waddesdon has the Diamond Jubilee Wood walk. Cliveden has a scandalous past. Chatsworth has grandeur. Little Moreton Hall has a bloody moat! When you compare Welldon to other manor homes in England, I am afraid we come up woefully short. Tourists want *Downton* bloody Abbey, not *Welldon* Abbey. They want the dowager countess to greet them as they enter and Mrs. Patmore to serve them a fresh scone as they exit. We can't compete with the illusion of Mrs. Patmore and the reality of Highclere Castle."

"I don't like to hear anyone sound defeated"—I link my arm through hers—"especially my fairy godmother turned real godmother."

"I *feel* defeated," she says. "We lost a substantial amount of our savings in the economic crisis several years ago, money we relied upon for the upkeep of Welldon. Knightley contributes most of his salary and his annual bonus to compensate for the loss, Brandon assists the groundskeeper with maintaining the gardens, and Bingley sold the Aston Martin he inherited from his father. Easton Neston, a country pile in Northhamptonshire, was rescued by a Russian clothing tycoon who invested forty million pounds to restore the estate to its former glory! We need a Russian clothing tycoon. We need a Max Leon!"

"I had no idea things were that difficult."

"We are hardly destitute," she says, tightening her scarf. "We aren't the Dashwoods, after all. We haven't been forced to vacate our family home because of England's ridiculously patriarchal primogeniture law. We haven't been reduced to accepting charity from a distant cousin."

Dashwood. Dashwood. I know that name. Agnes Dashwood. Isn't that the name of the girl who works at Call Me

Darjeeling? No! Wait! Elinor Dashwood is one of the characters in *Sense & Sensibility*. I saw the name when I was flipping through the pages to get to *Emma*.

"Thank God you aren't Dashwood-ing it. Still, there must be something I can do to put the Bibbity back into your Bobbity-Boo. A fairy godmother should float in a cloud of glitter, not slog along, head down, too defeated to sparkle."

Miss Isabella squeezes my arm.

"You have enough glitter for all of us, love. Truly, just being around you makes me feel happier and less burdened."

"Aw! Thank you." I drop my head on her shoulder and lift it again. "I believe you should spread joy like confetti, tossing it around by the handfuls. You have given me so much joy. I am glad to give you some in return. I just wish I could think of something to do to help"—I stop walking and squeeze Miss Isabella's arm—"Oh my lawd! I have just had the most brilliant idea!"

Chapter Nineteen

"Tell me your brilliant idea."

"First, have you heard of Rush Week?"

"No." She turns to face me. "What is a rush week?"

"A superexciting, superintense time at the beginning
of the school year when fraternities and sororities try to
recruit pledges." Miss Isabella frowns and I realize she
feels the way I feel when someone makes a reference to
classic literature. "A pledge is a potential member. Some
years, there are hundreds of potential pledges and all the
sororities are vying for the same select group of girls. I
learned early that a good recruiter must have a keen understanding of what makes their sorority unique. Then,

she capitalizes on that special thing—whether it be a designer-decorated day room or celeb alums—to woo the pledges to her sorority."

"I would wager you were brilliant at recruiting pledges."

"Aw, thank you." The enthusiasm for my idea is growing and I must shove my hands in my pockets to keep myself from doing cartwheels the rest of the way down the hill. "Think of visitors as pledges and offer them something unique, something that entices them to consider Welldon instead of, or in addition to, Highclere. It's true: Welldon Abbey doesn't have a safari park, it hasn't been a shooting location for a massively popular historical drama, but it has a unique feature."

"It does?"

"It does!" I say, grinning. "Do you want to know what that unique feature is?"

"Abso-bloody-lutely," she cries.

"Welldon was the setting for one of the most romantic stories of all time, the story of Sir Robert and Sister Helewise." I look back up the hill, at the graveyard silhouetted against the late-afternoon sky. "India has the Taj Mahal, a beautiful mausoleum built by a Mogul as a tribute to his first wife, and Welldon has an abbey built by a crusading knight as a tribute to his lost love. People from around the world flock to see the Taj Mahal, so why wouldn't they flock to see Welldon Abbey?"

Miss Isabella shields her eyes and follows my gaze, looking at the little graveyard perched at the top of the hill.

"Do you seriously think anyone else would be interested in Sir Robert and Sir Helewise?"

"Are you kidding me?" I cry. "We aren't the only hopeless romantics in the world. I'll bet there are loads of people who would get as weepy as I got when I heard Sir Robert's story. The problem is, nobody knows his story."

"The best way to tell his story would be to write a book, but we don't know enough about his life to support such an undertaking."

"I wasn't thinking about a book."

"What are you thinking?"

I look from the ruins to Welldon, judging the distance, envisioning what it would take to make my idea a reality. Designated parking spaces, permanent bathroom facilities, an easy way up the hill that wouldn't destroy the natural aesthetic, a commercial generator, a place to store chairs and supplies.

"Don't keep me in suspense, love," Miss Isabella says. "Tell me your idea."

"I think you should turn Welldon Abbey into a wedding venue!" I pull my hands out of my pockets, clapping them together, and bouncing up and down on my toes. "The most romantic wedding venue in all of England."

"But—"

"Wait!" I stop clapping and hold my hand up. "Before you tell me there are loads of wedding venues scattered all over England, consider that those venues do not offer the romantic history of Welldon Abbey. Sir Robert Welldon did not build an abbey as a tribute to his lost love in *those* locations. Archie Nickerson, the dashing nobleman who ran with Marie Antoinette's set, did not have secret rendezvous with his beloved in *those* locations."

"You make Welldon Abbey sound frightfully romantic."

"Take a look around," I say, sweeping my arm through the air. "The manicured gardens filled with flowers of every hue and variety, the cute little footbridges spanning the stream, the panoramic views of the Gloucestershire countryside, the historic manor home brimming with museum-worthy art, the thatched cottages in the distance, clinging to the sides of the hills. I don't make Welldon Abbey sound romantic; it *is* romantic!"

Miss Isabella gazes at the gardens—glowing in the golden light of gloaming, throbbing with the sound of buzzing bees—and a slow smile spreads across her face.

"Of course," Miss Isabella says. "Weddings at Welldon. It is a brilliant idea, Emma Lee. A bloody brilliant idea!"

"It is, isn't it?"

"It most certainly is!" She hugs me, laughing. "I can't wait to share the idea with Knightley, Brandon, and Bingley."

"Will you tell them tonight?"

"No." She continues walking down the hill and I follow, a step behind. "I want to have a clear and comprehensive vision before approaching them. Otherwise, they will dismiss the idea as another of *mum's mad schemes.* They will bombard me with questions—particularly Brandon; he is a stickler about details."

"I'll bet there are more stories buried in your archives, romantic stories of love found and lost."

"You do?"

"Yes, ma'am! If I were you, I would dig through all the old diaries and letters. I will bet you a pot of I Love You Oolong Time and one of Harriet's Nutella muffins you will find a few more stories. Deal?"

I hold out my hand.

"Deal," Miss Isabella says, shaking my hand. "Though, I am a trifle confused as to what we are supposed to do with these stories after we find them. I thought we were capitalizing on Sir Robert's story."

"We are definitely going to capitalize on Sir Robert's story, but we are living in the digital age, and millennials are distractible creatures. They have the attention spans of golden retriever puppies. They need loads of stimulation."

"You're saying one story is not enough to hook them?"

"One story might be enough to hook them, but we would need fab visuals to go with the story. You wouldn't happen to have any paintings of Sir Robert or Sister Helewise lying around your archives, would you?"

"I am afraid not," Miss Isabella says, sighing. "We do have a rather spectacular plaster relief of his tomb effigy that was done in the early eighteenth century by Lady Anne Welldon, when it was removed from the Abbey and brought into the great hall at Welldon."

"Tomb effigy?" I frown. "You mean a statue?"

"Precisely. A recumbent statue of Sir Robert, garbed in a tunic with a cross on his chest, hands pressed together in prayer."

"What happened to the statue?"

"Destroyed."

"No!"

"I am afraid so. The Nickersons fell on hard times after the Great War, like so many families. Sir Reginald Nickerson sold the effigy to a collector. Unfortunately, the statue fell out of the cart during transport and Sir Robert suffered irreparable damage." Miss Isabella raises her hand and makes a slicing gesture across her neck with her finger. "When I arrived at Welldon, Sir Robert's head was being used as a doorstop. Horrifying, that."

"Where is his head now?"

"Sitting on a shelf in my private library." Miss Isabella shakes her head. "Imagine, surviving the Battle of Hastings and numerous Crusades to the Holy Land, just so your effigy can take a tumble from a lorry and lose his head? Such an undignified and inglorious ending."

Even though the demise of Sir Robert's effigy is *saaad*, I am glad his head has found a safe resting place in Miss Isabella's library. I imagine the stone head nestled between a stack of Jane Austen books and a crystal vase of fresh peonies.

"Emma Lee?"

"Yes?"

"Once we have all the stories, what do we do with them?"

"I think we should give them to Bingley and ask him to write a short piece about each of the couples, something smart and romantic. Then, we post the stories on your website."

"But we don't have a website."

"Brandon handles marketing and publicity for Nickerson Publishing, right? I'll bet he knows loads of people who could build you a slick website."

"Of course."

"We will need glossy pictures of Welldon House and the Abbey ruins—the kinds you see in posh travel mags, like *Condé Nast* and *National Geographic Traveler*. Too bad Manderley is in France; she's a fantastic photographer."

"I believe I know a photographer."

"Great!" We step back onto the gravel path. "Ooo! I just had another idea. You said the DeMille cottage is empty and offers an unobstructed view of the Abbey, right?"

"Right."

"What if we made that the bridal cottage—you know, where the bride gets ready before the ceremony and the newlyweds stay after the reception?"

"I love that idea. Of course, it would need to be renovated, particularly the bathroom. We could add a freestanding pedestal tub with a telephone faucet, paint the wood paneling Oxford blue—"

"—add apothecary jars of bath salts made with lavender from Hayley Bartlett's farm and roses from your gardens."

"I love that idea!"

"We could get the whole village involved." I clap my hands. "We could ask Deidre to create chocolate bonbons or pretty, lace-edged cones filled with candy to be given out as favors, and ask Harriet to make a special blend of tea and name it Sir Robert's Promise or—"

"—Sophie's Secret Blend!" Miss Isabella claps her hands. "Mrs. Waites has a fancy embroidery machine. What if we hired her to embroider the cross that is on Sister Helewise's tomb on our guest towels?"

"Love that idea!"

"Vicar Parsons could officiate the ceremonies."

"I wish I had a notebook to jot down these ideas."

"I will send you an email later," I say.

"Mark it confidential," Miss Isabella says. "Weddings at Welldon will be our little secret. Just until we work out all the details. Promise?"

"Mum's the word."

Chapter Twenty

Emma Lee Maxwell's Facebook Update:
A team of neuroscientists studied dogs to determine
if they feel love. It turns out, dogs express their love
for you the same way your boyfriend expresses his
love for you. They smile, make eye contact, react
positively when they hear your voice, like your scent,
enjoy snuggling, and wag their tails.

"You have had a proper tour of the ruins and devised a
brilliant plan to get Welldon sorted, but you have not told
me about your matchmaking scheme," Miss Isabella
says. "I know it is early days, but surely you have had
some ideas. Who shall you match first?"

"Deidre."

"Deidre is a splendid choice." She nods her head. "Tell
me, Madame Matchmaker, who is Deidre's mate?"

I tell Miss Isabella everything I know about Johnny
Amor and why I believe he would make a good match for
Deidre, omitting my concerns about Johnny's potentially

unhealthy addiction to Tinder and Deidre's codependent relationship with her mother.

"Well done, you," she says, patting my back. "What about Bingley or Brandon?"

"I need to spend more time with Brandon, but from what you have told me, I think Hayley might be his match."

"Hayley? *Bartlett*?"

"Hayley is independent, works hard, and enjoys spending time outdoors. She makes like she's as placid as a pond, but I reckon there's a whole lot going on beneath her tranquil surface."

"Blimey!" Miss Isabella cries, stepping off the path and into the flower garden. "You just described Brandon."

"Right?" I blow on my fingernails and polish them on my jacket. "Matchmaking is my calling. I feel it, deep down in my bones."

"I am a believer."

"Thank you!"

"What about Bingley?"

"Bingley is a special case."

"Hear! Hear!"

"That came out wrong," I say, laughing. "I love Bingley. He is stylish, clever, and superfunny. Something tells me it is going to take me more than a few days to find the girl who can match Bingley's energy and dynamism."

"Bingley is certainly energetic and dynamic," Miss Isabella agrees. "Hang on, Emma Lee Maxwell! *You* are energetic and dynamic. Would it be a violation of the Matchmaking Code of Ethics if you matched yourself with my youngest son?"

"Me?" I laugh nervously. "With Bingley?"

"Too energetic? A bit too many sharp, snarky edges around his tender heart?" Miss Isabella chuckles. "Perhaps you are right. Perhaps Bingley isn't your type."

"No offense."

"None taken, love." Miss Isabella pauses before a peony bush, pinches a stem just below a withered blossom, removing the dead head with a quick flicking motion. "So, if not Bingley, who?"

"*Who*?"

"Who do you fancy, love? There must be someone you fancy. *A fine, tall gentleman with handsome features and a noble mien*, as Jane might have said."

I see a vision of Knightley striding through the airport in his beautifully tailored suit, Costa coffee cup in hand, and my tummy does a flip.

"I am not here to find a husband," I say.

"But if you were," Miss Isabella persists. "What sort of man would you search for?"

"I haven't thought about it."

"Right," she says, deadheading another withered flower. "Think about it now. Pretend I am the matchmaker and I have just asked you to describe your perfect mate."

"This is silly."

"Indulge me."

"Fine." I bend over to smell a peony the same shade of pink as the bow on my bottle of Viva La Juicy. "When I fall in love, I would like it to be with someone who is tall, dark, and as handsome on the inside as he is on the outside. He would need to have a good relationship with his family and love his momma something fierce. Daddy always said the best way to judge a man's true character is to watch how he treats his momma."

"Is that all?"

"Nope. Not even close."

"Go on."

"He needs to be a nonsmoker and a moderate drinker. I am not about that ashtray and beer-bottle life." I hold up my fingers, counting off the qualities I would want in a soul mate. "Kind, compassionate, intellectually and physically stimulating, mature, moral, and, above all, loving. If I settle down, it will be with a loving man, a man who loves me, loves life, loves everyone he meets. Life is too darned short to be saddled with a hater."

"Do you know who you just described?" Miss Isabella asks.

"Who?"

"Knightley."

Two gigantic shaggy dogs trot into the garden, tongues lolling, black eyes glowing, followed by Knightley Bloody Nickerson. I clutch Miss Isabella's arm, inching behind her as beast one sniffs my boots.

"Did I hear my name?"

Knightley steps into the flower garden. He strolls up to his mother and presses a kiss to her cheek.

"Hello, love," Miss Isabella says, patting Knightley's cheek. "I was just telling Emma Lee how fortunate I am to have such a loving son."

"Is that so?" He narrows his gaze on his mother. "What brought this on? I suppose you want me to pop into town for a loaf of bread? Change the oil in the Rover? Or do you want me to burn my fingers applying sealing wax to more Cheltenham Animal Shelter Benefit Tea invites?"

I imagine Knightley performing secretarial tasks for Miss Isabella, sprinkling glitter on lacy stationary, licking heart-shaped envelopes, and I bite my lip to keep from laughing.

"Bloody undignified way for the twenty-eighth Baron of Welldon to spend his evenings, pressing a paw-shaped stamp into a blob of molten wax," Knightley says, scratching beast two's head.

I laugh.

"Chin up, duckie!" Miss Isabella says. "You know the old saying, *What doesn't kill you makes you stronger.*"

Beast one opens his mouth, as if he is about to devour my leg, prole drift Hunter wellie and all, so I do what any sensible person would do; I scream and jump behind Miss Isabella.

"Relax, love. It is only Theodore and Adeline."

Knightley snaps his fingers, and both dogs drop to their bellies, massive front paws outstretched, tails frozen in midair.

"Emma Lee," he says, keeping his voice low and even, "these are my dogs, Theodore and Adeline. They look like wild beasties, but they are quite tame, I assure you."

"Theodore and Adeline?" Beast one (or is it beast two?) wags his/her tail when he/she hears me say his/her name. "You made a big mistake naming your dogs, Mr. Editor. You should have called them Sir Henry and Sir Charles."

Knightley stares at me, his expression unreadable.

In my head, I hear Benedict Cumberbatch exclaiming, *By Jove, Watson, I believe Miss Maxwell just made a literary reference.* I downloaded the Audible version of *The Hound of the Baskervilles* because Benedict Cumberbatch provides the narration. His voice is *soooo* soothing. A few minutes listening to him and I am out, dead to the world, limbs hanging off the sides of my mattress, eyes closed, mouth open; I only know this because Maddie secretly shot video of me sleeping when she was taking a film class. His voice is like Ambien, only without the side effects and risk of addiction. I have never stayed awake to hear how the story ends, so I am not sure if the hounds of Baskerville are real dogs or evil entities.

Great! The one time I slip a literary reference into a conversation, I insult Knightley by implying his pets are demonic hounds. I am about to apologize when Knightley laughs.

Beast one looks up at his master and thumps his/her tail against the grass. *Thump-thump-thump.* Beast two looks at me and licks his/her lips. I swear I can hear his/her stomach growling.

"Sir Henry and Sir Charles?" Miss Isabella asks.

"Emma Lee was making a reference to Sir Arthur Conan Doyle's *The Hound of the Baskervilles*, Mum." Knightley smiles at me, and I feel a warm tingle of satisfaction run through my body. "Sir Henry and Sir Charles Baskerville."

"Ah."

"Though I believe the hounds in that story were part-bloodhound, part-mastiff, and these great beasts"—he reaches down and scratches beast one's head and his/her tail thumps the ground more forcefully—"are Irish wolfhounds."

"Of course," I say.

Of course the CEO of one of the largest book publishing companies in the English-speaking world would trump my reference with an even more literate reference. Of course he would know what breed of dog the hounds in *The Hounds of the Baskervilles* were.

"You look properly happy, Mum," Knightley says, directing his attention to his mother. "You should visit the ruins more often."

"I should visit with Emma Lee more often."

"She does have that effect." With Miss Isabella looking on and beast one thumping his/her tail, Knightley picks a gorgeous red peony, the same shade of red as my favorite NARS lip liner, and hands it to me. "For making everyone around you smile."

"Thank you." I accept the flower with grace, but inside

I feel the way I did when Thomas Geoffries passed me a love note in middle of Algebra class. *What am I supposed to do with this? How am I supposed to respond?* "Red is my favorite color."

"Really?" He looks at the five different shades of red lipstick artfully applied to my mouth and his lips quirk. "I could not have guessed."

I stand there, holding the flower like a novice beauty pageant contestant accepting her first trophy, conscious of my posture, pose, and smile, wondering how I should hold my hands. Knightley continues to stare at me, a twinkle in his eye, and I wonder if he knows of his ability to turn a confident woman into a gawky girl with a single glance. I wonder if he is a major playah. The funny thing is: I have very good playdar and I have not had a single ping with Knightley Nickerson. Not even a blip on the playdar screen.

"Knightley?" Miss Isabella says, grabbing her son's hand. "You will not believe what Emma Lee has done."

"Hmmm." He rests his elbow on his hand and taps his cheek with his pointer finger. "Don't tell me! I know! Emma Lee found you a love match. Who is it? The man who delivers our post? Johnny Amor's granddad? A Russian businessman with forty million pounds?"

"Oh, behave, cheeky bugger." Miss Isabella nudges Knightley in the ribs, causing him to chuckle. "Emma Lee came up with a brilliant scheme to make Welldon more self-sufficient."

"She did?" Knightley looks at me.

"*I did?*"

"Weddings at Welldon," Miss Isabella says. "A brilliant scheme that will turn Welldon Abbey ruins into a premiere wedding venue and engage the services of several of Northam's small businesses!"

My mouth falls open. I stare at Miss Isabella in utter bewilderment.

"Close your mouth, dear," Miss Isabella says, touching my chin. "You'll catch flies."

"What happened to mum being the word?" I whisper. "I thought you wanted the scheme to remain our little secret until we worked out the details?"

"I do!" she says. "I promise I will only tell Knightley."

"We all agree," Knightley says, waggling his eyebrows. "You will only tell Knightley. So, tell Knightley."

Knightley releases his dogs from their frozen positions and they take off, bounding out of the garden. Miss Isabella gives Knightley the down and dirty about our plan—from the soaker tub to the embroidered towels. He listens intently, muscular arms crossed over his chest, dark brows knit in concentration. He changed out of his nicer clothes into a pair of worn jeans and a loose summer sweater tucked in his waistband, but still manages to look like an advert for a line of bespoke clothes for the country gentleman. Handsome, clever, kind, respectful of his momma. I can't figure out how he has remained single for so long. I searched for him on Facebook before I left Charleston, just so I could get a better understanding of the sort of women he might find attractive, but the search returned zero results. I got the sad magnifying glass face and *We couldn't find anything for* Knightley Nickerson.

I found Brandon's profile. What a boring News Feed! His last post—a photograph of him and some old military cronies at a benefit polo match—was posted a year ago. Bingley is a different story. His profile is public and updated several times a day, with funny stream-of-consciousness posts about fashion, pop culture, and politics, as well as iPhone snaps of Bingley living his fabulous Bingley life. Close-ups of a vintage Tiffany & Company silver-plated cocktail shaker, Hermès cuff links, the hood ornament on a Jaguar. Bingley at a fashion show, luxe hotel opening, swank cocktail party. There is even a selfie of Bingley and supermodel David Gandy posing in matching leather jackets.

I think it is strange I couldn't find the eldest and most intriguing Nickerson on Facebook—especially after what Bingley said about Knightley being Mr. *Town and Country* and all. Unless Knightley has his profile set to private. Why would Knightley Nickerson want to block strangers—and potential friends—from finding him on the world's largest social media platform? Who does that?

Celebrities. Terrorists. Playahs.

Funny, Knightley doesn't behave like a playah.

"Weddings at Welldon is a splendid idea," Knightley says, looking at me. "Capitalizing on the estate's unique romantic history and involving local businesses will set Welldon apart from the myriad of estates already operating as events venues. You gave Welldon a heart, a meaningful brand. Well done, you."

"In addition to being dead beautiful"—Miss Isabella nudges Knightley again—"Emma Lee is quite brilliant, isn't she?"

"Quite."

"You are a flatterer," I say, laughing.

"Never," Knightley says, his tone serious. "You will find I am incapable of giving insincere praise."

"It is true," Miss Isabella says, laughing. "Knightley is wholly incapable of flattery. Bingley, however, is quite another matter altogether. Bingley could charm the birds from the trees with his false praise—or chop the branch from under them with his sharp censure."

I remember something I saw on Bingley's Facebook News Feed, a scathing Who Wore It Best post, with a photograph of Cara Delevingne in a shaggy red faux fur coat beside a photo of a life-size Tickle Me Elmo doll, and find it difficult to believe he could ever flatter someone.

"Well"—My daddy always told me to look a man in the eye when I thanked him, but I look down at the peony clutched between my fingers, at the droplets of water still clinging to the red petals, because looking Knightley in the eye is just too much—"thank you for the compliment, Knightley."

"Is that Annalise?" Miss Isabella shields her eyes with her hand, staring in the direction of the main house. "Dear, I forgot I told her it would be all right if she photographed the Swinbrook's latest litter." She pulls her hand from her face and looks at me. "Excuse me for a moment, Emma Lee. I must pop over and say hello."

Miss Isabella hurries down the path and crosses the drive toward the main house, leaving me alone with the potential playah and his woman-eating dogs. I don't know why I am getting all weird about Knightley. A few compliments, a peony picked from his momma's gardens, and I am jumpier than a long-tailed cat in a room full of rockers.

"I am glad you are here, Emma Lee," Knightley says.

"You are?"

He moves closer. I crane my neck to look at his face. In this light, the flecks in his brown eyes appear golden.

"You are good for my mum," Knightley says. "She has kept busy since my father died, taking care of the estate, organizing her book club, and working with her many charities, but it has been a manic sort of busy. Weddings and Welldon will give her the focus she lacks and a purpose that is more personal than her other endeavors."

Beast one and beast two come bounding back into the garden. Beast one—it might be beast two—has a stick in his mouth—it might be a tree branch or Sir Henry Baskerville's femur—and beast two has a ravenous look on his furry face. I clutch my peony to my chest and duck behind Knightley. He turns around, smiling down at me, the late-afternoon sun shining on his dark head and broad shoulders.

"Relax," he says, grabbing my hand. "My dogs will not hurt you."

I'll bet having your femur bone severed from your body by a pair of gnashing teeth hurts something fierce, but I will endure the agony if you keep on holding my hand and staring into my eyes.

"Do you trust me?"

I nod. Beast one drops the femur on my feet, but I am too overwhelmed by the feeling of Knightley's strong, warm hand holding mine, the scent of his cologne teasing my nose, to care. Continuing to hold my hand, Knightley turns around to confront the panting, heaving beasts. With his free hand, he forms a fist. The dogs immediately sit. Knightley points at the ground, and the dogs drop onto their bellies, still, alert, eyes fixed on their master. Knightley squats.

"When you are comfortable, squat down beside me," he says, looking up at me. "The trick to greeting a strange dog is to remain relaxed and allow them to come to you."

I hold Knightley's hand and lower myself until I am squatting beside him, our knees touching, beast one's giant muzzle inches from the toe of my boot.

"Is this Adeline or Theodore?" I whisper, keeping my gaze on beast one.

"Adeline," Knightley says. "She is a pup still."

"A pup?" I look at Adeline's paw, as wide as Knightley's hand, and shake my head. "You are kidding me. You mean she is still growing?"

"She is a year and a half, so she has a little more growing to do. Adeline loves every human she meets, don't you, girl?" He scratches Adeline's head and I swear, the beast's eyes roll back in her head. "She is rather less friendly with four-legged creatures, though. We are working on her aggression toward other animals."

"How is that going?" I ask, keeping my eye on beast two.

"She is making strides. Adeline spent time with the Swinbrooks' new litter this afternoon and didn't devour a single Westie pup."

I look at Knightley, eyes wide. He laughs. Adeline stares at me with soft eyes, her massive tail *thump-thump-thumping* against the grass, sending a tornado of flower petals in the air. Aww. She *is* cute. With brown eyes and silvery-gray fur that sticks up on her head like an edgy punk-rock haircut. I hold out my hand. She sniffs my fingers, her wet nose and wiry fur tickling my skin.

"Awwee!" I giggle. "She is *sooo* sweet."

Adeline's massive pink tongue shoots out of her mouth and licks my hand until my fingers are dripping sticky dog saliva.

"Point your finger at her," Knightley instructs.

I point my finger at Adeline. She stops licking my hand and rolls onto her back, letting me rub her big gray belly. Theodore inches closer, finally nudging my hand with his head. I scratch his brown head and he closes his eyes.

Knightley stands.

"It looks like my gentle giants made you a dog lover."

I scratch Theodore's head and then give Adeline's belly one last pat before standing beside Knightley.

"I didn't *not* like dogs." Bravo, Emma Lee. Use a double negative when speaking to a bigwig book publisher. "I love dogs. I just haven't ever owned one."

"Why is that?"

I tell Knightley the synopsis of the Tragic Tale of Baby Dumpling, the precious bow-wearing, bloated Boykin Spaniel who broke my best friend's heart.

"I am sorry," he says, smiling softly. "It sounds as if Baby Dumpling's death traumatized you more than it did your friend."

"What do you mean?" I frown. "Ginger May was devastated."

"No doubt, but you said Ginger May adopted another dog."

"So?"

"So, losing Baby Dumpling did not stop your friend from opening her heart and home to a new pet. It stopped you, though. Why is that?"

Ouch! Knightley is probing into the deepest, most sensitive areas of my psyche. I am not stupid. I know loss has marked my life—my love life, or lack thereof—and I don't need this drop-dead gorgeous Englishman to remind me of it. I stare at him, trying to think of a polite way to mind his beeswax. Fortunately, he changes the subject.

"It is late. You must be famished." He snaps his fingers, and the dogs bound off again. "Would you like to clean up before dinner?"

"Yes, please."

We begin walking back to the main house.

"Miss Isabella said you named your dogs after characters from one of your favorite novels. Which novel?"

"Theodore and Adeline are two of the characters in the novel *The Romance of the Forest* by Ann Radcliffe. Have you read it?"

"No"—I consider telling a little white lie, but fibbing to Knightley feels wrong—"but if it's one of your favorite novels, I'll download a copy when I get back to Wood House."

"I think you will enjoy the story."

"Why is that?"

"You are a romantic, and *The Romance of the Forest* is, primarily, a romance. In fact, Ann Radcliffe was considered the first writer to pen a gothic romance novel."

"Girl, go!" I say, snapping my fingers.

Knightley chuckles. We walk onto the drive, our feet making crunching sounds on the gravel.

"I have a question for you," I say, changing the subject.

"I have an answer."

"Are you on Facebook?"

Knightley clears his throat. I can't tell if it is an uncomfortable, you-just-caught-me-in-my-playah-ways throat clearing or what.

"No, I am not on Facebook."

I stop walking.

"Are you kidding me?"

Knightley stops walking and looks over at me.

"I kid you not."

"Knightley Nickerson," I say, gently nudging him in the ribs. "There is a tree stump in South Carolina with a higher IQ than me if you think I am going to stand here believing that tall tale. We are more than a dozen years into the twenty-first century. Everyone has a Facebook page, except maybe that creepy little Kim Jong-un and his poor downtrodden people."

"I am not on Facebook, Twitter, or Instagram."

"Are you kidding me? You're not a sleeper agent, are you? Sent by Kim Jong to infiltrate the Free World's publishing industry."

"You got me." He laughs and makes a gun with his thumb and forefinger. "I am the North Korean James Bond, but with a much less exciting mission. The name is Nickerson. Knightley Nickerson."

"You do have a sexy car and a closet full of expensive bespoke suits."

"You think my car is sexy?"

I think *you* are sexy, Knightley Nickerson. *Lawd! What is happening to me?* My cheeks flush with heat.

"We weren't talking about your sexy car," I say, navigating the conversation out of the turbulent, sexually charged waters. "We were talking about why an editor at one of the largest publishing companies in the world doesn't have a social media presence."

"I am too busy to tweet."

"Cop out."

"I beg your pardon?"

"Tweeting is just socializing using one hundred and forty characters or less," I say, looking up into his handsome face. "You're never too busy to socialize."

"I socialize."

From what Miss Isabella told me, Knightley is an introverted workaholic who prefers to spend his downtime alone, reading or hiking with his dogs. She said he has loads of friends but isn't very good about staying connected.

"When is the last time you reached out to a friend, just

to say *hey there* or find out what was happening in their life?"

"I don't know."

"That's why you need a Facebook account."

"So I can find out what my mates think about the latest Ed Sheeran album, Marvel movie, or political scandal?"

"Exactly."

"What if I don't care what my mates think about the latest Ed Sheeran album or Marvel movie?"

"You have to care."

"Why?"

"Because . . . because . . ." I stare at Knightley, my mouth opening and closing, like I am a bug-eyed trout out of water.

"When I meet someone intriguing enough to make me want to ask such inane questions—*What are you having for lunch? Have you binged the new Netflix original?*—I will create a Facebook page. Until then, I am happy socializing using more than one hundred and forty characters, thank you very much."

I imagine Maddie's response if she had overheard Knightley's answer to my question. She would have snapped her fingers two times while saying, *Girl, hush.*

Chapter Twenty-one

Emma Lee Maxwell's Facebook Update:
Dating Tip from Emma Lee: Never snap your fingers
at a man, even if he acts like a dog.

When we arrive on the front lawn, Annalise Whittaker-
Smith is looking through the viewfinder of an expensive
camera, snapping photographs of a litter of West Highland terrier puppies. The puppies are standing on their
hind legs and have their front paws perched on the ledge
of a low stone wall. Five white furry faces with black button eyes focused on Annalise and her camera. Four of the
puppies have perky pink ears that stand straight up. The
fifth puppy has a wonky ear; one stands straight up and
the other flops over.

I notice Brandon standing behind Annalise, holding a
large round metallic disc so it bounces the dwindling sunlight onto the puppies. Annalise snaps her fingers and
Brandon raises the disc higher in the air.

Oh no, she didn't! She did *not* just snap her fingers at
that man, like she was scolding a naughty puppy. I won-

der how Annalise Whittaker-Smith talked Brandon into being her equipment biatch.

"There you are," Miss Isabella says, greeting us.

Four of the puppies become distracted at the sound of Miss Isabella's voice and begin chasing each other and rolling around the grass. The puppy with the wonky ear remains standing on her hind legs, front paws resting on the top of the wall, head cocked quizzically to one side.

"Are we interrupting?"

"Not at all," Brandon says, lowering the reflector. "Annalise was just taking her last shot."

Annalise slants a look in my direction. An unhappy look. Then she notices Knightley standing beside me. Her bottom lip turns down in a sexy little pout, making her impossibly angled cheekbones appear even more angled. I do not know which contouring kit Annalise Whittaker-Smith uses, but it is on point, ridiculously on point. She fashioned a headband from a silk Dolce & Gabbana scarf to keep her long, sleek chestnut bangs off her face while she shoots. I am not gonna lie, y'all. Annalise is arrestingly beautiful. With her hair swept off her face and the golden light of gloaming illuminating her perfect skin, she could be on assignment right now, shooting a fashion campaign. She looks like she just walked off the runway of a 1940s Gucci fashion show, looking trim and feminine in her high-waisted menswear-inspired trousers and crisp white shirt rolled to her biceps.

I hate Annalise Whittaker-Smith.

She hands her camera to Brandon and glides toward us, but the softly scented cloud of CHANEL Gardenia that seems to perpetually orbit around her arrives first.

"Hello, Emma Lee," she says, greeting me with gardenia-scented air-kisses. "You look dead gorgeous in red lipstick. What shade is it?"

I was wrong. I like Annalise Whittaker-Smith.

"Thank you," I say, smiling. "I love your headscarf. Very chic. I am wearing five shades, actually."

"Five shades? You borrowed a page from Marilyn Monroe's book! Well done! Clever, you. Her technique makes thin lips look fuller—not that you have thin lips. Your lips are quite lovely, actually."

"*Thank you.*"

"With your blond bangs and bright red lips, you remind me of Reese Witherspoon, circa 2007, when she wore that canary yellow—"

"—Nina Ricci cocktail gown to the Golden Globes?"

"Exactly."

Yaaas, queen! I barely spoke to Annalise Whittaker-Smith the night we met, so she has no idea how much I worship Reese Witherspoon, which means her compliment is sincere and organic.

I love Annalise Whittaker-Smith!

"Thank you," I whisper.

Annalise turns her attention to Knightley.

"Why, hello there, Lord Mucky Muck." She leans in, presses her chest against Knightley, and kisses his cheek. "I was just telling your mummy about that dreary day in Gstaad, when we were stranded at Bunky Davenport's chalet, and you taught me how to make a proper Gin Rickey, slicing the limes with your Swiss Army knife. Who knew fizzy water and lime juice would make gin so scrummy?"

Lord Mucky Muck? Stranded in Gstaad? I glance at Knightley, and an image of him dressed in a turtleneck, mixing gin cocktails in a luxe Swiss ski chalet flashes in my mind. James Bond, indeed! I return my attention to Annalise—or should I call her Pussy Galore? She rests her slender, perfectly manicured hand on Knightley's bare forearm in a familiar, proprietary manner, and a sharp pain stabs my heart.

I hate Annalise Whittaker-Smith!

Knightley looks at me. I imagine myself through his eyes and I do not like what I see, a jealous girl standing in her notice-me red prole-drift rain boots, clutching a peony like an obsessed Bieber fan clutching Justin's discarded chewing gum.

Wait a minute! *Jealous?* I am not jealous of Annalise Whittaker-Smith. *Sooo* not jealous. Sure, she is a semifamous model with silky hair, porcelain smooth skin, wide doe eyes, and a perpetual pout. It is true, she could be Keira Knightley's doppelgänger. And so what if she is one of London's Bright Young Things and starred in a splashy, trashy article about the most fabulous members of Britain's new aristocracy? What do I care? I am a bold, ambitious, outgoing American who rejects rigid class systems and aristocratic snobbery. I have naturally blond, silky-ish hair, sun-kissed, freckled skin, and porcelain blue eyes. What does Annalise Whittaker-Smith have that I don't have?

Knightley.

Brandon joins our little circle. He greets me with a warm hello and a perfunctory hug. I get the sense Brandon is not a hugger, another thing he has in common with Hayley. Annalise continues to rest her hand on Knightley's forearm while inching closer to Brandon, as if she can't decide which Nickerson she fancies. When I was a child and couldn't decide if I wanted to play inside or outside, my daddy would stand at the screen door with his hands on his hips and say, *In or out? In or out? Which is it going to be, Emma Lee Maxwell, in or out?* I want to stand between Knightley and Brandon with my hands on my hips and say, *Brandon or Knightley? Brandon or*

Knightley? Which Nickerson is it going to be, Annalise Whittaker-Smith, Brandon or Knightley?

The Swinbrooks join the group, and the conversation turns to the weather. I zone out and watch the puppies tripping and rolling around at our feet. Wonky Ear notices me watching her. She cocks her head to one side and stares at me quizzically, her black button eyes alert. Finally, she trots over and belly-flops on my right foot. Not by accident. On purpose. She just lays on my boot, one ear pointing up to Jesus, one ear pointing down to the devil. I am not gonna lie, y'all. Wonky Ear is giving me all the feels.

Knightley leans closer to me.

"I see you have made another furry friend," he whispers. "If you are not careful, you will leave here today with a dog in tow."

"Me? A dog owner?" I snort. "I don't think so."

"Why not?"

"Don't you like dogs, Emma Lee?" Annalise asks.

Everyone stops talking and looks at me. My cheeks flush with heat.

"I like dogs."

"Don't lie," Annalise says, her lips curved in a smile. "It's perfectly all right if you don't fancy dogs. Right, Mrs. Swinbrook?"

"Who doesn't like dogs?" Mrs. Swinbrook asks, in her clipped, upper-class British accent. "I mean, really."

"Emma Lee likes dogs," Knightley says, shaking Annalise's hand off his arm. "She suffered a traumatic event when she was very young that has made her leery of dogs. That is all."

"Were you maimed?" Annalise asks.

"Maimed?" Did I mention I hate Annalise Whittaker-

Smith? "No, I was not maimed by a dog, Annalise. I watched my best friend's dog die of bloat."

"Is that all?" Mrs. Swinbrook sniffs. "That was natural selection at work, wasn't it? The strong survive and the weak die off. The circle of life and all that."

"I am sure it was very traumatic," Miss Isabella says, rising to my defense. "A child doesn't understand natural selection. They only understand loss."

"You Americans are so strange." Annalise smiles sweetly. "The way you treat your pets is positively perplexing, infantilizing and sentimentalizing them. Can you see an Englishman dressing his terrier in a sweater and pushing it in a pram? Bonkers."

"I cannot!" Mr. Swinbrook declares.

Savannah warned me the British think Americans are flag-waving, dog-loving fatties with firearms, but I dismissed it. Some people see stereotypes, I see people.

I know I should take a deep breath and ask myself, *Now, Emma Lee, what would Jesus do?* but little Miss Gucci Pants is standing there looking fabulous, enveloped in a cloud of gardenia-scented perfume, staring at me with a smug smile on her face, and I snap.

"Sister, please." I smile and keep my tone as sweet as tea. "Don't *even* come at me with your anti-American shade. I watched *Downton Abbey*. I saw the episode when Lord Grantham's beloved Labrador died of cancer. That man wept like a child."

Miss Isabella laughs. Knightley laughs. Brandon chuckles.

"Poor Isis," Mrs. Swinbrook clucks. "Sad story, that."

"I have never watched *Downton Abbey*," Annalise says.

"Bless your heart," I say. "That's so *saaad. Downton Abbey* is such a great show."

"When you have a successful modeling career, you don't have time to lie about watching programs on the tellie. I am not complaining, though. Last month I was in Milan walking for Versace, this month I am shooting a campaign for Burberry, and next month I will be in Tokyo shooting the cover of *Vogue*."

"How nice for you," I say.

I hold Annalise's gaze and continue to smile my sweet-as-tea smile. If I learned one thing from living in a sorority and being part of a cheer squad, it is this: The best way to deal with a mean girl is to look her straight in the eye and smile sweetly. I call it the my-now-nice response. When a Southern lady says *my how nice*, she really means *eff you*.

When Annalise breaks eye contact, I look at Mrs. Swinbrook.

"Would you mind if I held one of your puppies?"

"Not at all," she says.

I bend over and lift Wonky Ear off my boot, cradling her soft, warm body in my arms. She is so relaxed, like a floppy rag doll. She nuzzles into the crook of my arm, her tiny snout resting on my elbow. I pet the silky fur on top of her head and she sighs.

"What do you think?" Knightley asks, leaning close.

"I think I am in love."

"That was easy."

"Look at her heart-shaped nose," I say. "How could anyone resist a sweet little girl with a heart-shaped nose?"

"How do you know it is a girl?"

"Do you think it is a boy?"

"Only one way to find out."

I hold the puppy up for Knightley to inspect.

"Girl. Definitely."

"Bit of a disappointment, that one," Mr. Swinbrook

says, staring at the puppy in my arms and clucking his tongue.

"A disappointment?" I look into the puppy's shining black eyes. "How could this little darling be a disappointment?"

"She has a lazy ear."

"Lazy ear?" I laugh. "You are kidding."

"Young lady, there are two things about which I never *kid*: horses and dogs. A Westie's ears should stand like a Buckingham Palace Guard, erect and proud, never faltering. A pup with a dropped ear is considered undesirable."

"But why?"

"Floppy ears are considered a defect and should be bred out of a litter," Mr. Swinbrook says.

I nuzzle the puppy with my nose and whisper in her ear.

"Don't listen to him," I whisper. "You are desirable. You are clever. You are sweet. You are special."

I kiss Wonky Ear's head before the Swinbrooks load her into a crate in the trunk of their Range Rover and take off down the drive, followed by Annalise in her sleek BMW convertible.

We eat an informal dinner of roasted chicken and garden salad in the morning room, a cozy but elegant space with dark wood floors, ivory painted walls, toile upholstered chairs, and built-in cabinets filled with delicate china. The wine flows as freely as the conversation. Military-bearing Brandon even cracks a joke.

We eat dessert—profiteroles—in Miss Isabella's sitting room and watch an episode of *Jeeves and Wooster* (Bingley gave Knightley the box set as a birthday gift). Miss Isabella's sitting room is so cozy, I want to snatch the cashmere blanket off the back of her overstuffed chair, curl up on her velvet sofa, and take a long nap. The scent of burning logs and sandalwood candles permeates the air like incense.

I say good night to Brandon, promise Bingley I will text him about our date with Johnny Amor, and give Miss Isabella a good-bye hug. Then, reluctantly, I follow Knightley through a maze of corridors, down a flight of stairs, through a massive Victorian kitchen filled with copper pots and crockery, and, finally, into the courtyard where his car is parked.

The air outside feels nippier after being in Miss Isabella's snuggly sitting room. I rub my arms to keep warm while Knightley unlocks the passenger door.

"Are you cold?" he asks.

"The plaid lining inside a Burberry trench coat looks fantastic, but it offers little in-insulation." I meant to make light of my discomfort—because that is the Southern way—but my teeth chatter on the last word. "I'll be f-fine."

"You're shivering," he says, shrugging out of his heavy navy peacoat and draping it over my shoulders. "Wear this."

His coat reminds me of Miss Isabella's sitting room, warm and tinged with a spicy scent.

"Thank you"—I lift his coat off my shoulders and hand it to him—"but I can't take your coat. You'll freeze."

Knightley does not argue with me. Instead, he takes his coat and wraps it back around my shoulders, his warm fingers brushing my cheek as he adjusts the collar. I shiver again, but it is a different sort of shiver.

We climb into Knightley's car, and before I know it,

we are turning into the drive leading to my aunt's cottage. Knightley parks by the garden gate and kills the engine. William Curtis looks out his window, recognizes us sitting in the car, and waves. We wave back.

"Would you like me to walk you in?" Knightley asks.

I forgot to leave a light on, so Wood House is creepy dark. Horror-movie dark. Psychopath-lurking-in-a-closet-waiting-to-stab-me-with-Aunt-Patricia's-knitting-needles dark.

"Would you mind?"

Knightley smiles, and then, as if it is something he has done a thousand times before, he reaches over and casually tucks a strand of my hair behind my ear. It is sweet, and it is tender. It is something a hero in a Nicholas Sparks movie would do just before he kissed the heroine. I hold my breath and wait.

But Knightley does not kiss me. Instead, he climbs out of the driver's seat, walks around the front of the car, and opens my door.

We walk up the path to the front porch. I stick the key in the lock, push the door open, and step into the dark foyer. Knightley stays on the porch.

"Thank you for the ride, Knightley."

"It was my pleasure," he says, smiling. "I must return to London tomorrow morning, which, regretfully, means I will no longer be able to act as your chauffer. Your aunt's car is sitting in the garage. Would you like me to come over next Saturday morning and acquaint you with the peculiarities of driving a British automobile on an English road?"

"That would be awesome. Thank you."

"Awesome," Knightley says, his lips twitching. "Shall we say half eight?"

"We shall!"

I remove his coat from my shoulders and hand it to him. Knightley takes his coat and drapes it over his shoulders.

"Good night, Emma Lee."

"Good night, Knightley."

He is halfway down the path when I pluck up the courage to create my own Nicholas Sparks moment.

"Knightley!"

I run after him. He turns around. I stand on my tiptoes and—I kiss him. A perfectly perfect whisper of a kiss. The sort of kiss that makes your teeth ache with the remembering because it is innocent and tender. It is a Disney kiss.

One moment my eyes are closed, my heart is thudding against my rib cage, my lips are brushing against his lips, and the next moment I am staring up at his face, lit by the silvery moon, wondering if our kiss really happened or if I dreamed it.

I wait—willing Knightley to say something tender, something I will remember forever and for always, but also wanting him to say nothing to break the spell of this moment. Another part of me, the naughty part, wills him to grab me by the back of my neck, pull me close, and kiss me as no proper English gentleman has kissed a girl while standing in a proper cottage garden.

Out of the corner of my eye, I see the golden light from William's window and wonder if the hypochondriac pharmacist is watching us. Tomorrow morning, when he stops for his Earl Grey and bran muffin, will he tell Harriet he saw the American girl kiss Knightley Nickerson, just as bold as she pleased, and then launch into a lecture about the various diseases that can be transmitted through a single kiss? Will he litter my front step with pamphlets about meningitis, gingivitis, or mononucleosis?

I look into Knightley's eyes and forget about William Curtis and his pamphlets on stopping the spread of infectious diseases.

Knightley does not say something tender or memorable. He does not kiss me with pent-up passion. He tucks a lock of my hair behind my ear, smiles softly, walks to his car, and drives away.

I stand on the porch and watch his taillights fade into the night, shoving my hands in my pockets and feeling the soft petals of the peony he gave me nestled against his handkerchief.

Later, after I have checked under every bed and in every wardrobe for knitting-needle-wielding psychopaths, I read about Mr. Elton traveling to London to have Harriet Smith's portrait framed on Bond Street. I applaud Emma for her success in matching her protégée with the amiable village vicar.

Which makes me think about Northam's village vicar, Ethan Parsons. Miss Isabella told me a bit of gossip about the good vicar. His mother is Irish, his father is English. His parents divorced just after he was born. So, he spent his childhood shuttling between Cork and the Cotswolds. Miss Isabella hinted that Ethan Parsons might have involved himself in *an impetuous youthful liaison with a publican's daughter, an indiscretion, as it were, that might have resulted in a nullius filius*. Thank God for Google! *Nullius filius* is a fancy way of saying Ethan Parsons has a baby momma back in Cork, y'all!

If things do not pan out between Hayley Bartlett and Brandon Nickerson, I might take a page from Emma Woodhouse's book and attempt a match between my protégée and the good vicar.

Because, if Miss Isabella's gossip is gospel, Vicar Parsons is no stranger to sin. All's I'm sayin' is, a man with a baby momma shall cast no stone at a girl born on the wrong side of the village.

I put the peony Knightley gave me between two sheets of wax paper and press it between the pages of my Jane Austen book, then switch off the bedside lamp and thank Jesus for delivering me unto Northam-on-the-Water.

Chapter Twenty-two

Emma Lee Maxwell's Facebook Notification: You have one new friend request from Knightley Nickerson. Confirm. Delete.

I accept the friend request and click on the red Notifications icon. Knightley Nickerson liked several of my photos and posted a message on my wall.

Knightley Nickerson ® Emma Lee Maxwell
May 26 at 6:02 a.m.
What are you having for lunch?

Chapter Twenty-three

Text from Alexandria Armistead:
   Cash is leaving for Pigeon Forge tomorrow and I have a big old knot in my stomach. I know you said to let him have his boys only weekend, but something feels off.

Text from Tara Maxwell:
   I am leaving for Ireland late next week. Aer Lingus Flight 122, Charleston to Chicago to Dublin. I was thinking about getting a pair of rain boots, but then I saw your Instagram post—the one you took of your wellies standing beside the front door of the cottage. What is prole drift?

Text from Bingley Nickerson:
   I Googled Johnny Amor. Found his Insta. Blimey! He's a gorgeous man. If I were a hen, I would go for Johnny bloody Amor.

Text from Roberta Hearst:
   He said he wanted to Netflix and chill—six months later I am flat on my back, stuck on bed rest, with two abnormally active fetuses practicing power yoga up in my

womb, 24/7. Knightley sounds gorgeous. Just promise me this: if he asks you back to his place to watch a movie and relax, run like a scalded haint.

Text from Madison Van Doren:
    That Barton boy shoved my Agent Provocateur Kendall thong in his pocket and promised to hit me up before I left Charleston, but he has been ghosting me ever since. Why didn't you warn me he was a major twat? On a more positive note, Cash's big brother invited me back down to Charleston to go crabbing with him sometime.

Text from Kristen Carmichael:
    Boo-yah! Guess who's crushing the squat challenge?

To: Emma Lee Maxwell
From: Manderley de Maloret
Subj: Re: Things that make you go hmmm . . .

Are you asking if I think it is a coincidence or divine intervention that you and Knightley Nickerson are named after the main characters in Jane Austen's *Emma*?

In the immortal words of M. Night Shyamalan, *See what you have to ask yourself is what kind of person are you? Are you the kind that sees signs, that sees miracles? Or do you believe that people just get lucky?* You know my answer to the coincidence question. There are no coincidences.

Why? Do you like Knightley Nickerson the way Emma Woodhouse liked her Mr. Knightley?

Love and miss you,
Manderley

Chapter Twenty-four

Emma Lee Maxwell's Facebook Update:
Maybe it won't work out. But maybe seeing if it does
will be the best adventure ever!

It is finally Saturday morning. Knightley will be here any
minute to give me a proper lesson on the right way to
drive on the wrong side of the road. I am, I believe,
dressed appropriately for the occasion in black skinny
jeans, black cashmere sweater over a white blouse, charcoal wool blazer, and Gucci riding boots. I have braided
my hair into a loose fishtail braid and am debating on
whether to add a supercute herringbone flat cap I found in
my aunt's dresser when I think I hear a car pulling up the
drive. My stomach tenses.

I look in the mirror and immediately recognize the
signs—ridiculous smile, flushed cheeks, eyes reflecting
excitement and terror.

Lawd have mercy! I have a crush on Knightley Nickerson, y'all. Just a teensy-tiny crush. He dropped me off
in front of the cottage six days and eleven hours ago.

Since then, I have only thought about him a few dozen times (per hour). I might have thought about him more often if I had not been so busy. I met with Miss Isabella three whole afternoons to work on our Weddings at Welldon scheme. I have had lunch with Deidre in her candy shop, met with Vicar Parsons about hosting a church-sponsored singles mixer, helped the Swinbrooks walk their puppies around the village, helped Mrs. Waites wash and set her hair, and met Bingley for Pilates in the Park.

I even visited with William Curtis. In an effort to strengthen our neighborly bonds, I invited him to Wood House for tea and cucumber sandwiches made with cucumbers picked from Hayley's garden (her stock boy called in sick, so I helped unload a truck full of fresh produce grown on her farm and she gave me bags of fruits and veggies to say thanks). It turns out, William is not as kooky as I first thought. He is an excellent conversationalist, once you make it past his dire warnings about environmental and ingestible hazards. I learned he attended medical school but realized medicine was not for him (medical practice, that is). When he discovered his fiancée *(I know! William Curtis was engaged! How does a germophobe even date—what with all the touching and macking?)* was having an affair with his physiology professor, he switched to chemistry and pharmaceutical studies.

The sound of the front door knocker striking wood echoes down the hall and a wave of sick rises in my throat. I think I am going to be physically ill. I can't spend the next three hours in a teeny-tiny car with Knightley Nickerson—not after the previous week. *What should I do? What should I do?*

I sit on the commode and take a deep breath. I could

send him a text and say I ate one of Harriet's Nutella muffins and now I think I have the Zika virus. Wait! Don't you contract Zika from a bite by an infected mosquito?

I could tell him I have a rare form of Tourette syndrome that causes me to kiss people randomly and spontaneously. Yes! That might work. Then we could go on as if I hadn't molested him in my aunt's garden. We could continue our big-brother/little-sister relationship, but with sexual chemistry.

Ew. Now that just sounds creepy.

I could climb out the bathroom window and catch the next bus to Heathrow. An eight-hour flight to JFK, quick hop in a puddle jumper to Charleston, and my stint as the Great Gloucestershire Matchmaker is nothing more than an impetuous youthful liaison, an indiscretion.

No. I cannot leave Northam. I promised Deidre I would read the first draft of her Queen Victoria child-rearing manual. I am meeting Johnny Amor in London next week. I must find Miss Isabella a Russian tycoon with forty million pounds in the bank and a little salt-and-pepper at the temples. I have people to meet and matches to make. And the girls are coming over tonight for our first ever makeup and mayhem (I am still working on the name of what is sure to become a regular event).

I stand up, spritz the air with Viva La Juicy, and twirl in a little circle. The knocking has stopped. I assume Knightley is sitting in his car or on the front step, so I am surprised when I step out of the bathroom and find him standing in the hallway. Dominating the hallway, really. His broad shoulders practically touching the walls, his head bent to avoid hitting the low ceiling.

"Knightley!"

"Emma Lee!"

The Viva La Juicy–scented air feels heavy and still, like it does back home before a hurricane. We stare at each other, and I wonder if *this* is what the romance novelists mean when they write about sexual tension, *this* terrifying feeling of being trapped in a mighty storm, your body humming with unspent electrical charges, the world around you growing darker by the second, fading away.

"Oh, bloody hell," he mutters.

I have one flickering moment of clarity, the calm before the storm, and then Knightley is pulling me into his arms, kissing me with a frantic, fevered kind of passion. It happens fast—like lightning bolting across a night sky—mesmerizing, breathtaking, the sort of kissing that leaves a body awestruck or devastated.

This is not a Disney kiss.

We continue kissing, sliding our hands over each other's bodies in a frenzied rush, until Knightley pulls away and draws a jagged breath.

We stare at each other, two survivors surveying the wreckage, wondering if they made it through the eye. I am not gonna lie, y'all, I would give my Kappa Kappa Gamma key to know if the look in Knightley's eye is regret. Is he trying to think of a plausible excuse for kissing me?

I expect him to say he is suffering from a rare form of Tourette syndrome or a Nutella-induced brain tumor, but the fictitious excuse never comes.

Instead, he smiles and reaches for my flat cap.

He lifts my cap off my head and sends it flying down the hallway with a flick of his tanned wrist. Then he unbuttons his shirt one button at a time until he is standing in the hallway as barechested as the day the good Lord made him. He lifts me into his arms and carries me to the closest bedroom.

What happens next would never make it past the Disney censors and leaves me thinking, *Flynn Rider? Flynn Rider who?*

"You are a natural at this," Knightley says.

"You don't think I am going too slow?"

"Slow is good, especially when you are just starting out."

I shift the car into a lower gear and follow the traffic through Stowe-on-the-Wold. After we—*you know*—Knightley suggested we drive to Stowe-on-the-Wold for their annual cheese and chocolate festival. He said it would give me a good chance to practice driving and expose me to local cuisine.

Knightley directs me to a parking lot and I pull into a free space, engaging the parking brake and switching off the engine.

"Well?"

"A little more experience mastering the roundabouts and you will be ready for the next Wales Rally."

"Get out," I say, thumping him on the arm. "Be serious."

"I *am* serious," he says, tucking a flyaway behind my ear. "I would let you drive me anywhere, Miss Maxwell."

"Thank you, Mr. Nickerson." I put my keys in my pocket. "I will remember that if I decide to start a motor-sport and need a navigator."

He laughs.

"Now, didn't you say something about lunch?"

We wander through the stalls, buying bottles of locally made cider, a jar of tomato chutney, pork pies, a loaf of Shepherd's Bread sprinkled with Cornish sea salt, a carton of juicy raspberries, and two different types of cheese: Double Gloucester, a hard, nutty cheese flecked with bits of onion and chives, and Wigmore, a creamy cheese that melts on the tongue. Knightley purchases two boxes of chocolate truffles filled with sweetened elderberry jelly—one for me and one for Miss Isabella. Then, we drive to a field between Nether Westcote and Little Slaughter and have a late lunch on a tarp we found in the back of my aunt's car.

Knightley picks a bunch of wild daffodils and presents them to me with a slight, Jane Austen–worthy bow, before dropping down on the tarp and popping a raspberry in his mouth.

We munch on soft bread and hard cheese and he tells me about his life in London, the long days spent managing a major publishing house, the after-hours press parties, book launches, and charitable events.

"What about after work?"

"What do you mean?"

"What do you do for fun? What do you do to unwind?"

He brushes the crumbs from his lap and then lays back on the tarp, closing his eyes and turning his gorgeous face to the sun. Sweet Jesus, but he is handsome.

"I do not relax when I am in London." He takes a deep breath and exhales slowly. "I jog in the park every morning to keep fit. Once a week, I meet my mates at the club for a session."

"The club?"

"The Thames Rowing Club." He makes a rowing motion with his arms. "Did you think I meant dancing?"

"Yes."

He drops his arms, chuckling.

"Do you like to dance?"

He grabs my arm and pulls me on top of him, my head resting on his muscular chest. I listen to his heartbeat and try not to shiver as he runs his fingers through my hair.

"I would like to dance with you."

"I am serious."

"Do you want me to like dancing, Emma Lee?"

I am a cheerleader. I love motion of any sort, especially dancing. I can't imagine dating a man who didn't like to dance.

"Yes."

"Then, yes, I love dancing."

"I don't believe you," I say, laughing.

"Are you questioning my veracity, Miss Maxwell?" he says, his lips grazing my forehead.

"I believe I am, Mr. Nickerson."

"Well then," he says, sitting up. "There is nothing for it. You force me to prove myself to you."

He grabs his iPhone and stands up. I watch him tap his phone screen, waiting, and a second later, the computerized xylophone beats of Ed Sheeran's latest love ballad begin playing. The same love ballad I use for my ringtone.

He grins and holds out his hand.

"*Here*?" I look at the nearby road, the cars puttering by on their way to Stowe-on-the-Wold. "Now?"

"Here. Now."

Chapter Twenty-five

Knightley Nickerson ® Emma Lee Maxwell
May 26 at 6:02 a.m.
What are you having for lunch?
Comments:
<u>Emma Lee Maxwell</u> I had the best lunch ever.
Chocolate and elderberry truffles. Ever had them?
<u>Knightley Nickerson</u> No, but I have had bourbon
balls ;)

Emma Lee Maxwell ® Knightley Nickerson
May 26 at 11:12 p.m.
I noticed you are in good shape. Any tips on how to
stay fit?
Comments:
<u>Knightley Nickerson</u> Consider dancing.

Chapter Twenty-six

"You look like a magic lantern," Deidre says.

"A magic lantern?"

"The Victorian version of a View-Master." She holds her hands up to her face as if they are binoculars. "Pictures on slides held in front of a bright light. You look all lit up inside."

"I do?"

I look at Hayley.

"You do."

Deidre drops her overnight bag beside the door and presses her cold palm to my forehead. She has arrived for the sleepover wearing a pair of flannel pajamas patterned with dancing sock monkeys and a long, chunky orange scarf wound tight around her neck. Her pajama top is unbuttoned, revealing a T-shirt with the quote, *The impor-*

tant thing is not what they think of me, but what I think of them.

"You do feel a trifle heated," she says.

"You were just outside," I say, laughing. "Your hands are as frozen as one of Queen Elsa's spells. Of course, my forehead feels heated."

"Hmm." She removes her hand from my forehead. "It's monkeys outside. Still, I hope you haven't caught a virus. William said a nasty stomach bug was going around."

"I am fine."

"Do you feel like you want to chunder?"

I look at Hayley, and she mouths the word *vomit*.

"My stomach is fine, thank you."

"What do you think, Hayley?" Deidre looks at Hayley, her eyebrows knit together in concern. "Does Emma Lee look a trifle peaky?"

"Glowing? Yes. Peaky? No."

"Do you feel light headed?" Deidre asks me.

"No."

"Dizzy?"

"No."

"Would you like me to pop over to William's cottage and ask him to come around?"

"Absolutely not! That would mean he would have to venture beyond his hermetically sealed walls."

"Just to ease our minds?"

"My mind *is* at ease."

"You are sure?"

"Quite."

"Well, then," she says, grinning. "If you are quite sure you are well, there can be only one reason for your glowing complexion and countenance."

"GlamGlow Flashmud Brightening Treatment?"

"No."

"Anastasia illuminating powder in Rose Gold?"

"Be serious!"

"I am serious," I say, winking at Hayley. "Never underestimate the power of a good illuminating powder, *darlin'*. Applied correctly, it makes a face appear as if it is lit from within."

"You are in love."

"*What*?"

"Barring illness, the first flush of love is the only thing I know capable of creating such a glow." Deidre grins. "When Prince Albert and Queen Victoria were courting, Albert said she stirred passions in him that burned brightly and filled his soul. You, Emma Lee, are burning brightly."

"Where are my manners? Would you like something to drink?"

I walk to the kitchen. The girls follow me. I open the refrigerator and begin grabbing bottles of water and soda.

"Ice tea? Orange juice? Coke?"

"Who is he, Emma Lee?" Deidre persists.

"I have wine." I toss the bottles of water back in the refrigerator and grab the bottle of rosé I picked up in Stowe-on-the-Wold. "How about it? Do either of you fancy a nice glass of rosé?"

Deidre and Hayley look at each other, smiling.

"*Emma Lee has fallen in love*," Hayley sings, moving her hips as if she is trying to keep an invisible hula hoop from falling to her feet. "*L-O-V-E. Love. Hang on, things might get a wee bit bumpy, before it's time for the rumpy-pumpy.*"

She thrusts her hips at the last word.

"Sweet Jesus!" I say, holding my hand up to block the image of Hayley's gyrating hips. "Weren't you going to make margaritas? You brought juicy-juicy mangoes from your greenhouse so you could make us margaritas. Get crackalackin', girl!"

Hayley peels and dices the mangoes before dumping them in the blender with fresh lime juice, orange juice, ice, and tequila. A lot of tequila. She pours the concoction into glasses rimmed with lime and sugar and we sit around the kitchen table, getting drunk off the margarita fumes and munching on some of the goodies I purchased at the cheese and chocolate festival, chatting like old friends.

We finish the first pitcher of margaritas—having shared our feelings about the serious (gun violence), the ridiculous (Meghan Markle saying she didn't know about the Royal Family before meeting Prince Harry), and the hilarious (the #DistractedBoyfriend memes on Twitter). Hayley makes a second pitcher and we move into the living room.

"So, who is it?" Deidre asks, looking at me over the rim of her sugar-rimmed glass. "Anyone we know?"

"No."

"Ah-ha!" Hayley cries, snapping her fingers. "You admit it! You are in love, just not with anyone we know. Does he live in Charleston?"

"Hang on!" Deidre says, pulling her iPhone out of the pocket sewn into the front of her pajama top. "Didn't you become friends with Knightley Nickerson on Facebook recently?"

"So?"

"So," Hayley says, waggling her eyebrows. "Is he your lover man? Your Mr. Rumpy-Pumpy?"

"Ew!" I wrinkle my nose. "I refuse to answer that question on the grounds it is offensive."

Hayley laughs. "What? The suggestion that Knightley Nickerson might be your lover?"

"No. That phrase: rumpy-pumpy."

"It is a British phrase," she says, hooting with laughter. "It means—"

"I know what it means!"

It feels good to be here, in this moment, drinking mango margaritas and laughing with my new girls. Meeting people and making new friends has never been difficult for me—Daddy used to say I could work a room like a Kennedy on the campaign trail—but I would be a bald-faced liar if I said I didn't fret about finding a group of girls in England that were as supportive and fun-loving as my KKG sorority sisters. Lexi, Maddie, Savannah, Kristen, Bertie—they are the OG, the Original Girls. In the words of the immortal Queen B, they are *irreplaceable*.

"He winky faced you," Deidre cries.

"What?"

"Knightley," she says. "He winky faced you."

My cheeks flush with guilty heat. It might be Hayley's eyeball-crossing mango marg, but for a minute I think *winky face* is British slang for . . . *you know* . . . doing the dirty, the rumpy-pumpy, or, as Tara would say, bumping uglies.

"I swear, he did *not* winky face me, y'all!"

Lawd, forgive me for lying to my NG (New Girls). I know the sister code requires complete honesty and candor about a few things, like weight gain, haircuts, and hookups with new boys. I swear, I am not trying to act shady. What happened with Knightley, what I am feeling about him, feels different.

Deidre holds up her iPhone, so we can see the screen.

"There, you see? Knightley said he had bourbon balls for lunch and then he put a winky face."

"OK." I sigh and drop my chin on my chest. "You got me. It's true."

Hayley and Deidre exchange looks.

"What's true?" Hayley asks.

"Knightley—" I sigh again.

"Yes?" Hayley squeals.

Deidre sits up so fast, her margarita splashes out of her glass and onto her scarf. Why she is still wearing her scarf, I do not know.

"Knightley—"

"What about Knightley?"

"He—winky faced me."

Hayley bursts out laughing.

"Cheeky cow," Deidre says.

"What?" I look at her all innocent-like. "He winky faced me hard."

Hayley keeps laughing. Deidre snorts and sticks the end of her scarf into her mouth, sucking the margarita out of the fuzzy orange fabric. I think Deidre might be a little bit tipsy. She is sucking a fuzzy orange scarf, y'all. No judgment here—but acrylic yarn can't taste good even if it is soaked in tequila.

"Knightley is too old for Emma Lee, anyway"—Hayley leans back in her chair and pushes her bare feet toward the fireplace, wiggling her toes against the warmth—"and he dated Annalise, which is *highly* suspicious. I am suspicious of any man who willingly dates my half sister. That's it! Knightley must have had a mini stroke—his advanced age puts him in the higher-risk category."

Thirty is not that old.

Deidre pulls her scarf out of her mouth and looks at me, squinting. "He is old, isn't he? Even if he is *dead* gorgeous."

"What about you, Hayley?" I change the subject. "There must be someone you fancy?"

Her cheeks turn bright pink and she turns her head so her long, curly bangs hide half her face.

"There is someone!" I say. "Tell us."

"Tell us!" Deidre encourages. "I promise we will not tell a soul. Will we, Emma Lee?"

"Cross my heart"—I draw an X over my heart with my finger—"hope to die."

"John Barrington asked me out."

John Barrington. The Cream of Wheat farmer in the rumpled-dad pants? Oh, really, Hayley, you can do much, much better than a discount Michael Fassbender in dirty work boots. Sorry-not sorry.

"It is about time!" Deidre says, leaning back and putting her slippered feet on the ottoman. "John has fancied you for a long time."

"He has?" Hayley says, flipping back her hair.

"Remember when we were kids? He used to follow you around the village to make sure Pippa Potts and her mates didn't take the piss out of you because of . . . you know."

Not helping, Deidre. So not helping.

"Pippa Potts! What a cow."

"Who is Pippa Potts?" I ask.

"A nasty cow," Hayley says, crossing her arms over her chest. "Her parents made a fortune selling cloth baby nappies over the internet. They are bloody rich, is what they are. Driving around in their fancy cars, putting on airs and graces. Pippa believes she is princess of Northam and she treats everyone in it as if they are her vassals."

"She was a nasty cow"—Deidre looks at Hayley and smiles sympathetically—"but for some reason, she was a massively heinous cow to you. I never understood it."

"Maybe she fancied John Barrington," I suggest.

"No, I think there is another reason," Hayley says, taking a big drink of her confession juice. "I think my mum had an affair with her dad before I was born—*nine months before*."

Deidre whistles and lets her feet fall off the ottoman.

"That would certainly explain many things," Deidre says. "Like why she was such a nasty cow and why you both have curly blond hair and cornflower-blue eyes."

"I am sorry Pippa Potts was so mean to you," I say, reaching over and squeezing Hayley's hand. "It sounds as if she was hurting something fierce and wanted to dump some of that hurt on you, even though you had nothing to do with your momma sleeping with her daddy."

"Hear! Hear!" Deidre says, raising her empty margarita glass. "Forget Pippa the Cow. Where did John say he wanted to take you on your first date?"

"The Three Counties Agricultural Show," Hayley says.

"Blimey!" Deidre whistles. "That is a tempting offer. What did you say?"

"I told him I would think about it," she says, laughing. "John is a lovely man, but sometimes he can be a bit of a one-trick pony. Farming. Farming. Farming. Don't get me wrong, I love farming, but I fancy a bit of adventure every now and again."

"Speaking of adventure," I say, smiling. "Did you know Brandon Nickerson climbed Mont Blanc last year?"

"Brandon Nickerson is fit," Deidre sighs. "Isn't he?"

"Yes, please," Hayley says, grinning. "Brandon is quite fit."

"You would go out with Brandon Nickerson?" I say.

"Sure! I will go out with Brandon Nickerson *and* Prince Harry, right after he gives Meghan Markle the heave-ho for saying she didn't know about the Royal Family."

"I am serious."

"So am I." She laughs.

"I have a great idea," I say.

I tell them about my nondate date with Johnny Amor and ask them if they would like to go with me to London to meet him and hear him perform at the swanky speakeasy club in Fitzrovia.

"A *shpeakeasy*?" Deidre is slurring her words. She closes her eyes and leans her head against the back of the velvet sofa. "I want to go to a *shpeakeasy* and meet a fit singer named Johnny Amor."

"Who said he was fit?" I ask.

"With a name like Johnny bloody Amor, he *hash* to be fit."

"Bingley found his Instagram feed and he is superfit," I say. "He is fit and funny and terribly clever. In fact, I was hoping to play matchmaker with him."

"Ooo!" Deidre doesn't open her eyes. "Who do you want to match him with?"

"You."

"Yippee." She tries to clap her hands but misses. "Deidre Waites and Johnny Amor. It *hash* a nice ring to it, doesn't it? If we get married, I will be Deidre Waites Amore."

For some reason, this strikes her as funny. She starts giggling. Her giggling turns into a fit of laughter that revives her. She sits up, wiping the tears from her cheeks.

"I'm Hank Marvin." She stands and wanders into the kitchen. "Do you mind if I make a cheese and pickle sammie?"

I frown at Hayley and she tells me *Hank Marvin* is cockney slang for starving and *sammie* is sandwich.

"Help yourself," I say, even though I think she will regret mixing her mango margarita with a cheese and pickle sammie. "The pickles are in the fridge."

"Anyone else want a sammie?"

"No, ma'am."

"No, thank you," Hayley says.

"Hayley," I say, "why don't I invite Brandon to join us?"

"It is your knees up."

"Knees up?"

"Party."

"What do you say, should I invite Brandon Nickerson to my knees up?"

"Are you playing matchmaker again?"

"Abso-bloody-lutely." I grin. "You are both hard workers who crave adventure. What do you say, fancy giving Brandon a go?"

"Fine." She sighs.

Deidre returns with a plate of pickle and cheese sandwiches on crusty bread sprinkled with Cornish sea salt. We munch the sammies and take turns doing each other's makeup. I spray Morrocanoil Mist on Hayley's wild curls and give her a full face, smoky eyes, red lips, and dramatic lashes. She looks glam. Deidre gives me thick baby doll eyelashes and bright pink, Betty Boop lips. Hayley gives Deidre an eighties makeover, with frosted blue eye shadow.

"Let's snap selfies," I say, grabbing my iPhone.

"I look dreadful in selfies," Deidre says.

"Not if we take one together," I say, holding the camera high in the air and tilting it so we are all in the frame. "It has been scientifically proven that individual faces appear more attractive when presented in a group. It's called the cheerleader effect."

Deidre and Hayley move in close and I snap a dozen photos.

"This has been mad fun," Hayley says, flopping back

on the couch. "Is this what it was like when you lived in your sorority?"

"Yes"—I flop on the couch beside her—"when we weren't going to classes, cramming for exams, or holding fund-raisers for our philanthropic causes."

"I think I would like to live in a sorority," Deidre says, squeezing in between us. "It sounds loads more fun than living with my mum. She treats me like I am still in nappies."

"My grands are the same way," Hayley says.

"I have a great idea!" I say, sitting up. "Why don't you both move in with me?"

"Are you serious?" Hayley says, sitting up. "Dead serious?"

"Why not? I have four bedrooms and a teensy-tiny fear of coming home to a dark house and being stabbed with a knitting needle by a psychopath hiding in a cupboard."

"What? How many margaritas did you drink?"

"Just kidding." I laugh, even though I am not kidding.

"How much would you want in rent?"

I wave my hand, dismissing her words.

"You have to let me pay something."

"Truth, y'all?" I look at both of my friends. "Normally, I would refuse your rent money, but I sold a piece of my momma's jewelry just so I would have the money to pay the estate taxes for this place. Until my matchmaking business takes off, I need to economize. Trust me, the word *economize* was not in my vocabulary until I moved here."

"So," Hayley says. "We would be helping you by moving in?"

"Yes," I say, my cheeks flushing with heat. "That's not why I asked you, though."

"I believe you, Emma Lee," Hayley says. "When can I move in? Would next week be too soon?"

"Next week would be great!"

"What about you, Deidre?" Hayley asks, nudging Deidre.

"I don't know."

"It's your mum, isn't it?" Hayley says. "You are afraid she wouldn't be able to manage on her own."

"Her eyesight isn't as bad as she pretends," Deidre says, her voice low, as if it is the first time she has ever spoken the words aloud. "She was gutted after my dad passed, stayed in her pajamas all day, staring at the telly. People were sympathetic for the first year or two, but she kept on with the grief, feeding it like a flame she didn't want to extinguish. I finally told her she was driving everyone away with her constant whinging and wailing. The next day, she said she thought she was going blind, that her vision was narrow and dark."

Deidre is quiet for a long time, and I sneak a peek out of the corner of my eye to make sure she hasn't fallen asleep, but she is just deep in thought.

"Mum will be fine."

"Does that mean you are moving into Wood House?"

"Abso-bloody-lutely!"

Chapter Twenty-seven

Emma Lee Maxwell's Facebook Update:
Remember when I had to take Biol 1030 and I moaned it did not make sense for a Communications major—who would end up handling public relations for a major social media outlet—to waste time learning about cellular activity (*not* cell phone activity)? I thought all scientists were atom-splitting geniuses. I saw an article today about two scientists who studied the behavior of four dozen couples over the course of sixteen years. Their findings: Kindness is the most important component in a successful relationship, and surprises are kindnesses that keep the relationship vitally alive. What a no brainer!

I am sprawled out across my bed, adding a string of hashtags (#picoftheday #mygirls #britishbesties #makeup) to the best shot from last night's makeover session, when I think I hear someone at the front door. It takes a moment to penetrate my consciousness because I am multitasking—hashtagging like a social media boss *and* fretting about Lexi. She hasn't added an update to her Facebook News Feed or answered my texts since Cash left for his Pigeon Forge foray and I am worried about her. First, she starts acting all insecure. Then, she falls off the grid. I might be fretting and clucking over nothing, but you must play momma hen every now and then when you have a bestie with a history of depression.

I cock my ear and listen. I hear Hayley's soft, gurgling snore coming from the room next door, and the white noise of the river whooshing outside my window. I am about to return to my hashtagging and fretting when I hear it again: a thud.

The sort of thud a psychopath might make if he were climbing in through a window or riffling through drawers in search of knitting needles.

Thud-thud.

Hang on! That sounds more like the thud of the front-door knocker. I look at the time at the top of my iPhone screen. It is just after eight—on a *Sunday* morning— when saints are making their way to church and sinners are sleeping off a night spent imbibing too many margaritas. (Sorry, Jesus! The mango made me do it!)

I climb out of bed, stumble into the bathroom, and gasp when I see my reflection. *Sweet Mother of Pearl!* I must not have removed all my Betty Boop–inspired makeup before going to bed last night because there are black marks around my eyes that make it appear as if I got tattoos to give me scary baby-doll lashes, and the skin around my lips is stained fuchsia. I look like Betty Boop about to take the walk of shame—I am even wearing a silky red babydoll!

Thankfully, the thudding seems to have stopped. I reckon it was a tourist looking for a bed-and-breakfast. I grab a fistful of makeup wipes and scrub away my hang-

over face. A few sprays of dry shampoo, some tinted moisturizer with illuminator, fresh mascara, brush my teeth, and
I have removed the shame from my game. I put on my
fluffy spa robe, the one with my loopy monogram embroidered in lipstick red thread on the pocket, slip my feet
into faux fur slippers, and pad to the kitchen to put the
kettle on.

Thud. Thud.

Sugar honey iced tea *(It's an acronym, y'all. Southern
ladies do not use cuss words—especially on a Sunday
morning)*! There is something banging away at the front
door.

I walk to the front door and look through the peephole,
but there is nobody there. No lost tourists. The drive is
empty, no cars or delivery vans.

I shuffle back to the kitchen and am pouring water into
the teakettle when I hear it again, the *thud-thud* of the
door knocker.

I walk back to the front door and peer through the
peephole. The image is slightly warped, like the reflection in a fun-house mirror. Warped rosebushes. Warped
garden path. Warped wooden garden gate. That is all. I
hold my breath and wait for a warped face to suddenly
pop up on the other side of the peephole or someone to
creep out of the bushes.

But—nothing.

I creep over to the window, pull the curtains back, and
look out, but the angle is all wrong to determine if someone is lurking beside the front door.

Back I go, into the kitchen to light the AGA and put
the kettle on the front burner. I am reaching for the kettle
when someone knocks on the back door.

"Son of a b"—I draw the b sound out for several seconds, willing my heart to start beating again—"*iscuit!*"

I drop the kettle onto the burner with a loud clang and walk to the back door. I turn the key in the lock and swing the door open to find Knightley Nickerson standing on the step holding a puppy in his arms—a puppy with black button eyes, a wonky ear, and a big red bow wrapped around her furry neck!

"You are a very difficult woman to surprise, Miss Maxwell," he says, grinning. "I have been knocking at your front door for thirty minutes. In the future, I will ring ahead to let you know I will be delivering a surprise. Though, I should imagine that would defeat the purpose."

I laugh.

"What are you doing here?"

"Hmm," he murmurs, raising an eyebrow. "Not quite the welcome I had imagined."

"Good morning, Knightley," I say, standing on my tip-toes and pressing a kiss to his cheek. "It is good to see you. I thought you would be on your way to London by now."

"So did I." He chuckles.

"Come in," I say, standing back.

He bends over and picks up a wicker basket lined in red-and-white-gingham fabric and filled with new puppy paraphernalia, before following me into the kitchen.

"What is all this?" I say, taking the basket.

"Bowls, toys, food, treaties, and a leash."

"I see that," I say, setting the basket on the table. "Why are you giving me a basket full of dog items?"

"You need them," he says, grinning.

Wonky Ear is staring at me, her little nub of a tail thumping against Knightley's arm, and I suddenly remember what Knightley said when I opened the door. *You are a difficult woman to surprise, Miss Maxwell!* Surprise.

"Oh my word!" I cover my hands with my mouth and bounce up and down on the balls of my feet. "Is this really happening? Are you giving me Wonky Ear?"

Knightley laughs. Wonky Ear wags her nubby tail faster. I bounce hard enough and fast enough to pull a backflip.

"Surprise!" He grabs the pup under her front legs and holds her out to me like a precious baby in a fur suit. "You are now the proud owner of a purebred West Highland terrier with a slightly lazy, though no less charming, right ear."

I stop bouncing and let out a squeal of delight. I take the puppy into my arms, hold her close, and nuzzle her soft white head with my chin. She smells like a puppy, sweet and earthy, with just the hint of Knightley's cologne. You know how parents always say they fell in love with their child the moment they laid eyes on them, the moment they knew that was their baby? Holding this puppy, looking into her trusting black eyes, I swear I feel the same way, filled up to bursting with love and terrified I don't have what it takes to protect and nurture my new little bundle. I am overwhelmed with emotion.

"You look as if you are about to cry," Knightley says, worry lines etched across his face. "Was this a good surprise or a bad surprise?"

"Good." I blink back tears and flash him a watery smile. "The best surprise ever. Thank you, Knightley."

"You are quite welcome." He leans down and presses a kiss to my lips. "You are sure you are happy?"

"Crazy happy."

Wonky Ear squirms in my arms. I let her down and she begins sniffing the legs of the kitchen table and chairs. She raises her head, looks me dead in the eye, and pees on the floor.

"Uh-oh," I say, grabbing a roll of paper towels off the counter. "Are you sure you want to leave Wonky Ear with me? I am a dangerously ignorant pet owner. I don't even know what signs to look for to know if my puppy needs to do business."

"I have every confidence in you," he says, pressing a kiss to my forehead. "You have only been in England for a few days and already you have learned how to light an AGA without singeing your eyebrows and operate a British automobile like a rally driver."

"Thank you."

"You're welcome." He grabs the paper towels from my hands, rips off several sheets, and attends to Wonky Ear's mess. "Now, I really must be going. The M40 is murder, even on a Sunday."

I scoop Wonky Ear into my arms and follow Knightley through the living room to the foyer. He steps out onto the porch and turns to face me.

"Remember," he says, scratching Wonky's head. "She will circle and sniff when she needs to go outside. Mrs. Swinbrook said to ring if you have any questions, and my mum said she will pop by tomorrow to check on you both. If you need anything else, I am just a Facebook post away."

"Circle and sniff. Got it."

"You will be great."

"Any other tips?"

"Only one," he says, grinning. "Reconsider her name. Wonky Ear seems rather insensitive, considering the hyperpolitically correct climate in which we find ourselves living."

I laugh.

"Right. New, PC name."

"Good-bye, Emma Lee." He kisses me again. "I will be back Friday afternoon."

"Good-bye, Knightley."

He strides down the path and turns in the direction of the walk leading to the stream. I watch until he disappears behind the hedges. I turn to go back into the cottage and practically collide with Hayley and Deidre, who are standing in the foyer, arms crossed, grinning like a pair of Cheshire cats.

Chapter Twenty-eight

Text to Alexandria Armistead:
   What's up, girl?

Text to Tara Maxwell:
   Prole drift is a stupid term used by uppity Brits to describe when an upscale product becomes popular with the nonaristo classes. Like I care. If Hunter wellies are good enough for Princess Diana, they're good enough for us. Right?

Text to Tara Maxwell:
   Right?

Text to Kristen Carmichael:
   Keep crushing it, crunch queen! We are not worthy!

Text to Madison Van Doren:
   Forget that Barton boy. He is a millionaire with no damned sense. You are worth a dozen Barton boys. (No

special reason. Just curious. Does Agent Provocateur deliver to the United Kington?)

Text from Bingley Nickerson:
    What are you wearing to meet Johnny Amor? Because we are meeting him at The Lucky Pig, I was thinking we could go Gatsby-esque. I am seeing you in a beaded flapper cocktail dress with loads of fringe and me in pinstriped trousers, suspenders, and fedora. Before you tell me you did not pack a flapper dress in your suitcase, I know just the place. What are you doing Wednesday next? Fancy a shopping trip with a gentleman of style and distinction?

Text to Alexandria Armistead:
    Are you okay?

Text to Alexandria Armistead:
    Check your VM. I left you a message.

Chapter Twenty-nine

To: Manderley de Maloret
From: Emma Lee Maxwell
Subj: Re: Re: Things that make you go hmmm . . .

Manderley de Maloret. Madame de Maloret. I don't reckon I
will ever get used to calling you *Madame*. You asked if I liked
Knightley Nickerson the way Emma Woodhouse liked her
Mr. Knightley. I am only on chapter eleven. So far, Emma
has treated Mr. Knightley like an older brother. Does she de-
velop romantic feelings for him? Ooo. I hope so, because
then this would be a case of life imitating art.
Love and miss you like crazy,
Em-girl
PS Do puppies always have to do business when they sniff?
Like every time?

Chapter Thirty

Knightley Nickerson ® Emma Lee Maxwell
May 29 at 6:09 a.m.
Have you thought of a kinder, gentler name for
Wonky Ear?
Comments:
<u>Emma Lee Maxwell</u> I have.
<u>Knightley Nickerson</u> Well? Is she to be Harriet Smith
or Jane Fairfax?
<u>Emma Lee Maxwell</u> No more fictional names!
<u>Knightley Nickerson</u> Well?
<u>Emma Lee Maxwell</u> Nether Westcote.
<u>Knightley Nickerson</u> Perfect.
<u>Emma Lee Maxwell</u> You think?
<u>Knightley Nickerson</u> I do. Someone beautiful once
told me remarkable adventures begin on the road to
Nether Westcote and Little Slaughter. I would have to
agree.
<u>Madison Van Doren</u> Please tell me you did not name
your va-jean Wonky Ear.

<u>Emma Lee Maxwell</u> Ew! You are nay-nay.
<u>Madison Van Doren</u> Me? You're the one who named your va-jean Wonky Ear. I do not even want to think about what must be going on down there for you to call it that.
<u>Emma Lee Maxwell</u> Stop!

Chapter Thirty-one

Emma Lee Maxwell's Facebook Update:
Relationships are like slipping on a pair of boots.
Some fit fabulously and make you feel like a million
bucks. Others pinch your toes and keep you from
walking the path you were meant to walk. Donate the
toe-pinchers to Goodwill, girl, and walk on!

A few days later, I wake to find another surprise waiting
on my doorstep—Lexi sitting on a Louis Vuitton rolling
bag and clutching a stack of papers in one hand and a
lump of damp Kleenex in another.

"Lex!"

Nether yaps and runs into the garden. I throw my arms
around my best friend. She lets out a sad little hiccup and
hugs me back. She looks like Betty Boop just before the
walk of shame—mascara ringing her eyes and lipstick
smeared on her perfect lips.

"What are you doing here?" I scoop Nether up in one
hand and grab my best friend's suitcase with the other,

walking into the living room and depositing them on the rug. "I was sooo worried about you."

"These were tacked to your front door." She sniffles, handing me the stack of papers, articles printed from medical websites: "Why You Should Be Taking Your Shoes Off at the Front Door," and "Sick Spot, Sick: Is Your Pet Making You Ill?" Thank you, William. "I would enjoy reading them if Cash hadn't broken my heart into a million pieces."

I take her coat and hang it on the hook behind the door, then grab her hand and force her to sit beside me on the sofa. Nether curls up in her basket. I made a cushion out of an old cashmere blanket and slipped my aunt's alarm clock in the basket. The puppy-rearing manual Knightley left is jammers with ideas for soothing and training pups.

"What happened?"

"Cash is m-m-married!"

"What?"

"He eloped."

I shake my head, like a cartoon character trying to clear the birds flapping around.

"Eloped? With who?"

"Charity Hawkins."

"*Who*?"

"S-s-some girl he met in Pigeon Forge." She sniffles.

"Charity Hawkins?" I cannot even wrap my mind around what is happening right now. Cash. Married. "What kind of name is Charity Hawkins? It sounds like a Stripper Name Generator name."

"Sh-she is a str-strippper!" Lexi wails, tears spilling out of her eyes. "He met her in a strip club. They flew to Vegas and got married at some all-night, drive-through chapel. Eloped! With a *stripper*! Could he have been more cliché? I don't think so!"

"Oh my word!"

I cover my hand with my mouth and stare at Lexi in disbelief. This is my cue to say something wise and comforting, but Cash and his lap-dancing bride have rendered me deaf, numb, and dumb-struck. What in the actual H-E-double L?

"He said our relationship was like that old U2 song."

"U2 song? What U2 song? How does Cash Aiken even know a U2 song? I thought he only ever listened to good old boys like Blake Shelton and Tim McGraw."

" 'I Still Haven't Found What I'm Looking For.' "

Ouch. I don't know the song well enough to recall the lyrics, but the title pretty much says it all, doesn't it?

"I couldn't remember the lyrics." Lexi wipes her tears with her soggy Kleenex ball and plum eyeliner smears across her temple. "I had to Google them."

"Bad?"

"Brutal."

I reach into the pocket of my robe and pull out Knightley's handkerchief, freshly laundered and folded with a peony petal inside, and hand it to her.

"Thank you." She sniffles, dabbing her cheeks. "It is about a man who has climbed the highest mountains, scaled huge walls, and run through fields to be with a woman, but after all that he realizes he still hasn't found what he is looking for. Pretty self-explanatory title, really."

"That boy is an ass." I am sorry for the cuss word, but I am so mad. There was no reason for Cash to do Lexi like that, to be cruel. Those damn lyrics will remain written on her tender heart for the rest of her life. "He couldn't find what he's looking for with somebody else's damn eyeballs. Look at you, Lex! You are beautiful, inside and out, and you don't need to get on a stage and shake your hoochie to prove it!"

"Thank you," she says. "I appreciate the pep talk. I swear I do, but . . ."

"But?"

"I don't want to talk about Cash Aiken and his pole-humping hussy. I am tired and smell like jet fuel. I just want to crawl into a hot tub and wash the stink off me."

"You smell like sunshine"—I clasp her hand hard and blink my eyelashes—"and you look like pine needles!"

She laughs at my intentional butchering of a funny line from the movie *Bridesmaids*. Lex loves that movie. Her laugh is a sad, broken little laugh, but I will take it.

"How long are you staying?"

She shrugs.

"Forever?"

"Deal!"

I hold up my pinkie so we can make a pinkie pact.

"Forever and ever, amen!" I say.

"Amen," she says, linking her pinkie through mine. "Now, you know what I really want?"

"A tub full of hot water and a bottle of Flowerbomb foaming bubble bath?"

"I could kill a venti vanilla soy latte with double Splenda," she says, handing me the handkerchief back. "Is there a Starbucks nearby?"

"No Starbucks," I say, laughing. "There *is* a fab little tea shop in town. We could walk there, if you are feeling up to it."

"Give me a few minutes to fix my face and brush my teeth." She stands and grabs her suitcase. "Where's the bathroom?"

"All of the bedrooms are en suite," I say, gesturing toward the hallway. "Take your pick. You can have any room you want. You want to know why?"

"Why?"

"Because you are *exactly* what I am looking for, Alexandria Armistead. Don't ever forget it."

"Never."

Lexi chooses the bedroom beside mine—the one with the twin beds and pale pink cabbage rose wallpaper. While she is unpacking and freshening up, I get dressed and pull my hair into a high pony. I take Nether Westcote to the garden, so she can do her business. I can't wait for the day when she can walk into town with me—I even ordered her a shiny red raincoat and matching boots—but her little legs aren't strong enough to make the trek, so I pop her into the kennel Hayley gave me as a gift, promising her a belly rub when I return.

We walk to the tea shop and drink three cups of I Love You Oolong Time—four sugar cubes for me, a splash of vanilla soy milk and two packs of sweetener for Lex— and Lexi tells me the story all over, about how Cash returned from Pigeon Forge with a skanky wife in tow, about how he stood on the porch at his momma and daddy's house and told her he did not love her. She tells me how her momma and Cash's momma got into an ugly crying and hollering match. When Mrs. Armistead threatened litigation for breach of contract, Lexi packed her suitcase, took the keys to Cash's truck, and drove herself all the way to the Atlanta airport, then boarded the first plane to London.

"Why Atlanta? Charleston is an international airport."

"The flight out of Charleston didn't leave for five hours and I didn't want to risk the chance of someone showing up and trying to talk me out of leaving. Besides,

I liked the idea of Cash having to get a ride all the way to Atlanta to get his truck back."

"Lexi!" I laugh.

"Bitch move?"

"Jilted fiancée move. It's better than taking a golf club to the hood of his car or burning his clothes."

"Tay-Tay did that in her 'Blank Space' video!"

"Let's not look to Taylor Swift as a model for how to behave in a relationship, dear." I mimic Taylor in the video, raising my arm and pretending to stab the air, eyes creepy wide. "She scares me."

We finish our tea, and I take her on a tour of the village. I decide to begin at the candy shop because I am eager for her to meet Deidre, because we will all be sharing a cottage soon. Along the way, I tell Lexi about Deidre and the delicate case of Mrs. Waites.

"Aw," Lexi coos. "The poor woman sounds sad and lonely. Imagine losing your husband after all those years together, building a business, a life? I am heartbroken, and I was only with Cash for two years."

"I am sorry, Lex."

Deidre must have reached into the bonbon box that is her closet and pulled out the nuttiest piece she could find. From the waist down, she appears normal in a swingy pink miniskirt, pink tights, and granny boots laced to the ankles. Above the waist? That is a different story. All the craziness is happening above the waist. She is wearing a cardigan over an ivory T-shirt with the silhouette of a crawling baby and the quote, *An ugly baby is a very nasty object.* Fastened to her sweater is a pin resembling the face of a porcelain Victorian baby doll, wide, unseeing eyes, round cheeks, and bow lips. She is wearing earrings that match. Victorian dolls are scarier than a haint, y'all. They do not become less frightening when worn as jewelry. Lexi and Deidre hit it off right away, but the true-love connection happens when Mrs. Waites shuffles into the room, squinting and waving her hands through the air in front of her face. The moment Mrs. Waites realizes there is a stranger in the shop—a stranger who is monop-olizing her daughter's attention—she starts complaining about the challenges of living with a degenerative eye disease, the feelings of hopelessness, uselessness, and isolation. Lexi listens with the patience and compassion of a true nurse. She validates the woman's suffering and then asks her if she would consider holistic alternatives to treat her condition. By the time we leave the shop, Lexi has promised to pop round to take Mrs. Waites on a daily stroll to the park, to improve her self-sufficiency. That's Lex. She has only been in Northam-on-the-Water for two hours and she has already made a friend and offered com-fort to a blind woman.

We meet Vicar Parsons on the sidewalk as we are leav-ing the candy shop. He seems particularly interested in Lexi's background, asking questions about her people. He invites her to attend a singles prayer group.

We visit the newsstand and chat with the owner, Mr. Egerton. We pop by the market but miss Hayley because she is delivering produce to a farm-to-table gastropub in Little Slaughter.

Our last stop is to Curtis and Sons Apothecary, so I can introduce my bestie to my neighbor. I forgot to tell Lexi about William's germophobia. I make the introductions and Lexi holds out her hand for William to shake. William hesitates. Lexi notices the hesitation, sticks her hand in her pocket, and asks William if he carries Ayurveda herbs.

"Which ones?" William asks.

"Triphala or Baheda."

"I am afraid not." William frowns. "Northam-on-the-

Water attracts an unsettling number of visitors, but we are a simple country village. Most of the tourists who wander into the shop have spent too much time in the pubs and require Nurofen or Panadol, over-the-counter tablets for head pain."

"I see." Lexi smiles. "Do you know where I could purchase Triphala or Baheda in powder form?"

"I can order any herbal powder you require, but they will take a few days to arrive."

"Would you mind?"

"Not at all," he says. "Would you mind if I asked you how you intend to use the powders?"

"I am making an oculus wash for Mrs. Waites. Triphala nourishes the nerves and can reduce the risk of damage from free radicals. Ayurvedic healers have used herbal eye washes to treat a variety of ailments, from glaucoma, myopia, cataracts, and conjunctivitis. So, why not macular degeneration?" Lexi looks up at William. "You think I am crazy?"

"Not at all!" William smiles. "Have you read Lasant Lashaki's book—"

"—*Ancient Ayurveda, Modern World*?" she cries. "Lasant Lashaki is brilliant."

"Bloody brilliant!" William moves out from around his counter. "I just finished reading *Divining the Science of Ancient Medicine*. Have you read it?"

"No," Lexi says. "I am reading *The Great Influenza: The Story of the Deadliest Pandemic in History* by John M. Barry."

"Fascinating read," William says. "Frighteningly fascinating. I could hardly put it down."

"Have you read *Germs: The Biological Weapons Outside Your Front Door, Stay Inside, Stay Alive*?"

William's eyes widen. He hurries back around the counter

and closes the book lying open beside the register, so Lexi can see the cover. *Germs: The Biological Weapons Outside Your Front Door, Stay Inside, Stay Alive.*

Lexi giggles.

Giggles!

What is happening? Something is happening here. William's posture has softened. Lexi is looking through her lashes. Sweet Mother of Pearl! Nurse Lexi and the germophobe are flirting.

My phone rings. William and Lexi look at me as if I just threw a bubonic plague–infested rat corpse at their feet.

"Sorry," I say.

I pull my iPhone out of my pocket, hit the Mute button, and hurry outside to answer the call, leaving my best friend and my neighbor to discuss oozing pustules.

I do not recognize the number on the screen, so I push the Talk button and say hello.

"Good morning, Miss Maxwell."

"Knightley!" I gasp. "This is a surprise."

"Good surprise or bad surprise?"

"Good." I look through the window into the pharmacy, at William smiling and Lexi twirling her hair around her finger. "Definitely good."

"You're sure? Did I ring you at a bad time? You sound . . . distracted."

"I am definitely distracted! Lexi just arrived."

"Your best friend?"

"Yes."

"Oh, I am sorry to interrupt," he says. "I only wanted to check on how things were progressing with Nether Westcote, make sure she hadn't piddled on your rugs or chewed your shiny red boots."

"Perish the thought!" I gasp, glancing at my boots. "Nether is great. My boots are great. The rugs—not so much."

Knightley chuckles.

"So, it is a match, then, you and Nether?"

"Are you kidding?" I think of the photo I posted on Instagram this morning, of Nether curled up on my pillow like a furry little bean, and my heart aches. "It is the best match ever! Nether is my soul puppy."

"I am glad," he says, laughing.

"Knightley?"

"Yes?"

"You are not going to believe what is happening right now in Northam-on-the-Water."

"—Deidre Waites is wearing an outlandish outfit?"

"Yes, but—"

"—Vicar Parsons is trying to recruit singles to join his prayer meetings?"

"Yes, but—"

"—William Curtis is—"

"—flirting with my best friend and she is flirting back!"

The line goes quiet.

"I thought you said your best friend was engaged to be married?"

I quickly tell Knightley about Cash's boys-only trip to Tennessee and his quickie Vegas wedding to a stripper from Pigeon Forge.

"Cash sounds like a tosser," he says. "Your friend is better off without him."

"She is," I agree.

"So, what does it matter if she chats with William Curtis?"

"William Curtis is sweet, but he could never make Lexi happy. She needs someone more dashing, someone who will force her to step out of her shell. Someone like—"

"Cash?"

"Be nice!"

"Forgive me," he says, adopting a mock-mournful tone. "It is too soon to make light of your first matchmaking disaster. It sounds to me as if you have someone in mind to fill Cash's unworthy shoes. If not William, who?"

"I don't know." I flip through headshots in my brain, mental profile photos, searching for my best friend's replacement mate. "What about Brandon?"

"My brother?"

"Sure, why not? He climbs mountains and plays polo with a bunch of burly, ex-military guys. He is just the type to pull Lex out of her shell." I see the sign for Hayley's market reflected in the window and groan. "Wait! That is not going to work. I have already matched Brandon with Hayley . . . of course, he doesn't know it yet."

"Hayley?" Knightley cries. "You mean to match Brandon with Hayley Bartlett?"

"What about Bingley?"

"You want to match Hayley Bartlett with Bingley?"

"No!"

"What about a match between Lexi and Bingley?"

"*Emma Lee.*" Knightley's voice is low with concern. "Perhaps it would be best if you focused your attentions on your Weddings at Welldon scheme."

"You mean, forget about matchmaking?"

"Not entirely," he says. "There is one match that definitely deserves your attention."

Chapter Thirty-two

Emma Lee Maxwell's Facebook Update:
If he is stupid enough to walk away, be smart enough to let him go. You should never have to chase a true love, darlin'. Just sayin'!

Knightley said I should focus my attentions on helping Miss Isabella launch Weddings at Welldon, but I truly believe it is my calling to be a matchmaker. A divinely inspired calling. Patti Stanger said you get credits in heaven for being a matchmaker, and I believe her. I believe her with all my heart. What duty is more divinely inspired than paving the way for two people to be able to travel to the altar together?

Unless a host of heavenly angels suddenly appear in the garden at Wood House and tell me to quit my meddling, I am going to keep on doing God's work.

I must be doing a few things right, because Vicar Parsons took my suggestion to start hosting single's mixers, Deidre is superamped to meet Johnny Amor, Hayley has not said another thing about going to the hogs and heifers show with boring old John Barrington, and Brandon has agreed to join the evening of Amor! Now, if only I could find a Russian millionaire for Miss Isabella and a fun guy for my bestie.

Then again . . .

. . . I'm not so sure Lexi is looking for a fun guy. She arrived on my doorstep Tuesday morning. She returned to the cottage Wednesday and Thursday morning after walking with Mrs. Waites, put her pajamas back on, and climbed back into bed.

Friday, I convinced her to ride with me to the Tesco Superstore in Stowe-on-the-Wold. I told her I was terrified to drive by myself and needed dog food for Nether Westcote. We had a blast cruising down the aisles and seeing who could find the most unusual items—brown sauce, salad cream, English roast beef and Yorkshire pudding–flavored potato chips (sorry, crisps), pork scratchings. We both agreed Lexi was the clear winner with Aunty's Spotted Dick steamed puds. She seemed superhappy when she found a Tesco-brand Zesty & Zingy body wash in Mexican lemon and lime she said smelled like Tara's Key lime pie and when she found Stem Ginger ice cream made with double Devon cream, but then we got home, and she put her pajamas back on and ate Stem Ginger ice cream out of the bright yellow carton.

Saturday Knightley invited me to go to the Ashmolean Museum in Oxford, to see an exhibit titled Romance Through the Ages. I asked Lex if she wanted to join us, but she would rather stay in her pajamas, read her influenza book, and eat the rest of her Stem Ginger ice cream.

The Romance exhibit was breathtaking. How could it not be? Dreamy watercolors and bold oil paintings depicting people in various stages of love and lust. We ate lunch at a posh hotel, Belmond Le Manoir aux Quat'Saisons. I ordered braised beef—in French—which surprised Knightley. He said my accent was *parfait* (the chef agreed). I am not gonna lie, y'all, I was superpleased with myself. Thank you, Jesus (and Clemson) for requiring communication majors to study a foreign language.

We took a long, circuitous route back to Northam-on-the-Water because we were enjoying each other's company, so it was dark when he pulled up in front of Wood House. The lights were out, which made me imagine all sorts of things. Lexi sprawled out on the sofa clutching an empty bottle of sleeping pills or hogtied with a knitting-needle-wielding psychopath standing over her.

You will never guess where I found her. Sitting on the bench beside the stream—with William bloody Curtis! She wasn't clutching a bottle of sleeping pills and she sure wasn't hogtied!

After that, the days passed with a steady rhythm. Lexi walking with Mrs. Waites or meeting William at the bench by the stream to talk about pandemics and flesh-eating bacteria, while I worked on training Nether West-cote to walk on a leash and met with Miss Isabella to continue our work on our scheme to turn Welldon Abbey into a luxurious wedding venue. Bingley turned in several sigh-provoking pieces about Welldon's most romantic residents and Brandon helped us find a brilliant brand developer who created eye-catching brochures and a slick, user-friendly website.

I even finished reading *Emma*—a feat that left me with mixed emotions. I was wrong about Mr. Elton. What a horrid man. And his wife! Ugh!

However, I was pleased to discover Emma's feelings for Mr. Knightley, her dear Mr. Knightley, altered by the end of the novel, from brotherly affection to all-consuming passion. They even got married! Sigh.

I can only hope—in this—my life truly will imitate Jane Austen's art.

Chapter Thirty-three

Emma Lee Maxwell's Facebook Update:
Nothing brings me more joy than bringing friends together.

It is happening. It is finally happening!

I am walking through the Oxford Circus tube station with Deidre, Hayley, Lexi, and Bingley. I am wearing a sexy, speakeasy-inspired dress and Bingley is wearing pinstriped trousers with suspenders and an au courant fedora set at a rakish, Gatsby-esque angle.

We are only minutes away from meeting Johnny Amor!

My stomach is twisted in knots. I wonder if Patti Stanger feels this anxious before her millionaire mixers? I wonder if Johnny will see Deidre from across the smoky speakeasy and fall head over heels in love with her? I wonder if silly old Bingley is the man to put a permanent smile on my best friend's face? I wonder if Hayley and Brandon will make the love connection they have been unable to make back in Northam?

A lot is riding on this evening. The romantic futures of six people. My reputation as a matchmaker. Honestly, the stakes could not be higher.

We meet Brandon outside the station.

"Hello, Brandon," I say, smiling.

"Hello, Emma Lee. You look lovely."

"Thank you!" I hug him. "I am so glad you decided to join us. We are going to have the best time! And Hayley is here." I grab Hayley's arm and pull her closer. "Doesn't she look fab?"

I tamed Hayley's wild curls into soft waves that frame her face and give her a sexy, smoky eye. If there were a runway in Oxford Circus, Hayley would stomp the sugar honey iced tea out of bony old half sister. Annalise who?

"Hello, Hayley," Brandon says, smiling. "You look lovely, too. I have never seen you in a dress."

That's right, darlin'. Get an eyeful of all that!

We walk the short distance to The Lucky Pig, and I swear, I feel the heat from the sparks of attraction passing between Hayley and Brandon. It's chemistry, y'all! Bring me a bucket of water because I'm on fire!

Johnny Amor said he would meet me out front. He did not tell me what he would be wearing, so I am searching the street for a man in a pink velvet suit. Which is ridiculous, really, because Bingley has sent me dozens of screenshots of Johnny's Insta feed, and I know he owns many suits and they are not all pink.

"Hello, love," a voice purrs in my ear. "You must be Emma Lee. I would know you anywhere. Who else but an angel has hair the color of moonbeams?"

"Johnny Amor!"

I spin around, and my breath catches in my throat. Johnny Amor is more gorgeous in person than on his Instagram feed. He is wearing big white oval sunglasses that remind me of a pair Mick Jagger might have worn when he was courting Jerry Hall, and his dark brown hair is combed into a cool, updated pompadour. He is wearing a black tuxedo trimmed in black velvet and a black-and-white, silk-polka-dot shirt open to expose a sprinkling of dark hairs. On his fingers, chunky silver rings one expects a rock star to wear.

"I am Bingley," Bingley says, thrusting his hand between us. "Knightley's brother."

"Knightley?" Johnny asks. "Who is Knightley?"

"Emma Lee's boyfriend." Bingley frowns at me. "At least, I think he is your boyfriend. Have you two shagged yet? Are you a thing or what? He bought you a dog and took you to a posh French restaurant."

Sweet Mother of Pearl! Is Bingley cockblocking me? He knows I am not interested in Johnny Amor, that I am trying to make a match for Deidre, so what is he doing?

"A dog and a posh French restaurant in the Cotswolds?" Johnny Amor whistles. "They're a thing, mate."

"Coveting your glasses," Bingley says to Johnny. "Versace, Style Rebel."

"Thanks." Johnny grins, and I swear I think I feel the heat from a spark of attraction passing between them. "I am feeling your fedora."

"Johnny Amor!" I pluck the sleeve of his tuxedo jacket. "Let me introduce you to my other friends."

I start with Deidre, who is wearing a little black dress with stripy tights and black Mary Janes, which, I think, is tame for her. Deidre smiles. Johnny smiles. I swear, I do *not* feel the heat from a single spark of attraction pass between them.

Once all the introductions have been made, we go into The Lucky Pig. Johnny reserved us a booth near the stage. We slide in and he orders us all a round of gin cocktails.

I am wondering where Knightley is when Brandon leans over and whispers, "Knightley might be a little late. Annalise was not pleased with the artwork on her cover flat, so they are meeting to see what can be done to make her happy."

"Annalise?"

"Annalise wrote a novel about the modeling industry."

Of course, she did. Supermodel. Photographer. Why not add published novelist to her Wikipedia? Yes, she has a page, I checked.

"Did she?"

"It's brilliant!" Brandon gushes. "The next *Devil Wears Prada*, but sexier, snarkier."

Of course it is.

I try to spark conversation between Johnny Amor and Deidre by asking Deidre about her favorite bands, hoping she will name a few of Johnny's favorite bands and they will discover they are soul mates. Deidre is in to electric dance music. Johnny hates electric dance music.

I try to spark a conversation between Hayley and Brandon by asking Brandon to tell us about his latest adventure; turns out it was a three-day boating trip in the Mediterranean with a group of friends and—gasp—guess who was there? Annalise bloody Whittaker-Smith!

I turn back to Deidre and Johnny only to find Bingley and Johnny deep in conversation.

". . . pseudo-intellectuals who sit around quoting *Finnegans Wake* and *Atlas Shrugged,*" Bingley says, looking at Johnny beneath the rim of his fedora. "Nobody reads *Finnegans Wake*, not by choice anyway. It's a grudge read."

"Grudge read?" I ask.

"A book you read to punish yourself, because you feel

guilty for wanting to read something else, something sexier. It's like a grudge shag," Johnny explains.

"Grudge shag?"

Bingley sighs and whispers in my ear. "When you have sex with someone you're really angry at or to get back at someone else. It's a mad way of thinking, really. Massively mad."

My cheeks flush with heat.

"Grudge shags serve their purpose," Johnny says.

"Abso-bloody-lutely," Bingley agrees.

We finish our gin cocktails and order a second round. The bartender keeps pouring cocktails and the conversations around our table keep flowing—in the wrong directions. Brandon talks to Deidre about her idea for a Queen Victoria–inspired child-rearing manual—and he seems genuinely interested. Brandon talks to Johnny Amor about Irreverent, the indie book publishing company Johnny helped his best friend launch—and Brandon seems genuinely interested. Lexi talks to Deidre about Victorian medicinal practices. Hayley talks to Bingley about the organic gastropub trend. Bingley talks (and talks) about Bingley, his mad, fab life as a lifestyle (emphasis on style) reporter—and everyone is genuinely interested.

Then, Annalise arrives looking like she just walked off a runway, of course. Flawless makeup, flowing hair, towering knee-high boots, and on-point, clingy, metallic minidress. Anyone else would look like Charity Hawkins in that outfit, but not Annalise. She does not look like a pole-twirling, rainmaking stripper from Pigeon Forge. Nope. Not Annalise. She looks like a glamazon, a real-life Wonder Woman.

Of course.

"Hello, Emma Lee," she says, smirking. "Knightley has been detained."

We all shift to make room for Annalise (of course) and she scoots in close beside Brandon (where Hayley had been sitting).

Fortunately, we are spared from hearing about how Annalise has become the first woman to land the cover of every *Vogue* around the world while winning a Pulitzer for her snarkier-than-*Devil-Wears-Prada* novel, because the live performances have begun.

Johnny Amor says he must head to the dressing room to get ready for his set and asks Bingley if he would like to watch the performance from backstage—*Bingley*, not Deidre!

I shoot Bingley a withering look, which he ignores.

He blows me a kiss and slides out of the booth, disappearing into the darkness with Johnny bloody Amor.

This evening is not turning out at all as I had imagined. Hayley doesn't really seem interested in Brandon. Bingley hasn't spoken a word to Lexi. Johnny obviously isn't feeling Deidre. And who in the H-E-quadruple L invited Annalise Whittaker-Smith to this party?

The thing is, everyone is having a great time. They are laughing, connecting—even if they aren't love connecting.

Johnny hits the stage and you know what? He is good. Very good. He has a unique sound—the voice of an old-school crooner with a little Mick Jagger flash and naughtiness added in. I can't decide if he is a more pop, rock, or indie. He is ambiguous—in more ways than one. He puts out seriously mixed signals—winking at girls and guys alike. Not that it matters. He is funny and clever. Loads of fun to talk to and easy on the eyes (and ears).

I excuse myself to go to the loo, and when I return,

everyone is dancing. Annalise and Brandon are dancing together, and Hayley, Deidre, and Lexi are all dancing with the guys from the booth across from ours.

I am the odd man out.

And I feel like sugar honey iced tea.

The more I stand here, watching my friends laughing and having a fab time with their nonmatches, the worse I feel.

I hate The Lucky Pig. There's nothing lucky about it. I just want to leave. I want to be home, snuggling with Nether Westcote.

It's not as if this lot requires my matchmaking skills.

What matchmaking skills?

I try to get Lexi's attention, but she has her back to me. Finally, I can't take it anymore. I have to leave. I send a quick group text, saying I have a crushing headache and am headed home, then run out of the club—and right into Knightley.

"Emma Lee," he says, grabbing my forearms. "What's wrong? Where are you going?"

"Home," I cry.

"Why? It's still early."

"I am a lousy matchmaker. The worst."

His lips press together, and I can tell he is trying not to laugh, which only fuels my self-pity fire, and I begin to sob. He hugs me tight and waits for the tears to subside, then asks me to tell him what happened tonight. I tell him about my intention to match Lexi with Bingley, Hayley with Brandon, and Deidre with Johnny, and how it all went horribly, confusingly wrong.

"I thought being a matchmaker was my divinely designed purpose, but I am a terrible, awful, rotten matchmaker."

I stop talking and wait for him to say something, to refute my self-deprecating assessment.

"You are a bad matchmaker, Emma Lee"—he pulls me close and kisses my forehead—"but you are an excellent match."

"I am?"

"Abso-bloody-lutely," he says, looking into my eyes. "You're *my* excellent match."

Chapter Thirty-four

Emma Lee Maxwell's Facebook Update:
Dear Facebook Friends, Today, I tried not to think about bespoke suits, red peonies, the whiff of a cologne that turns my knees to jelly, a dance in a daffodil field. Today, I tried not to think about the way he makes my tummy do backflips every time he looks at me. Today, I tried not to think about how much I love Mr. Knightley Nickerson. *My* Mr. Knightley.

Epilogue

Hey y'all! Remember earlier, when I asked you if you thought it was romantic when two halves came together to form a whole? I talked about that scene in *Jerry Maguire*, when Tom Cruise told Renée Zellweger that she completed him. Maybe we aren't supposed to find the person who completes us; maybe we're meant to find the person that accepts us just as we are and use their love as motivation to complete ourselves. That's my thought anyway. Hugs!

**LOVE ISLAND: WHY ENGLAND HAS
BECOME *THE* WEDDING DESTINATION
T O W N & C O U N T R Y**

**The Most Romantic Wedding Venues on this
Sceptered Isle**
From Bamburgh to Bath, the most
romantic places to say I DO
by BINGLEY NICKERSON

As the brisk winds of winter nip like hunger pangs in a Dickensian orphanage, relentlessly, endlessly, we turn our thoughts to the English spring: the annual Easter-egg hunts, the walks through the cobalt mists of a bluebell wood, the weekend jaunts to the Lakes District to behold the seas of daffodils that inspired Wordsworth to ejaculate prose with prepubescent fervor, the *weddings*.

The idyllic Austen-esque villages, great country piles, and romantic ruins scattered throughout the country have made England the premiere wedding destination. Late springtime—those magical weeks *after* septuagenarians have mothballed their pastel fascinators and *before* the Chestertons-set have unpacked their perfect whites and military-style blazers—is the perfect time to hold a wedding in England.

With breathtaking views of the Gloucestershire countryside, the eleventh-century Benedictine ruins at Welldon Abbey near Northam-on-the-Water have become the venue of choice for couples wanting a bespoke nuptial experience. Welldon Abbey features a stately Georgian manor home, romantic gardens, spa facilities with indoor swimming pool in the converted stable block, and sumptuously appointed cottages. The Bespoke Package allows guests exclusive use of the home and grounds.

Supermodel Annalise Whittaker-Smith and publishing executive Brandon Nickerson spoke their vows at Welldon Abbey in a

splashy ceremony that was filmed for BBC
One's new reality show, *Close Up, Please* . . .

PRESS RELEASE
Welldon Weddings
WeddingsAtWelldon.com

Knightsbridge-based wedding and lifestyle brand
Anghel Antonescue has teamed up with Welldon Weddings to produce an exclusive collection of wedding
gowns and bridal gifts inspired by the uniquely romantic
history of Welldon Abbey. Anghel Antonescue, a Roman-
ian-born designer, business tycoon, and seven-time winner of the Bridal Designer of the Year award, is known for
his innovative, glamorous designs. Committed to working
with "burgeoning talent," Antonsecue cherry-picked sup-
pliers and artisans from around Gloucestershire to help
produce the line. Antonescue says he eagerly anticipates
a long and intimate collaboration with Isabella Nickerson, managing director of Welldon Weddings.

PRESS RELEASE
Nickerson Publishing

Nickerson Publishing is pleased to announce the acquisition of Fitzrovia-based independent book publisher,
Irreverent Press. Irreverent was founded in 2015 by
Adam Quirk and Johnny Amor, and quickly gained a reputation as a cultivator of unique literary voices. Through
the deal, Irreverent retains its name, and founder Adam
Quirk will become managing director of the imprint.

GLOUCESTERSHIRE GAZETTE
WEDDING ANNOUNCEMENTS

Hayley Bartlett and John Barrington, both of Northam-on-the-Water, were married in an intimate ceremony officiated by Vicar Ethan Parsons and held in the gardens at Welldon Abbey, Saturday. The bride is the granddaughter of Alfred and Edith Bartlett, Bartlett Farms, Northam, and the groom is the son of John and Mary Barrington, Barrington Acres, Northam. The bride wore her grandmother's Chantilly lace wedding gown and veil and a shocking lack of cosmetics. The joyful but placid couple will make their home in Northam.

GLOUCESTERSHIRE GAZETTE
ENGAGEMENT ANNOUNCEMENTS

William Curtis of Northam-on-the-Water is pleased to announce his engagement to Alexandria Armistead. The bride is an American, born and raised in Fairfax, Virginia, and holds a nursing degree from Clemson University. Mr. Curtis is the proprietor of Curtis and Sons Apothecary. The couple plan to wed in a small ceremony later this year.

@bingleynickerson
London, United Kingdom
Bingley Nickerson Town & Country / Man of Style & Distinction / Rock Star Wife

@**bingleynickerson** When you are unable
to share monogrammed luggage, shirts, sta-
tionery, or handkerchiefs, you get matching
tattoos on your ring fingers. @johnnyamor
#love

Text from Madison Van Doren:
    I am in love, love, love! Crabbing is a damn fine way to
get all sweaty on a lazy afternoon. I love it! (BTW, Chase
Aiken has shown me a few more ways to get all sweaty
on a lazy afternoon. What-what!)

Text from Deidre Waites:
    BLIMEY! I know you are trying to enjoy your holiday
with Mr. Knightley, but my agent just rang. Guess what?
We Are Not Amused hit the top-ten list for trade sales in
the United Kingdom, and Lucy Worsley's people have
reached out to say she is interested in a collaborative
project! I love Lucy Worsley! She has a fantastic lisp and
she wears tights with high-heeled Mary Janes!

Text from Ethan Parsons:
    As vicar, I find myself in the unusual position of need-
ing guidance. It is of a nonspiritual nature, I assure you.
Years ago, at a vicarage luncheon, over bowls of celery
root soup, I developed an ardent fondness for Miss
Deidre Waites. Recently, I shared my feelings with her.
She did not take me seriously. You are an authority on
dating. What do you suggest? How might I woo and win
Deidre Waites? God bless.

Text from Isabella Nickerson:
    Hello, love. I hope you are having a splendid time in
Rio. Sun, sand, and samba! I have just heard the most

scrummy gossip about Vicar Parsons that simply would not wait for your return. Remember the story I told you about his youthful indiscretion? Well, the girl he had the indiscretion with won eighteen-million euros in the Irish Lotto three months ago! The good vicar has made several trips to Cork these last few weeks. I have it on good authority he proposed to her yesterday, but she turned him down.

Text from Tara Maxwell:

I am as big as a whale—and I did not get this way from eating boxes of Feckin' Faddle! I blame a feckin' eejit Irishman with eyes as blue as the sea, one too many Bánánach Brews, and a hot and heavy session of bumping uglies in the cider barn. Remind me: Does your Mr. Knightley have blue eyes? If he does, promise me you will not look directly into them. Ever.

Text from Manderley de Maloret:

I am wearing a Dior gown to the Cannes Film Festival gala. No, you may not borrow it.

THE END
(or as we like to say in Charleston, That's All, Y'all)

**Love the Maxwell sisters?
Be sure to check out
DREAMING OF MANDERLEY
And
YOU'LL ALWAYS HAVE TARA
And don't miss
Leah Marie Brown's
The It Girls Series
Available now from Lyrical Press**